I0537116

Virgin at the Speedway

BARBIE O'CONNOR

Copyright 2016

Copyright

Copyright © 2016 by Barbie O'Connor. All rights reserved. Please do not participate in or encourage piracy of copyright materials in violation of the author's
rights. In accordance with the U.S. Copyright Act of 1976, the scanning, uploading,
and electronic sharing of any part of this book without the permission of the author
constitute unlawful piracy and theft of the author's intellectual property. If you
would like to use material from the book (other than for review purposes), prior
written permission must be obtained by contacting the author at barbie@barbieo-
connor.com. Thank you for your support of the author's rights.

All Rights Reserved
Published in the United States
by Zunné Group Racing, Inc.
Racing Resort Ranch is a registered trademark of
Zunne Group Racing, Inc.
Library of Congress Cataloging-in-Publication Data
O'Connor, Barbie
Virgin at the Speedway/Barbie O'Connor
ISBN 10: 0-9975767-0-7
ISBN 13: 978-0-9975767-0-2
eBook ISBN 13: 978-0-9975767-1-9
Cover design by Eli Miller

Virgin at the Speedway is a work of fiction. Names, characters, places, and incidents
either are the product of the author's imagination or are used fictitiously, and any
resemblance to actual persons, living or dead, businesses, companies, events, or
locales is entirely coincidental.
While the author has made every effort to provide accurate telephone numbers
and Internet addresses at the time of publication, neither the publisher nor the
author assumes any responsibility for errors, or for changes that occur after publication. Further, the publisher does not have any control over and does not assume
any responsibility for author or third-party websites or their content.

For Toby

Thank you for the ride of my life.

PROLOGUE

The tires shrieked as the car crashed against the wall. The shrapnel of the carbon fiber wings and side pods exploded as it hit the outside of turn 4 and then ricocheted across the track to the pit road. There, like a pinball, it bounced from wall to wall, destroying everything in its path, until it finally rested, a smoldering shell, flames invisible, as the methanol burned. The fuel left its shadow in the form of a smudge of black smoke as the last of the oil burned away, leaving the remains of two cars in its wake.

It wasn't a dream, exactly. Luz had woken up to these images and lived through the crash every day since it happened. So much was on the line then and so much was on the line now. Entrusted with a business she knew nothing about by friends she loved like family, she made each decision along the way with the same care and deliberation she employed when she managed portfolios: looking towards the future, considering the past, and then with no turning back, a determined strike to get the best outcome. In a few hours she would know her fate and that of others who were her responsibility and in her care. Today was the beginning or the end of her time in this exotic world she wanted for her future. Today was the Indianapolis 500-mile race.

CHAPTER 1

As she looked out her office window, Luz Maria Dane saw the river walk waking up. Restaurateurs sprayed the sidewalks clean, set out chairs, wiped off tables, and prepared for the day. Luz turned up the volume on her squawk box to hear the morning call from the European and Asian markets.

"European stocks are in a selloff on speculation that the dollar will strengthen after the Federal Reserve meeting today."

Taking a sip of decaf from her "Go Girl!" mug, Luz looked at the call sheets of her best clients and reviewed the list. She made every effort to call her clients regularly to review their portfolios. She felt that this way she got to know her clients and their needs better than anyone else and could therefore advise them more appropriately on what to do with their money.

Luz started in the investment field with Emerson York

right out of college. She nurtured her local clients, mostly widows and conservative businessmen, while she helped her international clients looking for a safe haven for their money to understand the intricacies of the financial marketplace. Her fluency in Spanish was a blessing bestowed upon her by her mother, while her father, a rancher, instilled in her a belief that she could accomplish anything if she worked hard enough and long enough. From childhood, when her father first taught her how to read the stock pages, showing her how her college savings was growing, Luz had been fascinated by the investment world.

While Luz made her first call of the day, chatting with an elderly client about her nieces and nephews, she heard her manager, Mark Sloan, whistling as he walked down the hallway towards her office. The whistling stopped at her office door, and Mark came in and took a seat on the edge of her desk.

Luz finished her call, then asked, "And what have I done to deserve this unexpected visit?"

"I just wanted to thank you for the way you treated the very wealthy prospective clients I referred to you yesterday," Sloan said, his voice dripping with sarcasm. "Not only did I introduce you to them and set you up in the luxurious conference room overlooking the river gardens, but I practically closed the account myself. What the hell happened?!"

The angry edge in his voice sharpened as he continued. "You really messed up this time. I hand you a multi-million-dollar account and you do everything in your power to piss them off, and out the door they go taking their money with them. Ricky was so mad he said he would never step foot into another Emerson York office again."

Luz listened quietly as she watched Sloan rise from her desk and stand over her, pounding his fist in his palm as he made each point about her performance. She waited patiently until he was finished, and then she said, "Ricky? So you were on a first-name basis with Ricardo Delgado after what? Only ten minutes of visiting with him?"

"Yes, we got along great! Talked about hunting in South Texas, since he asked about the trophy buck I have on the wall in my office. By the time he left my office before you met with him, I could have closed that deal. He was going to transfer millions of dollars into his accounts today!"

"And probably transfer them right back out again. Did you ask him anything about his business? About why he wanted to set up an account with Emerson York? About his sources and uses of funds?" Luz stood up, crossed her arms, and looked pointedly at her manager. "No, of course not, you just wanted to be buddies, hang out together. That expensive suit, the Hermès tie, the gold cufflinks and the gold Rolex, had you starstruck. Not to mention the perfectly groomed mustache and goatee, styled hair, and the recently manicured nails. Made you think he had lots of money, right?"

"Yes, but what about the other guys with him?" Sloan asked defensively.

"The two little old men with him who said they were his uncles were great camouflage too, since they were charming and so willing to share information with me when I spoke with them in Spanish. I'm sure I'll open those accounts later in the year when they return at Christmas. But Ricardo Delgado? No! He avoided answering every profiling question, and he was not happy I was asking for that kind of information. I can't prove it, but I would bet he was looking for a place to launder money."

Sloan glared at Luz, shrugged his shoulders, and left her office, whistling again as he walked down the hallway.

Luz returned to the call sheets on her desk. An hour later her assistant appeared at the doorway. "Michelle Amberson on line 2. She says it's urgent."

Luz promptly picked up the phone. "Michelle, what's going on?"

"Clint is in the hospital. He's had a stroke. Oh, Luz, I don't know what I am going to do. He's been working so hard prepping the team for the 500. The doctors say he will have his strength back eventually, after a lot of physical therapy and care, but . . . I need to see you, to talk to you," Michelle said, her voice catching.

Luz listened to the sadness pouring from Michelle as she recounted the details of the stroke her husband, Clint, suffered the night before. Luz felt hollow and empty; tears welled up in her eyes as she imagined Clint losing the use of his right hand and leg. Since her parents died, Michelle and Clint had treated Luz as if she was their daughter, and now they really needed her.

"Sure, Michelle, however I can help," Luz said, her voice soft and consoling. "Let me wrap up a few things here at the office, and I'll be right out to see you."

"I know it would be asking a lot of you, Luz, but the Indy

500 is only six weeks away and I need someone I completely trust to oversee the team while I stay here to care for Clint. Luz, I need you to do that for me and especially for Clint." Michelle sniffled through her words, her voice rough from crying.

Luz was stunned. She didn't know anything about running a race team, but she knew Michelle wouldn't ask if she knew someone else who was suitable. Luz felt proud that Clint and Michelle had enough faith in her to put her in charge during such a difficult time in their lives. She knew she had to say yes to this unusual opportunity, and it might be the best move for her own life too: After her most recent discussion with her manager, she wanted a break, far away from the office.

"Michelle, you know I'll do anything to help you and Clint, anything at all," Luz said. "I'll work something out here at the office, and I'll be there for you and Clint. See you a little later. Love you."

After she hung up, Luz spent the afternoon going over client accounts and reviewing her calendar for the coming weeks. She knew the Indy 500 took place over Memorial Day weekend, which was only six weeks away. But she didn't know how much time she would have to spend in Indianapolis; Michelle would fill her in on the details tonight.

For the next hour Luz focused on the portfolios she reviewed each quarter. Her concentration broke when the phone rang and kept ringing. Looking up, she saw her assistant motioning that she couldn't answer it because she was on the phone with a long-winded client, so Luz grabbed the receiver. "Luz Dane, how can I help you?"

A silky tenor voice asked, "*Preciosa, cómo estás?* My precious, how are you?"

Startled by the bold familiarity she remembered from the years they'd gone out together, Luz caught her breath. Why was he calling her now, after they hadn't spoken in so long? She responded guardedly: "*Bien*. I'm good."

She wanted to sound more confident than that, she realized, but still to avoid sharing anything real with him, so she spoke again. "Work is busy. And you?" She hoped her feelings didn't reveal themselves as they talked.

"You are still focused on your work. That's good. It always satisfied you. That is why I called you. I need some advice on where to put some money from my real estate investments I just cashed out. Maybe you could help me?" His voice practically purred with sensuality. It was the same tone he used on her whenever he wanted anything, and in the past, he usually got it.

Listening to him, she was transported back five years when she was tumbling-down-the-stairs in love with him, and in so deep she could not see him for what he was: someone who loved her so he could use her. When they'd broken up, she had made so many lists of why he was wrong for her. She kept one by the phone, one in her purse, one in the car, one at her office, just so she could remember that he did not have her best interests at heart. Now he was calling, and his flattery was not what she needed now, but as she'd learned the hard way, turning him down flat only made him come on stronger, so she'd just have to string him along somehow and hope he'd lose interest before she reached a breaking point.

"Mauricio, I'm on a tight deadline right now. Let me refer

you to someone else who has the time to help you," Luz said, hoping she could pass him off to somebody else in the office.

"*Preciosa*, I can wait. I won't have the money for a few weeks anyway, so there is plenty of time. I'll call you back then. *Ciao, mi amor.* Goodbye, my love." He hung up.

With her mind swirling and her gut churning, all Luz wanted to do was run out of her office and get far away. Years before, Mauricio would just appear out of nowhere, walking into her office unannounced, when minutes before he'd been talking to her on his cell phone; he'd pretended to be far away while he was right outside the door all along. She was glad she'd be away for a few weeks at Indy; there he couldn't stalk her usual haunts or drop by the office to invite her to lunch on the spur of the moment.

Before she left for the day, she quickly reviewed the Amberson portfolio, checked the cash balance, and looked to see that the power of attorney documents were on file and everything was in order. Luz knew she could help Clint and Michelle at Indy, and at the same time, with the web and cell phones and fax machines, she could take care of her clients no matter where she was.

CHAPTER 2

The drive through the Hill Country to the Amberson ranch was one of the prettiest in Texas. On both sides of the highway the wildflowers bloomed in brilliant blue, hot pink, and sun yellow, speckling the countryside like Easter eggs in a basket of green grass. As the little red Mustang GT embraced the curves over the thirty miles Luz drove to Boerne, she felt the warm, fresh air brush against her cheeks.

How many times had she taken this trip in her life? After her parents died, she came here for solace. Open to her night and day, whenever she needed comfort, love, and the feeling of being with family, Michelle and Clint welcomed her. Now they needed her, and Luz was ready to make this time easier for both of them.

Luz first met them fifteen years ago. Clint was a friend of her father's; the two men had met as students at Texas A&M. After college Clint went to work for a major oil company, and when his father died, he returned to Boerne to manage the family estate. By that time, he oversaw the oil company's sponsorship relations with various race teams in NASCAR, Indy Car, drag racing, and Formula One. When he left to manage his family's business, he started his own race team and made a name for himself and his team manager, Roger Schneider, with their efforts at the Indy 500. Clint was such a colorful personality that Luz could not imagine him drained of energy and vitality by a stroke.

The familiar row of mailboxes appeared on the left side of Highway 46, and at the top of the hill Luz made the turn into the crushed limestone driveway, which wound through the ranch like a long snake. When Luz reached the house, the garden of native plants surrounding the entrance gates seemed to be exploding with color. Bluebonnets reflected the color of the open sky, and Indian paintbrushes' brilliant pink petals echoed the sunset in the western sky. Through the large wrought iron gates, originally from a hacienda in Mexico, Luz entered the courtyard, where Michelle waited for her, sipping a margarita. Candles in hurricane torches and on the table glowed warmly. A southeasterly breeze passed through the patio as darkness settled on the horizon.

Michelle got up and gave Luz a hug, then pulled up another chair and poured her a margarita. Toasting to Clint's recovery, each took a sip of the cold, tart drink, and the fresh lime juice, tequila, and triple-sec made Luz feel she was in Mexico. Despite the sad circumstances that now brought her together with her old friend, Luz was glad she could be there to comfort Michelle. A former Miss Winston, Michelle Amberson had taken Clint for a wild ride during their courtship. Once married, she settled down and became the perfect corporate wife. Their marriage was a partnership on all levels; Michelle was an active participant in all decisions that affected their personal and business lives. Her thoughtful acceptance of Luz as a surrogate daughter was an expression of that partnership with Clint.

Michelle, her green eyes filled with tears, told Luz, "More than anything else in the world, Clint wanted to win the Indy 500. When he submitted the entry a few weeks ago, he said, 'This is the year we could win Indy.' He talked on and on about it. It was an obsession of his to win that race. It means so much that you are going to be there for us at Indy."

"But I've never done this before," Luz said cautiously. " I don't know where to begin."

"Oversee it like it was your own race team. You manage money that way, and you are very successful. Think about what you want, and of course, what the sponsors would want. You will be acting in Clint's place. Hopefully the other team owners will have the good manners to accept you. You are familiar with a man's world, Luz, a tough man's world. I'm not saying it will be easy, but I believe you can handle it."

Luz sighed and took another sip of her margarita. She stared into the candle flame reflected in the glass of the hurricane lamp, taking her back to another time of loss, confusion, and change in her life. Hesitantly, she asked, "Michelle, is there anything else I need to know? About Clint, I mean. Is he going to make it through this okay? I thought he was pretty healthy."

"He's going to be fine. If you want to know what brought on the stroke, I can't say. But I think Roger Schneider, the team manager, created more worry and problems for Clint these last few weeks than ever before, and that didn't help anything," Michelle said angrily.

"What kinds of problems?"

"Every time he talked with Roger Schneider on the phone, there was always some piece of equipment missing or some part gone astray. One week Roger said he had no wheel guns, even though the computer inventory showed there were eight wheel guns warehoused in the storeroom at Indy. Then parts were ordered that Roger claims were never received, but we have records that indicate the package was signed for at the shop by one of the mechanics there," Michelle explained. "That's another reason we want you at the track, at the shop, at Indy: to watch our back. We don't know who is causing us problems, but you are the only one I can trust at this point."

"I'll do my best, Michelle." Luz felt her mind racing through various possibilities behind the events Michelle described.

The two women talked more about what Luz would be doing at Indy: the events she would attend, where she would stay, how she would continue her investment advisory business while she was there, and when she would start—in only two weeks. Luz had a lot to learn. She set up time to go over the computer records for the team, the rule book for the racing sanctioning body, and the team roster and jobs each member executed. Before she left for the evening, Michelle asked her, "You remember Jeff Harwood, from the Orlando race?"

"Oh, right; tall, handsome, twinkling green eyes. Who

could forget him?" A slight smile played on Luz's lips, and a faint blush tinted her cheeks. "He worked for Clint for a few years, didn't he?"

"Yes, but now he has his own team. He'll meet you at the airport, help you get situated at your apartment, and give you a quick orientation at the track when you first arrive."

Looking at her watch, Luz said, "It's getting late. I have a full day of work ahead of me, plus all this homework." She held up a tote bag full of books and computer printouts. "So I'd better be going."

As she drove away passing the courtyard gate, Luz waved goodbye. Michelle managed a hint of a smile, a Kleenex still in her hand. Since her parents' death, Luz had made every effort to live life to the fullest, knowing that any day could be her last. She had always balanced responsibility and risk in her everyday life and her profession. Now she would do the same in her work for Clint and Michelle, running the race team for the Indy 500—the chance of a lifetime. She hoped she would never regret it.

CHAPTER 3

Settled into her seat on the Lear jet bound for Indianapolis, Luz reviewed the calendar for the days leading up to the Indy 500 taking place the Sunday of Memorial Day weekend. It all began this coming weekend for Luz, opening day, with the first weekend of practice for all of the teams, starting the month off. So much to do once she arrived at the track: get credentials, order a fire suit, find her way around, meet the sponsors. It reminded Luz of her first days at Emerson York: she felt like she was jumping into a new world, with its own language, dress code, and internal regulations. She knew she could survive and excel, hopefully long enough to get the team to the finish line.

Anxious about soloing this first week at the Speedway, Luz put aside the files she'd glanced at and realized what she needed to know was not in front of her, but at the Speedway itself. Exhausted from a two-week whirlwind of tutorials about racing, as well as catching up with her top clients before she left, Luz closed her eyes for a moment and thought about what had brought her to this point in her life. When had the world of racing opened up to her? What had led to this job, this huge opportunity? Would her skills translate to another world: the world of fast cars, big money, and life-and-death decisions?

Auto racing came into her life in 1995, when Clint made the decision that the Amberson team would compete in the Indy Racing League series, after many successful years at the Indianapolis 500. Luz remembered how they realigned his portfolio to provide the seed money for the team to participate in the new series.

When all of the teams came to Indianapolis, the Ambersons' two-car team usually qualified in the two front rows, with at least one car finishing in the top five. Teams often worked around the clock to prepare their cars for qualifications, and then for the big race itself. With the largest purse in racing, the Indianapolis 500 was the race to win.

Luz thought about the time she had been invited to join them at the inaugural race at Walt Disney World, soon after her breakup with Mauricio. At that point she was still skittish about formal dating, so the convivial atmosphere of the race garage and pit row suites was comfortable for her. It was in that setting that she met Jeff Harwood, who at first glance was a mechanic with dirt under his nails, but through that weekend impressed her with his gentlemanly ways, his intellectual sophistication, and the ease with which he gained the respect of his teammates. Jeff would be the one picking her up at the airport and introducing her to the Indianapolis Speedway.

"Ms. Dane, we are beginning our approach to the Indianapolis airport," the copilot announced.

Reflecting on all her preparations to be away from the office for the month of May, Luz recalled that just two days ago her manager, Mark Sloan, had done everything in his power to block her from taking on this challenge of doing two jobs at the same time. To get him off her back, she compromised by announcing she was taking the four weeks of vacation she was entitled to, even though she would continue to work with clients and stay in contact with the office. She knew if one of the men in the office went to Indy to work on a team, Sloan would be eager to buy tickets and attend the race. As it was, she was lucky to outmaneuver him this time.

When she placed the files back into the briefcase so stuffed with documents she could barely close it, Luz came across the copy of the *Autoweek* with the red Ferrari on the cover. She remembered how in the hospital the sight of that magazine made Clint so agitated that his heart monitor went off. Rushed out of the room by an officious nurse, Luz hadn't yet had the chance to read the issue. Now she flipped through the article and scanned the photos of each of the new teams, the list of new team members, and the short team histories. When she saw Roger Schneider, Clint's team manager, listed as the owner of one of the new teams, Blackbird Racing, Luz was perplexed. How could Roger own his own team and manage another race team at the same time? Maybe that was what bothered Clint. Luz would have to look into it once she was settled at the speedway.

Thinking about her other carry-on bag made her laugh.

A fairly good cook, Luz had on occasion brought friends she visited a plate of cookies or a cake, but this time she felt like a caterer. By special request, inside an insulated case, she had packed two dozen flour tortillas, tamales, refried beans, and hot sauce to give to Jeff Harwood, who missed Mexican food from his favorite San Antonio restaurant, La Fonda. Whenever he came to visit Clint and Michelle, Jeff looked forward to a trip to this restaurant, which served cold margaritas made in the Mexico City tradition along with authentic Tex-Mex food.

Looking out the window during the approach to Indianapolis, Luz saw the track as they flew over it, so big it was easily spotted from the air. A two-and-a-half-mile track, it was classified as a super-speedway, encompassing five hundred acres, built in the city of Speedway, Indiana. As the plane taxied down the runway, Luz saw row after row of private jets: each one brought sponsors, team owners, and fans to the illustrious site.

As she walked off the plane, she looked around for a familiar face and saw no one in the private lounge. The pilots helped her with her luggage, while she handled the carry-on bags, with their precious cargo. While waiting she noticed a bright red Indy car chassis emblazoned with the name of Barbar Beer on display to her left. In a glass case beside it were model cars, autographed photos, replicas of the starting lineup, leather jackets with the speedway logo, and more. The walls held prints by famous artists that depicted heated competition from past Indy 500 races. Luz carefully studied the show car on display and reviewed the mechanical parts and their names. Reflected in the glass of one of the framed prints was a face she knew, one she had thought of many times since the Disney World race. Before she turned around, she heard Jeff Harwood's Texas drawl: "Studying up won't help you now. You're about to take the ride of your life, Luz." Laughing, he grabbed both her carry-on bags, threw his left arm around her shoulder, and said, "Welcome to Indianapolis!"

Luz gave him a hug. "Thanks for picking me up, Jeff. It's so good to see you. I'm so glad you're here. Michelle said you might meet me, if you weren't too busy at the track."

"Sorry I was late, or maybe you were early. Either way, it's great to see you, too! You're looking good," Jeff said, his green eyes glimmering mischievously. Then he motioned towards the show car. "Don't bother studying that thing: it's about four years old. A lot has changed since then."

"I'm afraid if I don't study, I'll make a fool of myself. I've been reading the rule book for the last few weeks to learn the basics."

"Why bother with that? Your crew chief worries about those details. What a waste of time!"

"You never know when it might be important to at least understand the rules," Luz countered. "But then again, maybe you're right. My job is purely decorative. Just go to the car owner's meetings, attend cocktail parties, and make sure the sponsors get the benefits outlined in the sponsorship contract."

"There's more to it than that, but you'll learn after a few days. What about grabbing a bite to eat? Thought we'd go to one of my favorite haunts here, then move you into your apartment," Jeff said as he walked her out the door. "The phone lines, cable, and Internet are connected and working already. And your rental car is waiting for you at the speedway garage area."

"Aren't you efficient? I'm impressed."

"Don't be. Michelle sent me the details. Tomorrow we'll pick up your credentials. Clint's team worked out of their race shop at Gasoline Alley this week. They don't want anyone to steal their speed secrets."

"Speed secrets?" Luz asked.

"Yeah, everyone wants to qualify here. They don't want the other teams to know what they are doing to the tires, engine, or chassis. I think it's a lot of hooey—Schneider just wants to make a grand entrance tomorrow for opening day." Jeff hoisted her bags into the truck.

"I'm a little anxious about being here. I've been briefed on everything, but there have been some communications problems with Roger Schneider. Evidently Schneider has given Michelle the run-around for a while, and they haven't talked for weeks. It's been a game of phone tag ever since Clint had his stroke."

"Everybody has problems with Roger Schneider. Don't let him get to you. Have we got everything?"

"Yes, we've got it all, including your Mexican food fix, which is in this little cooler," Luz said, patting that bag on the top.

"Yum." Jeff's face lit up with a broad smile. "I'll save that for later this week. Thanks for bringing it to me. You know how much I miss good Mexican food. How is ol' Juan doing down there in San Antonio?" Jeff asked as they walked towards the forest green SUV.

"Making those killer margaritas, as always. I know you don't visit the Ambersons as much as you used to, but it would be good to see you in San Antonio more often," said Luz, a soft blush creeping over her cheeks.

Jeff looked at her, smiling shyly, then cleared his throat as he looked her up and down, admiring her long legs and trim waist, accented by the very business-like pencil skirt. "You know the dress code for the garage area and pit road. I hope you're not planning on wearing that get-up at the track," Jeff said as he opened the door for her. "You can if you want to, but I don't think you will be very comfortable." He looked at her pointedly when she stepped awkwardly into the SUV's cab, her high heels and fitted skirt making it hard for her to swing gracefully into the seat.

"Look, I came straight from the office to the plane." Luz laughed. "Don't worry about me. I'll be in uniform. They ordered some team shirts in my size. I brought the required black pants with me, and comfortable walking shoes. Sometime this week I need to go to Simpson to be measured for a fire suit."

"Oh, those guys are going to have a good time with you. They get tongue-tied when women come in for a fitting. Especially when they measure your bust, waist, and inseam. I'd like to be there for that. What a hoot!" Jeff slid into his seat and started the car. "It's too late to take you to the track. The garage area closed at eight. The rules are strict now, since the accident a few years ago, where a mechanic was injured at two in the morning during a golf cart race around the garage buildings." They drove out of the airport onto the freeway.

"A golf cart race? It sounds almost funny, except it's sad, since someone was hurt."

"Yes, it was a real shame. When the garage area was open twenty-four hours to crew members, we would sometimes stay till three or four in the morning, barely getting to sleep before it was time to wake up again. We might horse around some, but most of the time we spent working. The new rule leveled the field for the smaller teams, because with so few people, there was no second shift to come in late at night. The eight o'clock rule even hurt the big teams. One team needed the extra time to work on their chassis before the last day of qualifying, and was turned down. They didn't make the race that year," Jeff said soberly.

"When I hear about making the race, it gives me chills."

"That's what is so great about Indy. Everybody has to work hard, big teams and small teams. And everyone has a chance. The race isn't as much about competing against the other teams as it is about man and machine mastering the track over a five-hundred-mile distance in three to four hours. After you get your credentials tomorrow, I'll show you around."

Jeff took the freeway to the Crawfordsville Road exit, then turned left, and they wound their way to a restaurant called the Union Jack.

CHAPTER 4

"May I speak with Mr. Roger Schneider?" he asked, the words tinged with his Spanish accent.

"Mr. Schneider is in a meeting. May I take a message?" the perky receptionist responded. "I was told not to disturb him. If you tell me what this is in regard to, maybe I could help you, sir?"

"This is a private matter, and *no*, you cannot help me. Get Schneider on the phone, *now!*" His deep voice now had a threatening edge.

The receptionist pulled the phone away from her ear as he thundered. She was tempted to hang up on him, but then she'd have to listen to Roger Schneider's tirades, so instead she punched the hold button and stepped towards the door leading to the huge shop area directly behind her. In all the years the receptionist worked at Amberson Racing, no one had spoken to her that way before.

She walked quietly through the cavernous warehouse space and joined a small group of Japanese men crowded around a balding overweight man pointing out the changes his specialists had made in gearboxes. She waited until Roger Schneider finished his explanation, then tapped him on the shoulder, bowed politely towards him and his guests in the Japanese tradition, and whispered in his ear about the man with the Spanish accent waiting on hold. As if he'd been struck with a cattle prod, Schneider straightened upright, bowed to his guests, and motioned to his crew chief to finish the tour. He ran upstairs to his office overlooking the shop. The receptionist had never seen him move so fast.

CHAPTER 5

From the outside, the Union Jack looked like an English pub, with beveled leaded-glass windows and woodcutter's-cottage gingerbread trim. Once inside the entrance vestibule, another door led to the restaurant, where the honey-colored oak paneling was juxtaposed with the bright primary colors of racing memorabilia. Mounted up high along the edge of the ceiling were racing helmets, most of them signed by the drivers who'd raced at Indy. Photographs of winning cars and drawings by well-known artists hung on the walls. Drivers' fire suits were in display cases with die-cast models of various cars displayed alongside them. TV monitors in every corner showed footage of racing on all the major networks.

Opposite the old-fashioned rectangular bar, with its brass footrail, was a fireplace, and to the left of that was a glass enclosure, accessible from the outside by a huge garage door. This big glass case held the show car of the winner of last year's Indy 500. Dramatically liveried in poppy red with white accents, its sponsor's name on the side pod, this car was polished to perfection, the display lights reflecting off its finish.

The three sides of the bar were crowded with people dressed in bright team shirts of yellow, red, green, blue: colors of the rainbow. A medley of conversation and laughter filled the room as team members enjoyed an after-work beer with their friends and competitors.

The hostess, Debbie, greeted Jeff as an old friend, telling him there was a ten-minute wait for a table. He introduced her to Luz, then they went to the bar. A few guys in the crowd yelled hello to Jeff as he and Luz made their way to two barstools. Shortly after they sat down, a slow, deliberate migration of people came over to say hi to Jeff and to meet Luz.

"The way news travels around the garage area, by tomorrow morning you won't have to introduce yourself to anyone. They will all know who you are and why you're here," Jeff said. "Don't be surprised if a few of these guys snub you. They aren't used to women being a part of the team. Some don't even think women belong here at all. Just ignore them."

Jeff ordered potato skins to share, since the line for tables was longer than expected. While they waited he told her, "We'll be starting early, around six-thirty in the morning. Get donuts for the team, then hit the credentials office early, show you around a bit, and go over any questions you have."

"Great! Maybe we could leave right after we finish these potato skins. I still have to unpack and set up the apartment. I'm wired being in new surroundings, but it's time to call it a night."

They argued playfully about who was going to pay the bill, then agreed that Jeff would pay this time and Luz would owe him another trip to the Union Jack on her. Jeff said goodbye to his friends as they left, then escorted Luz to the car.

From the Union Jack parking lot, Jeff crossed Crawfordsville Road, then turned into an apartment complex built of white brick. He drove around to the back, settling in front of a row of two-story townhouses.

"Here's your home-away-from-home. It's pretty cozy. Let me show you around," he said as he unlocked the door. "Since you'll be working and living here, Michelle made sure there was plenty of room. Upstairs are two bedrooms and two baths, and a full bath down here, along with the living room, dining room, kitchen, and breakfast room."

Luz and Jeff walked through the downstairs. When they reached a curtain covering a sliding glass door, Jeff pushed the curtain aside, slid the door open, and ushered Luz outside.

"This little terrace has a great view of the pond. You can see the duck's nest over in that corner." He pointed to the left of the window, where a cluster of reeds protruded into the pond.

"It would be a great place for coffee in the morning, or even a glass of wine at night," Luz said, smiling at his interest in the ducks.

From where she was standing, she could see the twinkling lights of the other apartments reflected in the mirror finish of the water. Walking back into the spacious apartment, Luz was pleased to see it was decorated in cool mauves, grays, and soft sage greens. The furniture looked brand new, and the carpet had been freshly cleaned. Placing her purse on the dinette table, she walked upstairs to take a look at the two bedrooms.

New sheets were stacked on the double beds in each of the rooms. Towels were already in the bathrooms. A simple chest of drawers and nightstands on each side of the bed completed the furnishings in each room. One of the rooms had a connecting bath, while the other one opened onto the hallway. Big walk-in closets provided plenty of room for clothes or storage. A washer and dryer were stacked in a closet at the top of the stairs.

Luz walked downstairs, where she found Jeff sitting on the sofa, surfing channels on the television in the living area.

"It's perfect! It's bigger than my apartment at home. There is definitely plenty of room to work, and it feels very comfortable. Oh, and the fax machine, computer and printer are plugged in and ready to go." Luz plopped down on the sofa next to Jeff.

"Yeah, we tested the fax, phones, and Internet connection this afternoon. The cable works, too. This channel broadcasts live from the speedway," Jeff said, showing her the number to select for up-to-the-minute race coverage.

Luz watched footage from an earlier practice on the screen.

"I took the liberty of stocking your fridge with some things so you could wait to go to the store. It's getting late. I assume you want both of these bags upstairs?" Jeff asked.

"Yes, please. Put them on the bed in the second room. I can unpack later," Luz said to Jeff's back as he carried the bags awkwardly up the stairs.

When he turned to go back downstairs, she was facing him at the top of the landing, blocking his way down the stairs.

Jeff put his hands on her shoulders, turned her around, and marched her down the stairs. At the bottom, he turned her around, kissed her on the forehead, and walked swiftly to the door. "Gotta go. See ya at six-thirty in the morning. Remember to lock up before you go to bed. Sleep tight!" The door closed behind him.

Watching him leave, Luz touched her forehead. Sweet, she thought. Still excited about all the new places she'd been, people she'd met, and the new experiences yet to come, she wanted to stay up and wished he'd stayed a bit longer. Luz guessed he was right about getting a good night's rest, though. Tomorrow was the beginning of a new way of life for Luz, and she wanted to be at her best.

CHAPTER 6

Luz's hand groped its way over to the clock, pushed the snooze button, and silenced the annoying alarm. As she snuggled into the pillows and pulled the covers over her chin, she slowly woke up. When she grabbed the alarm clock and saw it was five forty-five, she jumped out of bed. If Jeff was on time, she had less than an hour to shower, dress, and clear her mind.

After a quick shower, Luz padded downstairs to the kitchen to see what, if anything, was available for breakfast. Opening each of the cupboards, Luz was glad to see the oatmeal chocolate chip cookies, oatmeal, and organic whole-wheat crackers Jeff had bought. In the freezer she found what looked like freshly ground French roast coffee, along with some vanilla chocolate chip ice cream. The refrigerator held milk, apples, hummus, whole-wheat bread, cheddar cheese, orange juice, eggs, and butter. For someone who didn't know her at all, he had bought the same staples she regularly kept at her own apartment.

Luz started the coffee; the aroma of the fresh-brewed coffee was irresistible. After adding sugar and cream to a blue ceramic mug, she walked upstairs to dress. Luz pulled on her khakis and polo shirt and laced up her shoes. While she was braiding her black wavy hair, Luz thought about how this first day at the track would be a big step for her. She knew that it was the beginning of a new chapter in her life, an adventure she would always remember, and that whatever skills were required of her she would master them.

As she set her backpack on the kitchen table, the doorbell rang. It was six-thirty: Jeff was exactly on time. When she opened the door, she saw he was wearing a navy blue all-weather jacket and a beige Stetson. One hand covered his mouth, stifling a yawn.

"Not enough sleep for you either, I see," Luz said good-naturedly.

"Never enough sleep this time of year," he said, shaking his head and grinning. "It's May. We work the full month, all day and some of the night, spending as much time as we can at the track. You'll see, after the race, you'll know what I'm talking about." Jeff he looked at his watch. "Time to go. I have to stop to get my crew their donuts."

Luz picked up her backpack and followed Jeff out the door. A flash of lightning highlighted the eastern sky, where dark clouds obscured the morning light. It was the beginning of a stormy day. As the wind increased, more drops of rain fell. She pulled the door shut and locked it.

"Ready to make a run for it?" Jeff asked, his head motioning towards the car, only fifteen feet away.

They both ran towards the car, hoping to move faster than the raindrops. Luz jumped into the truck, laughing, and asked, "Does every day start with a race?"

"No, just this one. It's another cold snap. Practice this week will be interesting."

"What do you mean?" Luz held her hands in the warm air streaming from the vents.

"The rain washes all the oil, rubber, and debris off the track so it's real clean, making the track surface slick. Also, the outside air is colder, making the tires less sticky. So after weather like this, drivers have to be extra careful on the track because the tires have less traction against the clean asphalt, and there is a greater chance of accidents."

Jeff drove out of the apartment complex and stopped at the light at Crawfordsville Road. He reached into the back and grabbed a file folder an inch thick, filled with legal-size paper with charts printed on them. He handed the file to Luz.

"I thought you might want to learn to read the run sheets from practice. These are from last year. Knowing this year's times when your team qualifies is essential. You can get these in the pressroom or online. Look over them now. I won't have time later to explain them. We'll both be too busy."

Jeff turned left and drove about four blocks to the donut shop. "I'll be just a minute," he said, then he ran in.

The wind blustered outside while the rain beat against the windshield. Luz opened the file and looked over the charts. Each page listed the best practice times of each driver, starting with the name of the fastest driver at the top of the list. Below were the others listed in order of speed, with the slowest at the bottom of the page. Reading from left to right, the columns listed the driver name, the car chassis, the engine type, the tire brand, the name of the sponsor, the time per lap, and the top speed of the day for each driver.

Luz knew the track at Indianapolis was two and a half miles long: its length and design made it a super-speedway. Cars commonly clocked over 240 miles per hour on the back straightaway and averaged speeds of 217 miles per hour per lap. Reviewing the charts, her forehead creased in concentration, Luz looked for the relationship between practice and qualifying times.

Jeff returned to the car and placed the pink-and-white box on the back seat, with the small pile of napkins on top. "I got napkins in your honor. The guys are going to razz me about it. They may not know what to do with a napkin in the garage area. Normally they use a shop rag or wipe their hands on their pants."

He took a bite of a still-warm glazed donut and washed it down with coffee. Motioning to the papers in her lap, he asked, "So, what do you think?"

"To tell you the truth, I really don't understand why this is important. More information, please?"

"Each car has three chances to qualify. To determine whether the car owner will take the qualifying run or not, he has to know his competition. He has to know the range of speeds from highest to lowest, so hopefully his car will make the race and won't be bumped out of competition on the last day of qualifying," Jeff said, wiping his mouth with a napkin.

"Oh, okay," Luz said, still reviewing the sheets in front of her. "What's this other sheet, 'Entries'?"

"That one is from this year, listing all the car owners, along with the car numbers, the drivers, and the sponsors of each car. It also lists the crew chief and sometimes the chief mechanic. Each team may have more than one backup car, just in case there is a wreck."

Luz studied the list carefully, looking for the Amberson listing. The car number was there; even the backup car was listed. Roger Schneider was listed as the crew chief, with Blake Miller as the chief mechanic. Luz remembered that Miller was the crew chief and Schneider the team manager, and she wondered why that wasn't reflected on the official list.

She spied the listing for Jeff's team, Harwood Racing, at the top of the third page. Something below it caught her eye: an entry for car 66 for Blackbird Racing also listing Roger Schneider as the crew chief and Blake Miller as the chief mechanic. Puzzled, Luz wondered how Schneider and Miller could work for two teams at the same time.

"Jeff, do they ever make any mistakes when they print up these lists?" she asked. "Schneider is listed as the crew chief, and Miller as the chief mechanic, but I thought Miller was the crew chief and Schneider the team manager."

"Sometimes team members do double duty. It could be that Schneider is both the crew chief and the team manager. And there are some special contingency awards given out after the race based on how a team qualified and/or how the car finished. Maybe Schneider wanted to give Miller a chance to be recognized, or maybe Schneider wanted a shot at some of that extra money."

"So can a crew chief work on two teams at once?" Luz asked, continuing to study the pages.

"When a team has a backup car, sometimes the crew chief does double duty during qualifying, but during the race that would be hard on everyone. The crew chief normally communicates with the driver during the race and makes all the calls on the pit stops. Usually the crew chief and driver work together. Some have worked together since they were teenagers racing go-carts."

"If a crew chief goes to another team, does the driver go too?"

"Not always. Sometimes it's the other way around, unless a driver wants a change or they disagree. Some crew chiefs stay with a driver until he wins, and then they find another rookie to make into a winner. Others stick together like glue. Some fight like cats and dogs. A race team is like a family, with a lot of the same dynamics," Jeff said as they reached the parking lot labeled the Red Lot, next to the garage area.

Once they were parked, Jeff leaned over the seat to grab a folding umbrella, then rooted through the center console glove box and handed Luz a lanyard with a plastic card hanging from it.

"Wear this for right now to get into the garage area. From there we'll take the golf cart to credentials. It's easier to get around the speedway in that than in a car."

Luz pulled the chain over her head so the tag was visible over her red jacket. Jeff carried the donut box and his briefcase. As they walked by the security detail, know as the Yellow

Shirts, all three of the old men dressed in yellow rain slickers carefully looked her over, checking her credentials and her compliance with the dress code. As they waved her through into the fenced garage area, Jeff told them, "She's with me. Now, y'all will be seeing a lot of her. She's a friend of Clint and Michelle Amberson, and she'll be checking up on things for them while Clint's recuperating from his stroke," he said in his heaviest Texas drawl.

"Oh, well, is that so? Pleased to meet you, Miss," said one of the Yellow Shirts, tipping his gimme cap to her. "Anyone who is a friend of Clint Amberson is a friend of mine. If you need any help, you come find me."

The other two men tipped their hats and smiled, nodding at Luz. Before Jeff introduced her, she felt they viewed her as an enemy intruder. Now they treated her like an old friend who had been a member of the same club for years.

When they walked into the garage area, Jeff pointed out Firestone, to the left, where stacks of tires were mounted on rims waiting for each team to collect them for use later in practice. To the right was Indiana Oxygen, its doorway filled with the nitrogen canisters used to fill tires and operate the air jacks on the car. Directly in front of them were four rows of buildings, the first three labeled with a large letter: A, B, and C. The last row was barely visible from the entrance to the garage area. It housed suppliers, the pressroom, gift shops, and concession stands. Opposite that building were grandstands crowned by luxurious corporate suites.

Jeff led them to the left, between the first two buildings, C and B. Each garage space was about fifteen feet wide and about twenty feet long. Equipped with a standard-size heavy-duty metal garage door to allow for easy access to the cars, each garage also had a separate steel security entrance to allow team members to go in and out when working behind closed doors. The driveway running between the buildings was close to four cars wide, about forty feet. Above some of the garage doors were long two-foot-wide signboards in the livery colors of the cars, with decals of major sponsors displayed prominently along with the car number and qualifying speed. A drain ran down the middle, catching rainwater as it flowed off the two buildings. Jeff walked up to the third security entrance on the left and punched in a code, and the two entered the garage space for Harwood Racing.

CHAPTER 7

As the door opened, Luz saw the mechanics, all in the same uniform, hovering around the rear of the car, like bees swarming around a hive. When the door slammed shut, they all looked up. "Hey, Jeff! How ya doin', Jeff? Mornin', Jeff." These morning hellos were sprinkled with Texas accents. When they spied the pink-and-white box, they slowly followed Jeff to the workbench at the back of the garage.

"Good time for a break," said a paunchy fellow with a handlebar mustache who was reaching into the donut box. He was Tommy James, the tire specialist on the Harwood team.

"It's only seven-fifteen. When did you start, five in the morning?" Jeff countered.

"Now, boss, you know we start the minute we get here," Tommy said with a smile.

"Start what? Drinking coffee? Telling stories about the knight fighter you picked up last night?" Jeff laughed as he poured sugar into his coffee.

"Are you, by yourself, gonna use all five pounds of the sugar I bought? I hoped it would last at least half the month," snapped a skinny guy named Jay Jennings, the team engineer, who wore his short black hair parted on the side. Grabbing the sugar shaker away from Jeff, Jay continued, "You're on rations, son."

Luz joined them, leaning on the bench out of the way. The mechanics, seated on plastic lawn chairs, sipped coffee and munched on donuts. She watched everything, realizing how much this reminded her of the computer jocks she knew in college. Even though she stood there for over ten minutes, no one said hello to her. She'd had the same experience her first day at Emerson York. If they ignored her, maybe she would go away and leave them alone, content in their male-dominated world.

While she waited, Luz looked around the garage. Along the perimeter were red, rolling toolboxes, each one open, immaculately clean and organized, the tools lined up like surgical instruments. On one of the workbenches, a three-inch-thick notebook was open to a page of diagrams. One of the mechanics carefully compared the part he held in his hand to what he saw in the book. In front of one of the garage doors was the Indy car they were working on when she and Jeff walked in. In front of the other garage door was a rectangular metal box lying flat on the floor. It appeared to be made of thick steel, about sixteen feet long by eight feet wide and four inches deep. Two ramps led up to the box from the garage floor. Luz remembered seeing something like it at Clint's shop in Boerne. As she walked towards it to get a better look, Jeff touched her forearm and guided her to the center of the garage space. "You can look at the setup pad later, when someone can explain it to you," he said. "Now it's time to meet the guys."

Jeff tapped a screwdriver against one of the toolboxes to get everyone's attention.

"Now that we've all eaten a little something and taken away that early-morning cranky feeling, I want you to meet Luz Dane. She is overseeing the Amberson race team while Clint is recovering from his stroke and Michelle is at home caring for him. Hopefully he'll make it for the race. In the meantime, I promised both Clint and Michelle I'd do what I could to help Luz. I expect the same from you fellas too."

Luz watched as all faces turned towards her. A few rolled their eyes when Jeff mentioned helping her. She had gotten the same response when she started at Emerson York. Luz was in all-male territory; she wasn't wanted there. She knew the rules: listen, ask questions, triangulate, and watch your back.

"Joe Kerr is our crew chief," Jeff said. "He works with Christi Cole when she's racing." A tall blond guy tipped his hat to her, his Dutch boy haircut swinging when his body moved.

"You've already heard from Tommy James, our tire man. He never thinks we get enough coffee breaks." The beefy man with the handlebar mustache toasted her with his coffee cup to say hello.

"And the guy who is our adopted mother, Jay Jennings, will keep track of every teaspoon of sugar I use this month. He should have been an accountant, instead he's our engineer." The tall lanky sugar monitor waved hello.

As Jeff finished the introductions, the security door opened and two people walked in. One was a petite girl, about five foot two. She had short platinum blond hair and a face like a pixie, with fair skin and green eyes. The other was a fair man about the same height, with brownish red hair and brown eyes. Both were slim, with broad shoulders for their size. Each was carrying a helmet and a workout bag. They were chattering to each other, using words like "loose in the corners," when they saw Jeff waving at them.

"Just in time! Luz Dane, may I present my drivers, Mark Miller and Christi Cole."

Luz and Christi smiled at each other. Luz was thankful there was another woman inside at the track. Christi came up to shake her hand.

"Nice to meet you. Welcome to the show. I'm a rookie this year. I've been racing Indy Lights for the last few years, and Jeff is giving me my big break," Christi said.

She looked at Jeff like she had a huge crush on him.

"Let me know if you have any questions. Some of these guys I've known most of my life. I'll do what I can to help you."

"Thanks. This is my first day. Jeff is showing me around, but I may need some help later. I really appreciated the offer."

Just as she started to ask Christi a question, Jeff walked purposefully over to them and touched Luz on the shoulder to get her attention. "I've planned a short team meeting before we get your credentials, just fifteen minutes or so. You can sit in on it if you want."

Overhearing Jeff's invitation, Joe Kerr, the crew chief, asked, in a serious tone, "What about our speed secrets? Do you really think she needs to know those? What if she's really a spy?"

Stifled laughter broke out into huge guffaws as Luz turned to Jeff with a perplexed look on her face.

"What speed secrets? We don't have any speed secrets, unless you count that runner who helps push the car onto the track after each pit stop," Tommy James said.

Joe Kerr was red in the face from laughing. He patted Luz on the back. "You must be a good sport, Luz, since our inside jokes don't bother you at all." He shook her hand and smiled. "Yes, ma'am. Luz Dane, you ought to do just fine here at the speedway. Why don't you have a seat here while we have our meeting?"

Joe found a chair for her to sit in and placed her backpack on the workbench behind her. Luz sat down, and everyone else settled into a comfortable spot. Some people perched on stacks of tires; others leaned against the workbenches or sat in chairs. All paid close attention to Jeff. Some even took notes.

Jeff led the meeting with humor, praise, and constructive criticism. After each team member reported on his work, he took questions, which included hands-on demonstrations on the car. The meeting ended with his marching orders and words of encouragement.

Looking around the room, Luz watched the team members start their assignments and noticed the smiles as they worked together. Jeff was a great leader, with a common touch that made his crew members feel respected and comfortable. She felt happy she had met this fine group of people.

BARBIE O'CONNOR

CHAPTER 8

To get to the Amberson team garage, Jeff walked across the driveway that ran between the buildings and into a hallway that cut through building B.

"The men's and ladies' rooms are in these hallways. I'll meet you outside, between B and A buildings, near the Amberson garage spaces. See ya in a minute." Jeff slipped into the men's room.

Luz took advantage of the opportunity to look at the women's facilities. Inside she found cinder-block walls, a large shower with dressing area, two stalls, and two sinks. As she checked her hair and applied lip gloss, Christi Cole came in, carrying the bag she had with her earlier.

"How do you like our fancy dressing room?" Christi asked, scrunching up her nose. "Most of the male drivers just dress in a corner of the garage, but somehow I don't feel comfortable doing the same."

Laughing, Christi sat on the bench that ran along the wall opposite the sinks, and pulled her Simpson driving shoes out of her bag.

"I'm surprised they have facilities for women at all, much less a shower," Luz said.

"The speedway owners are very progressive. Each of the three buildings has this same setup. This is the only sports facility in America I've ever seen where the men have to wait in line for the restroom, instead of the women," Christi said. Luz giggled, thinking of how many times she missed the beginning of the second half of a ball game because the restroom line was too long.

"Maybe we can get together sometime to have a bite to eat," Luz said.

"Yeah, that would be great. Maybe next week, once I get through with rookie orientation."

"Okay, I'll check with you then. See ya later. Good luck!"

Luz left the restroom and followed the hallway to the next garage building. She saw Jeff waiting for her outside. The hallways in each building provided a shortcut to get from one building to the next.

Exiting the hallway, Luz and Jeff turned right and found themselves in front of Amberson Racing. Four signboards displayed the sponsor names and logos of the Amberson teams. All four of the garage doors were closed. Looking through the window of the middle security door, Jeff saw people inside. When he waved, no one responded, so he knocked on the door. A few minutes later a balding man with a substantial beer belly and a face like a bulldog's opened the door.

"Look what the cat dragged in," he said. He was wiping his hands on a shop rag, which he stuffed in his back pocket. He extended his right hand to Jeff, chuckling. They shook hands, then gave each other a big bear hug.

"Sid, I didn't know you were with Amberson now," Jeff said loudly, and then he turned to Luz. "Luz, I'd like you to meet an old racing buddy of mine, Sid Fury. Is Roger here?"

Wiping his hands on his pants, Sid extended a hand to Luz apologetically. After she shook it, he pointed to the back left corner of the garage, where two partitions made a small room in the corner.

"Nice to meet you. If you're looking for Roger, he's back there, probably on the phone. I know he'll be glad to know a pretty girl is waiting for him." Sid sniggered as he walked away.

Luz thought about how much this reminded her of an investment firm. She was just another pretty face, someone they could flirt with and push around, or so they thought. Luz felt an undercurrent of hostility as she waited. What she saw of racing piqued her curiosity. She knew there was more to it than was readily apparent.

As she waited for Roger Schneider, Luz looked around the garage. It was obvious more money was spent here than at Harwood Racing. Instead of only two garage openings, this team took up four garage spaces. The wall partitions had been removed between the different spaces, making one large room that seemed long enough to be a basketball court. The team colors—red, white, and black—were displayed in banners touting different sponsor names and logos. Cardboard cutouts of the team drivers were positioned strategically behind the cars in each garage space so they would be visible to the public when the doors were opened. At one doorway was a small monitor that replayed the team story, complete with rousing Sousa marches. Behind it was an Indy car painted with the team livery of Barbar beer, looking ready for race day. A cardboard cutout of driver Matt Locke branded with his Twitter handle and Facebook page was positioned to the right of the doorway. This was an organized marketing machine that made the most of every opportunity to sell their sponsors' products.

Luz thought it was strange that the image of Matt Locke showed him in a yellow-and-white driving suit, completely different colors than the car, with a different sponsor name embroidered on the uniform. She jotted down a note to herself to check the sponsor contracts and then coordinate these promotions with the marketing people for both the fan club and the team.

Just then a loud voice rose from behind the partition in the corner. "That's the way I want it, so do it the way I tell you. Don't make me tell you again!"

With each sentence the voice grew louder. Whoever was talking was not a happy man. From behind the partition came a stocky man, about five foot ten, with brownish-black hair and a matching mustache trimmed closely above the top lip. The mustache made him look like a plumper version of Hitler. His eyes were brown and looked worried. Wringing his hands, he approached Luz, Jeff, and Sid.

"You must be Luz Dane. I understand you are here to see

me? Is this about the cocktail party where you want my drivers to make personal appearances?" Schneider asked.

Luz shook her head no, but he continued, "Please understand we make those arrangements at least a year in advance, and I don't think we can make any exceptions at this late date."

Before Luz could say a word, he turned around and walked away.

"Mr. Schneider, um, I think you may have me confused with someone else," Luz said in a firm but quiet voice.

With an audible sigh, he turned back towards her. "Please understand, Miss Doe, I am a very busy man. I have two cars to get out on the track within twenty minutes, over fifteen men to supervise, and a myriad of problems to resolve before then. The owner of this team is not available now, and all this responsibility is on my shoulders. I don't have time to deal with you," he concluded emphatically.

Luz listened intently, watching the frustration expressed by Schneider's hand movements as he pointed to the cars and the men and hunched his shoulders to show the weight of his responsibility.

"Didn't anyone call you and let you know I was coming?" Luz asked.

"Look, I already told you, I'm busy," Schneider said, his face red as a beet, like a balloon ready to explode. He strode towards the door. "I can't be bothered with you now."

The door slammed behind him.

Luz looked after him, puzzled, wondering what was going on.

"Gee, I'm sorry he was so rude," Sid said. "He's normally

not like that. But he's under a lot of stress right now. One of the car's not running right, and I guess he's a little edgy."

Luz raised her right eyebrow. "A little edgy? I'd hate to see him when he's really upset."

Glad she wasn't a sponsor representative looking for a chance to spend the company advertising budget on a decal on an Amberson race car, Luz felt Schneider had acted like a narcissistic jerk.

"C'mon, Luz. We'll come back later. Let's get your credentials," Jeff said, cupping her elbow in his hand and leading her towards the door.

As she left the quiet, darkened garage, Luz was surprised by the bright sunshine, after the early morning rain and wind. She squinted and put on her sunglasses. With the change in the weather, teams towed their cars to the pit road in their brightly colored livery while the fans gathered around the garages that were still open. One by one, the doors closed as the remaining cars were towed to the track. And the crowds followed, looking forward to the engines starting once again on opening day.

Jeff led the way back towards Harwood Racing through the hallways that cut through the garage buildings. Luz was lost in her own thoughts, preoccupied by the puzzle of the yellow-and-white driver's suit. She wondered if Matt Locke was a driver of the car for Blackbird Racing: that would explain the mismatched driver's suit. Checking the entry sheet she'd looked at earlier might reveal if he was the driver of the number 66 car.

Then she heard Jeff's voice. "Beau Williams will take you

to the credential office. Practice starts at eleven, and the team likes me to be on the track when the car is out."

"Sure, Jeff, you've been great! We're not on the same team, and you've spent all morning with me. Thanks for all your help."

"I'll see you later, probably out on the pit road. Make sure Beau shows you where everything is. Once you get your credentials, that silver badge will let you in almost anywhere. So I expect to see you this afternoon. I promised Michelle I'd get you through your first day safely."

At the end of the building, they walked by a long row of motorcycles parked next to the chain-link fence separating Gasoline Alley from the motor home parking area. Harleys, Ducatis, BMWs, and Buehls were lined up like a row of showgirls decorated with the fancy paint schemes and shiny chrome accessories every rider dreams of. These bikes were a worthy distraction from the race practice on the track.

As Luz and Jeff approached the Harwood garage, the wide bay door was open. Fan access was limited by crowd-control barriers: the barriers' elastic arms stretched across the wide doorway, allowing the curious to peer into the inner sanctum of Indy Car racing, the garage. Inside the doorway was a life-size cutout of Christi Cole dressed in her blue-and-white ABC Mobile driver's suit. Beside it was a table covered with a black-and-white-checkered tablecloth and strewn with brochures. The long driveway separating the garage buildings looked like an open-air street market lined with displays in all the colors of the rainbow.

"The guys are packed to go out," Jeff said, taking a look inside the ice chest sandwiched between tires and tool chests on the cart awaiting a trip to the pits.

Jeff beckoned to a tall, olive-skinned man who was closing the heavy steel doors to secure the garage while the team was on the track. "Beau, please use your charm to help Luz get her credentials. Since the women in that department find your Cajun accent charming, the two of you will be back in no time."

Beau chuckled as he recited his laundry list of responsibilities. Jeff knew the two of them would get along fine. Jeff turned towards Gasoline Alley, where he hitched a ride on a cart going out to pit road.

Beau motioned Luz over to a golf cart with six seats: two in front, two in back facing forward, and another two facing backward.

"You ever driven one of these things?" Beau asked Luz.

"Yeah, an electric one, at one of those charity golf events the company I work for sponsors," Luz answered.

"Then you'd better drive. It's easier to find your way around if you've driven there yourself."

Beau handed Luz the keys and walked around to the passenger side.

"I want you to back this up just a little ways, then pull it forward to edge of the building, then turn left and go through the gate that leads out to the transporters."

Luz followed his instructions, the cart making its *beep-beep-beep* sound as she backed up.

They drove through the chain-link gate she remembered from earlier. "This is the same way I walked in this morning," she said.

"Once you pass all these transporters, turn right. Now stay right. Watch it—some guys come around from the other side and they cut it close. We don't want to have a wreck before we get you to the track."

As he said this, up ahead, Luz saw another cart darting around the big transporter truck.

"See what I mean?" said Beau.

She made it through the turn and approached the main road through the infield.

"Which way?" Luz asked.

"Left, and in another hundred yards turn left again, to-wards the track. The tunnel under the track is the fastest way to the other side. If you were going to the FanFest, the medical center, the motor homes, or the museum, you'd turn right."

It had become a balmy, sunny day, and cars lined up to enter the infield parking area. As Luz turned on the drive leading to the tunnel, pedestrians crossed the road sipping drinks, holding children by the hand, and carrying coolers. Closer to the tunnel, Luz heard the engines thunder as the race cars started. Looking ahead, she saw a pedestrian tunnel, with walkways at the sides for foot traffic and two lanes barely big enough for golf carts in the middle.

"Keep right, just like you do when you're driving at home. I was with this English guy here once, one of the engine reps, and he started to go left, like in England. He almost ran into another cart with some big shots on it. Lucky we didn't." Beau grinned.

As they drove under the track itself, Luz heard the *thump-*

thump of the cars passing over her head. The high-pitched engine whine sounded muffled, like it was wrapped in cotton. As she came out the other side, Beau told her to turn left again, as they drove underneath the outside stands edging the front straightaway and Georgetown Road. As they came out from under the stands, near the first turn of the oval track, Luz saw a mirrored building in front of her slightly to her left, with a fleet of golf carts parked in front.

Beau led her toward the door over to the left, where another Yellow Shirt was sitting and reading the paper. Beau waved and greeted him.

"Turned out to be a pretty day, didn't it?" Beau said, opening the door for Luz.

"Yep, looks like they'll get a few laps in today after all. This morning I was sure those cars would stay in the garage all day. But not now, not with the sky clearing this way. Where ya going?" asked the older man, resting his paper on his paunch, looking straight at Luz, but asking Beau.

"Credentials. She's with the Amberson team. Meet Luz Dane."

Luz shook hands with the old man, who smiled and said, "Clint and Michelle—great people. What a shame about his stroke. You let me know if I can help you. My name's Buck Marshall. Be careful, now, and good luck. You'll slip right in; the line is short."

When they reached the counter for team credentials, Beau asked to speak with the head of the department, Gena Newman. An attractive brunette came out of one of the side offices, wiping her fingers on a paper napkin and swallowing before she introduced herself.

"Hi, I'm Gena Newman. I heard you specifically asked for me." She smiled.

"Sorry to interrupt your lunch," Beau said. "Luz here is new to the Amberson Team. She's watching over things for Clint."

Gena listened attentively, looking from Beau to Luz. Without saying a word she pulled out a file, opened it, and asked, "So how are Clint and Michelle? Heard he'd had a stroke."

"Yes. Hopefully they'll be here for the race, assuming Clint's doctor okays it. Right now he's under strict orders for bed rest and supervised exercise," Luz told her.

"That'll drive that old buzzard crazy," Gena said. "Clint was only happy here when he was out on the pit road. Hated to be in the stands or up in the suite hobnobbing with the sponsors."

Luz handed her the envelope from Michelle with the liability forms, credential documents, insurance papers, medical forms, and a notarized letter giving Luz power of attorney in all things regarding the team: everything she needed to establish herself at the speedway.

"So how were you so lucky to get this job?" Gena asked in a gently sarcastic tone, emphasizing the word "lucky."

"I've known Clint and Michelle for years, as friends and as clients. When this happened, they turned to me. I spent a little time going over some things. The team is so important to Clint, and, well, I couldn't say no. Besides, it will be an interesting challenge. If you have any helpful hints, or if there is anything you think I ought to know, I'd sure like to hear from you," Luz said earnestly.

Gena looked at Luz directly, paused as if she was about to

say something, and then stopped, looked at Beau, and looked down at her papers. Luz waited.

Finally Gena said, "Let me see what you've got in the way of paperwork."

"I have so many forms that look alike. I think I've signed all of them and completed the ones requiring more information."

"Looks like everything is here. Let me see . . . Oh, wait, there's something missing, something you may want to read later and bring back to me this week, or later tomorrow. And there's one final thing." Gena went back into her office, and came back out in about five minutes. "Here's the silver badge. It will get you in anywhere, except the competition's garage, unless you're invited," she said wryly. "Roger Schneider picked up the twenty-five sponsors' credentials and signature sheets for Amberson. For a fee any other guests or dignitaries can purchase bronze badges at the ticket sales counter next door that allow access to the garage area everyday but race day. There are some other things you may want to call Michelle about, so take a look at all this when you're through for the day. I put my number in there in case you have any questions. Feel free to call me," she said, looking directly at Luz, an easy smile on her face.

"Okay, thanks for your help. See you later," Luz replied, tucking the envelopes under her arm before she turned to walk out the door. Beau was flirting with one of the other clerks, and they were laughing about some story he had told her. Luz waited outside in the sunshine in the golf cart until he came back out.

"Hey, we're not finished yet. We've got to check on a table

for the banquet," Beau told her.

"When is the banquet?"

"It's always the night after the race, usually the Monday night of Memorial Day weekend. Jeff said to check the reservation for the Amberson table. Needs to be paid ahead of time. Michelle usually does that, but we have to be sure."

He led her down a long hallway past the credentials office, past the Safety Patrol counter, where the security staff of men and a few women checked in and received their yellow shirts and their list of rules and regulations for this year's race. Beau and Luz turned left and walked over to the ticket area. He waved to a young blond woman sitting at the third desk behind the counter. She came up to the counter. "What are you doing here, Beau? Why aren't you out at the track?"

"I'm here doing a favor for Jeff Harwood, and Clint and Michelle Amberson. Paula Everett, meet Luz Dane. She's new to the Amberson team. Paula is the assistant department head for ticket sales."

"What can I help you with?"

"Has Amberson reserved a banquet table this year?" Beau asked.

"I was just looking at those records when you walked up. They have a table reserved and already paid in advance. Oh, Luz, let me get the Amberson suite tickets for you and the other block of tickets on the front straight, near the start-finish, that Michelle insisted on buying," Paula said, as she riffled through a file cabinet behind her and pulled out two large manila envelopes, both labeled "Amberson."

"Great! I have some other things to go over with Michelle,

so she'll be glad to know I have them in hand."

Luz added the two new envelopes to the one she'd picked up at credentials and jotted a note on the front.

"You've got quite a lot of envelopes there. Here's a rubber band so you can keep them all together," Paula said with a grin.

"Thank you! I'll see you around." Luz and Beau left the counter.

They walked by the main entrance as a big group entered the building. Squeezing through the crowd, they walked down the long hallway, and out the door, saying goodbye to their friendly Yellow Shirt.

"Bye, Buck. See you next time."

CHAPTER 9

As they hopped on the golf cart, Luz said, "Beau, thanks for helping me find my way here, and for getting Paula and Gena to help me. Being an owner of one of these teams sure involves a lot of paperwork. These envelopes are packed full." She placed the stack on the seat between them. "Do I go back the same way I came? Or is there some shortcut?"

"Go back the same way. See if you can do it without my help," Beau challenged her.

Luz drove out of the golf cart parking lot and found her way around the tents, under the stands, and back through the tunnel that ran under the track. When she got to the inner loop road, she made a right turn, and soon they reached the lot where the transporters were lined up, one after the other. Carefully she maneuvered around the crowded curves, narrowly missing another cart going the opposite way and making a wide turn.

When they arrived at the gate where the Yellow Shirts waited, Beau prompted Luz to flash her silver badge. The men's faces lit up with smiles as she showed them. She drove into the garage area, turned left at the B building, and parked in front of Amberson Racing. As she hopped off the cart, Luz watched as a pit cart towed the blue-and-white Harwood car into Gasoline Alley towards the garage in building C.

"Is that Jeff's car?" she asked Beau.

"Yeah, looks like they're bringing it in for some adjustments to the setup. That's mostly what we do around here. Take the car out to the pits, start it, run it around for a few laps, check the tires, make a few minor adjustments, run it a few more laps, look at the engine data, talk to the driver, run it a few more laps, check the tires, and then tow it in to make major adjustments. And we do that for days."

"Sure seems like a lot of time. And sounds really tiresome," Luz commented as she watched the parade of cars through the garage area.

"We never know how race day is going to turn out, so we collect lots of data. If we qualify on a sunny day but we race on a cloudy one, we still can set up the car so it will run well no matter what the weather is like," Beau said. "Um, I know you are a bigwig with Amberson Racing, but this cart belongs to Jeff, and I want to return it to him."

Luz laughed and handed him the keys she had mindlessly pocketed moments before.

"I don't know what belongs to who at this point. Maybe you can straighten me out. I'll ride with you, if you don't mind."

Both of them rode in the cart, with Beau driving. He went

the long way around, passing the motorcycles near the fence at the edge of motor home parking. As they approached the garage, the Indy car was being pushed up the ramps onto the metal platform Luz now knew was a setup pad. Once on the pad, the car was positioned on a rectangular box that recorded the weight of each tire. With this information, the mechanics could set up the car's suspension to be the most comfortable for the driver, who could then drive faster on the oval track. After the chassis was in position, the mechanics took off their gloves and stopped for lunch.

Luz waited by the garage door while Jeff finished giving instructions to one of his crew members.

"Ready for lunch?" he asked.

"Yes, I'm starving. Where do all these crew members eat? This is a lot of people to feed at one time."

"I happen to know of a cozy bistro just around the corner, very exclusive. The chef knows me." Jeff chuckled.

"Oh, wow, I didn't think there was anything like that around here. All I've seen are the concession stands and the hamburger stop across the street," Luz replied, suddenly realizing how hungry she was.

"Follow me." Jeff turned to the left, entering one of the cross-through hallways that ran by the restroom facilities for garage building C. He took the shortcut through all three buildings and finally stopped in front of several storefronts opposite the A building. Signs on those storefronts were emblazoned with the names of the different companies housed inside: Canon, Loctite, Bosch, Bell, IBM, and a few others. Jeff opened the door to the Loctite space and ushered Luz inside.

A television in the corner aired a midday racing show. A few tables in the center of the room were filled with mechanics dressed in their different multicolored uniforms. On one table by the door were cans of various soft drinks arranged in rows, plus plastic cups and a bucket of ice. Along the side wall, directly in front of the door, was a counter where a hot dog machine toasted buns and heated plump wieners. Behind another counter, opposite the door, was a mustachioed man with a mop of dark hair who was trading quips with the different team members stopping by to pick up a cookie or two on the trays in front of him. Shiny new tools were on display on a wall rack behind him, tempting the diners as they came in for lunch.

Helping himself to a paper plate, placing two buns and then meat on them, Jeff turned to Luz, paper napkin over his arm, like a waiter, and said, "And what will you have, miss? Mustard, catsup, relish, chili, or plain? As this is the specialty of the house, I recommend it highly."

"Everything but chili. And of course I want some of those chips, too," Luz said with a laugh.

"Certainly, mademoiselle. And over there"—Jeff pointed to the drink table—"we have fine cuvées for your enjoyment."

"Hmm. Which one would you recommend?" she asked.

"I prefer the one in the red can, but then again the green one is good too," he responded playfully.

"Hey, Jeff, how's it going?" yelled the Loctite man. "Sharing any speed secrets with anybody today? I hear Blackbird Racing's got a fast car. Wonder where he got all his parts? When the cat's away, the mice will play. Heh heh."

"I told you I knew the chef," Jeff said, looking at Luz. Then he taunted the fellow behind the counter: "Bruce, you never change. I can always count on you to keep me up to date with the latest goings-on around the speedway. I was going to introduce you to this fine lady, but I think I'll skip it now."

He guided her to the table the farthest away from the counter, close to the door, and said, "Let's sit over here."

They sat down, at a table with two other guys Jeff knew. The three of them exchanged comments on the track, how their drivers were running. All of them had cars in the garage on the setup pad. Luz ate her track dogs, enjoying every bite. She couldn't remember when she'd had one that tasted so good. After she finished she sat quietly, looking around. When she asked how much lunch was and where to pay, Jeff explained that Loctite provided food as a service to the mechanics.

"Sometimes I think the food is bait to get us in here to look at the tools. When I am missing a tool, or don't have the right one, everything I need is here for me. If it's not in stock, it's shipped overnight," Jeff said.

They both thanked Bruce for the grand cuisine, and he invited Luz to drop in any time.

"Remember, we have coffee and sweet rolls in the morning. Come by and I'll let you know what's happening around here," Bruce said, winking at Luz as they left.

Outside, the bright sunlight forced them both to don their sunglasses.

"As you may have guessed, Loctite is gossip central for the garage area," Jeff told her. "Bruce knows things before anyone else. Be careful, though. He talks to everyone about everything, and he wants to know everything about everyone."

Luz looked at her watch. It was almost one o'clock.

"I wonder if I can pin down Roger Schneider sometime today. Do you think I can find him now?"

"Why don't you forget about Roger for today? It's your first day at the track. The weather is beautiful. Whatever you need to talk to him about will wait for the next rainy day. Come on out to the pit road, watch practice, and find out what really happens to make the cars run. It's a great day for it. Besides, he's probably going to be out on the track too, so maybe you'll run into him there."

Luz looked up at the robin's-egg-blue sky, squinting as she felt a cool breeze against her cheek, and laughed. "Why not? It's Saturday—I normally have the day off. Besides, I need to learn something about this sport from experience, and you are the perfect teacher."

She hooked her arm in his, and together they walked out to the track.

CHAPTER 10

On the pit cart as it towed the race cars to the pits, seated next to stacks of tires, a couple of toolboxes, and an ice chest, Luz took in the sights, smells, and sounds of the racetrack during her ride. The sunny day enlivened the crew members. With the fans in the stands enjoying the clear skies and soft breeze, the brightly dressed mechanics strutted proudly for the audience that awaited the upcoming performance in the pits. The men in the stands happily removed their shirts in the sunshine; likewise, the women in halter tops hoped for an early tan. The whine of the engines captivated the opening-day crowd as the cars flashed by at over two hundred miles per hour.

Holding a stopwatch and a clipboard, Jeff asked Luz, "Would you time and score for me?"

"Um, okay. I don't know what that is, but I'll do my best. What do I do?"

Jeff opened the clipboard, folding the cover back. The aluminum case gave her a firm surface to write on. Enclosed were fill-in-the-blank forms requiring the date, the wind direction and velocity, the air temperature, and the track temperature. Words to describe weather conditions were listed at the top as well, prompting the user to identify the condition for that particular day and time. Column headings below the top margin were labeled "lap number," "lap time," and "tire set number."

"Fill in all the blanks at the top," Jeff said. "Get the track temperature and air temperature readings from Tommy James, our tire guy, as well as any of the other information you're missing. He's the one who looks like a young Santa Claus. Sit on the scoring stand up high, where you can see turns 1 and 2, along with pit road and the front straightaway. Pick a place where you can easily watch for the car, and each time it comes around, press the button on the stopwatch and write the time down for that lap. The stopwatch is already set for this two-and-a-half-mile track.

"Okay, it sounds simple enough. Let me give it a shot."

"Great! It's easy to get distracted, so do your best to focus. Remember: pick a point to watch for the car, and focus!"

"Key word is focus. Okay."

Luz walked to the right of the scoring stand, where there were four stacks of tires. Tommy James leaned over them, looking at the grease pencil marks on the sidewalls, jotting down data in a skinny notebook he normally kept in his back pants pocket.

"Tommy, would you please help me fill in the blanks at the top of the scoring sheets? I know I need the track temperature and tire temperature and other weather-related data," Luz asked.

"Sure, I can look at the lap times while I'm helping you with the rest of it. My records serve as the backup data for later."

Tommy looked over her shoulder at the form on the clipboard and noticed that the date was already filled in, along with the overall description of the weather.

"Looks like you've already got the hang of it. Now it's time for you to get on that stand, 'cause I just heard we're about to go green,"Tommy said.

Luz looked puzzled, but climbed up to sit on the bench on the scoring stand.

"Going green signals the track is open for practice. In a race, it means drivers are permitted to go full speed, that the track is clear and ready to race. When the track goes yellow, that means caution, slow down. The red flag is used to stop the race due to rain or a serious accident."

"Thanks, Tommy."

He gave her a thumbs-up sign as he smiled, then put on his headset.

Luz stuffed her earplugs into her ears. Earlier in the day, when they fired up the engines in the garage area, Luz realized that any time spent on the track near these motors would leave her deaf if she didn't wear ear protection. From the scoring stand, she saw all of the cars lined up on pit road ready to go out. Each one was in different livery, with its crew bent over the tires, side pods, and rear of the car, waiting for the track to go green. Most of the drivers were already in the cars; helmets on, gloved hands gripping the steering wheel, ready to go out.

Others sat on the pit wall, sipped water or Gatorade, and waited for last-minute adjustments.

"Are you daydreaming already?" She heard Jeff's voice from down below. "We're about to go green. It's easier to see the car when the nose is lined up with one of the catch fence posts. Note the time quickly because you have less than a minute till you do it for the next lap. Oh, I forgot to tell you, time the pit stops when we bring in the car. We're practicing like it's the race. Make a note: the driver for these laps is Mark Miller. Later today, we'll run Christi Cole. Use a separate sheet for each driver."

Before she could answer, Jeff turned around and talked to the team engineer to review the morning's data on the computer.

"We're going green," shouted Joe Kerr, the crew chief, making a winding motion with his hand over his head where the entire team could see it.

At that moment, the sound of ten engines filled the air. A few of them initially sputtered but finally they all reached a full thundering roar. Revving the engines as they left their pit stalls and drove onto pit road, some drivers laid rubber with smooth control, leaving smoke where the car once stood. Adrenaline filled the air. Luz felt the energy everywhere around her. The crowd cheered as the cars came to life; afternoon practice was under way.

For the next hour the team followed a routine: The car ran about four to eight laps of the track, then returned to pit road. The tire man, Tommy James, took the temperature of each of the tires, talked to the adviser for Firestone tires, made notes in his little book, and passed some of the information to Luz. The team engineer, Jay Jennings, plugged a computer cable connected to a laptop into a little port behind the car's roll bar and waited for engine data to download. Joe Kerr, the crew chief, talked to the driver about adjustments to make, then removed either the front suspension cover or the engine cowling to look at some part or make some adjustment. Wet towels covered the side pods, cooling down the headers and preventing the paint from scorching during the stops. Sometimes they changed the tires, and Luz noted that in her records. As she watched for the car to come around again, Jay, with his computer, keyed in some of the numbers she had, comparing them to the data from the program. Shortly after the fifth round of laps, Jeff signaled to the crew to take the car into the garage area. He turned to Luz in the scoring stand. "The car is going in for setup changes. Why don't you take a break? Now might be a good time to visit Roger Schneider. See him sitting in the scoring stand in pit row near the Gasoline Alley opening to pit road, where the red-and-white Barbar Beer car is in its pit stall? I'll give you a lift."

Jeff helped her down from the scoring stand and took the clipboard out of her hand. "You won't need this while you talk to him, but I'll need it to make changes to the car. We'll be back out on pit road in about half an hour. Don't go away. I still need your help."

He smiled and walked around to the driver's side of the pit cart. Luz sat next to him, feeling the cool breeze on her face as they drove.

Right in front of the Amberson pit, he stopped. "Here you

go. See you in a little while."

Luz stopped to talk to the Yellow Shirt who was directing traffic. He motioned Jeff into Gasoline Alley and took a break to talk with her.

"You're new here, right? Are you with Jeff's outfit or what? I'd heard you're helping Clint and Michelle, so give me the real story."

"I'm helping Jeff today, since he's kind enough to give me an orientation. Mr. Schneider's been difficult to talk to, but that's why I'm here now. Hopefully he'll have time for a little chat before the day is through. See ya!"

Luz waved as she walked the fifteen feet to the pit wall and slowly climbed over it, careful not to sit on the wall's chalky top, which left many an imprint on the dark black pants most of the team members wore. She hoisted herself up the scoring stand and sat next to Roger Schneider, who leaned down the opposite direction talking to his tire man.

"I don't care what the problem is with the new compound, and I don't care that everyone is having the same problem," Schneider shouted. "It's your job to figure out the tire stagger so we can get the speed up." His yelling could be heard over the engines as the few cars left on the track continued to practice. When he sat up, he bumped into Luz.

Surprised, he said in an imperious tone, "And what are you doing here? What do you want?"

Luz felt a visceral surge of fear. Her gut was usually right about people, and it was telling her Roger Schneider was a bad guy. How could Clint and Michelle work with a man this self-important and egotistical?

"I really want your autograph, Mr. Schneider. Clint and Michelle Amberson have told me so much about you, and of course they send their regards."

Luz controlled the tone of her voice, but sarcasm crept into the last comment.

He looked at her with confusion. Hesitantly he asked, "H . . . how do you know Mr. and Mrs. Amberson?"

So it was Mr. and Mrs. Amberson? Luz wondered if that was for her benefit or if that was how he really addressed them. He certainly was a bit more contrite than a few moments before.

"I've worked with Clint and Michelle for years. You obviously don't remember me. I'm Luz Dane. I met you in Orlando, at the Disney World race."

She held out her hand for him to shake. Schneider didn't budge. He kept looking at her searchingly.

"Still confused? Let me see if I can help. Mr. Amberson had a stroke. So since they needed someone in place to mind the store here at Indy they asked me, their trusted financial adviser, to do the job until Clint feels better."

Luz thought she heard Schneider gasp. Then again, she was wearing earplugs, and there was a lot of engine noise around—maybe she was mistaken. She continued, "You know, help you out, and make sure everything is on the up and up. Be their personal liaison at the track until they arrive." Luz watched for his reaction.

Schneider kept staring at her. Finally, he sat up straight and said, "What makes you think you can possibly represent Clint and Michelle Amberson? This must be some kind of joke. I represent Clint and Michelle Amberson wherever and whenever I damn well please."

Luz was surprised by his response. Maybe he was trying to scare her away. But from what?

"Look, Roger. I'm not going to take your job away from you. I'm only here to look over things, observe things. Very simple, this is a great holiday for me. Let's be friends," Luz said casually, a sweet smile on her face, her hand extended again.

He ignored the hand hanging in mid-air. Incensed, he stood up and looked down at her. "I don't think we will ever be friends. I don't have time to talk to you. My secretary's at the shop most mornings, and she comes here in the afternoon to help with hospitality. You can observe. You can look over things. Just make sure you don't get in my way." With that he turned around, climbed off the scoring stand, grabbed his clipboard, and stalked into the garage area.

Luz had learned from experience that when people overreacted, it usually meant she had struck a nerve. Was Roger Schneider a self-absorbed jerk with an overgrown sense of importance, or did he have something to hide? Luz looked at her watch. It was almost four o'clock, time for the team to come back to the track. Would the rest of the Amberson team treat her the same way, and if so, what did that mean?

Shortly the Amberson car appeared on the pit lane. The two mechanics that brought the car squinted at Luz, but said nothing to her.

"Who the bloody hell is sitting in our scoring stand?" The loud, belligerent voice she now heard belonged to a rat-faced man with thinning hair and a Cockney accent. He swaggered towards her, his bulky biceps and forearms tensed as he approached her, slamming his clipboard down on the desktop of the scoring stand. Luz jumped. He'd missed her fingers by a few inches.

"What are you doing in our scoring stand? Did you pinch anything?" Rat Face looked her up and down. He opened some of the cupboards in the back, quickly glancing at their contents, then glared at her again. "Hmm, looks like everything is here."

Luz sat calmly waiting, watching to see how the others would react. A tall, swarthy man with longish black hair and a black mustache walked up to Luz and said, "I'm Carl Robins. Don't mind Blake—he's like a guard dog. Territorial. We don't mind your sitting on our scoring stand, but our boss, he's not going to like it one bit. So you may want to come down from there. And I know he'll ask to see your credentials." Robins looked athletic, like a professional weight lifter.

"Thank you, Carl. I'm Luz Dane. I've met your boss, and I bet you're right about him."

As she spoke, Luz noticed the Harwood car moving towards its pit stall over fifty yards away, close to where the cars entered pit road from the track. She waved at Jeff, hopped off the scoring stand, and caught up with the pit cart that waited while another car edged into place in the pits. As she perched on the edge of the cart, grabbing onto a tire, she waved at her new acquaintances Carl and Blake. Blake gave her an angry look; Carl waved back.

"So, you met Blake Notson," Jeff said with a wry smile. "A real charmer, isn't he?"

"I can't figure out how all these people are on the Amberson team! These aren't the kind of people I usually find around Clint and Michelle," Luz told him, not bothering to hide her frustration.

"Some of those guys are new, like Blake. Roger hired him. Others have been around for a while, like Carl, and they like the bonuses. Everyone is looking for a good mix of people, and sometimes you get it and sometimes you don't. Blake, as the crew chief, interfaces with the drivers. It takes a prick like him to deal with a prick like Matt Locke. I'm glad I don't work with them."

CHAPTER 11

Luz clambered up the scoring stand, opened her clipboard, and prepared for the rest of the afternoon. Christi Cole waited for her turn to practice while Mark Miller ran a few laps in the car with the new setup adjustments. She joined Luz on the scoring stand, where the wind ruffled her short blond hair.

"What kind of time are they doing?" Christi asked.

"Forty-seven seconds per lap, around 217 miles per hour," Luz told her.

"Much better than yesterday. They must have made some adjustments in the setup, maybe even the tire stagger."

"I keep hearing about setup and tire stagger. What are they talking about, and why does it matter?"

"These adjustments make it easier for the driver to control the car. On an oval the left-side or inside tires sustain more wear than the right side or outside tires. Some adjustments to the suspension automatically help the car turn left. On a speedway like this, throttle control is paramount. How a driver does or does not press on the accelerator pedal determines if the team takes advantage of the natural forces of physics to move the car around the track," Christi explained.

"And what does it mean when the term 'loose' or 'push' is used?"

"When the car is loose it means the rear end wants to swing the car around, kind of like when you are driving in mud, or on slippery streets right when it starts to rain—it kind of fishtails."

"Oh. And when it pushes?"

"When it pushes, the car wants to go straight, even when you are turning the wheel to the left."

"Okay. So the adjustments to the suspension take care of those problems?"

"There are a lot of factors involved: the temperature of the tires, the temperature of the track, traffic and dirty air, how much fuel is in the car, and the crucial suspension adjustments. Taking into account your data, the dashboard data, and the suspension and setup notes we can re-create the best setup for the chassis when the weather changes," Christi said. "It's an art, not a science."

All the while she explained these details to Luz, Christi kept her eyes on Jeff, watching him converse with the chief engineer. Mark Miller climbed out of the car. Christi knew it would soon be her turn at the wheel, so she grabbed her helmet and joined the crew chief to look over his notes before her practice laps.

Jeff yelled up into the stand. "Luz, change to a new form.

Put Christi's name in the driver's slot. Fill in the rest of the blanks and be ready to start in about five more minutes." He turned away and rushed around the pit issuing staccato instructions to one crew member after the other.

After Luz readied the paperwork, she watched the rest of the cars on the track and in the pits. Looking towards the entrance to Gasoline Alley, she noticed that the red-and-white Amberson car was not on the track or in the pit box. Instead, a yellow car with a black bird on the engine cowling was in that space. Watching for the Harwood car each lap sharpened her spotting abilities, and she was sure of what she was seeing. But why would another car be in the Amberson pit box? Luz was sure it was the Blackbird Racing car she saw on the list that morning as number 66.

"Ready, Luz?" she heard Jeff ask. "You're not daydreaming, are you?"

Jeff stood to her left by the scoring stand. She had no idea how long he had been there.

"No, I was watching the other cars—so many to look at. Being here is anything but dull," Luz answered, smoothing the paper on the clipboard and resetting the stopwatch for a new series of laps.

For the next hour and a half, Luz followed the car, wrote down the times, and watched the crew as they changed tires and made adjustments to the suspension. When the car went to the garage for a slight adjustment on the setup pad, she stayed in the scoring stand to watch the Amberson pits. On a spare piece of paper she noted the lap times for the yellow car. Later the red-and-white Amberson car was in the same pit box where the yellow car had been. Luz saw the same team members, same uniforms, but different cars.

"You sure seem distracted," Jeff commented as he slid onto the bench beside her.

"I've been watching the other cars as they come in and out—noticing how the different teams work," Luz said. "I've been lucky to get your insights on the race teams. It's impressive to be here, especially when I can see how hard everyone works just to get out on the track. With the weather as nice as it is today, there's no other place I'd rather be."

Jeff looked surprised, then took a deep breath. "Thanks for the help today. The forecast is for cold and nasty weather the rest of the week, and we needed to get data for this kind of weather. We'll only be out another half hour, then you can ogle some more of the guys on the other teams."

Grinning, Jeff slipped out of the scoring stand, hopped over the pit wall, and leaned down towards the cockpit to say something to the driver. After he walked over to the crew chief, he gave the wind-it-up signal with his hand, they started the engine, and the car roared out of the pits.

As she timed the blue-and-white Harwood car, Luz noticed that the yellow Blackbird car and the red-and-white Amberson Racing car were never on the track at the same time. Either one or the other was visible, but not both.

Toward the end of the afternoon, Jeff tapped on the top of the scoring stand to get her attention. "Luz, we're calling it a day. Can you bring the clipboard to the garage when you come in? I'm going by the press room to pick up the run sheets."

"I'll go with you," Luz said as she closed up the clipboard, stowing the pencil inside.

She followed Jeff through the crowds of crew members, visitors, and Yellow Shirts who closed the pits for the day. When they reached the winner's circle, they walked across the black-and-white checkerboard flooring and through an outside arcade area bordered by gift shops and snack bars. Reaching the entrance to Gasoline Alley, Jeff and Luz waited with the crowds of fans watching the cars as they rolled into the garage area. As they stood there, the red-and-white Amberson pit cart came through towing the yellow Blackbird Racing car. Jeff watched Luz's face cloud as she turned her head to follow the car before the crossing crowds blocked her view.

At the door of the pressroom another yellow shirted man greeted them at the door and asked to see their credentials. Jeff introduced Luz and then picked up the run sheets.

Along the wall opposite the door was a whiteboard. Listed on it in order of the fastest speed were the drivers, their teams, and their speeds in miles per hour. The board also held a list of press conferences scheduled for the pressroom under the stands by the entrance of Gasoline Alley. Rows of long tables were set up in the room, each seat marked with the name of a different newspaper, television station, or news service. Each table had its own telephone, electrical, and computer outlet. In the center of the wall closest to the track was a magazine stand full of press kits and press releases from different teams.

The daily run sheet, the report compiling data gathered by the speedway's electronic system, listed lap times, total laps run, and total time on the track for each team was stacked on the top shelf of the stand. Also available was an entry list of all the teams and cars entered for the race, along with the names of the crew chiefs, chief mechanics, the car entrants.

Jeff handed her a copy of each. Luz glanced at the timing and speed sheet and noticed that the Blackbird Racing car ran ten seconds faster per lap than the Amberson car. Looking at the entry list, Jeff said, "It seems impossible to qualify this year, with seventy-three entries to compete against, but I know from experience that only a little more than half will try to qualify."

As they headed for the exit, Stan Green, the director of the pressroom, stopped Jeff to say hello. He invited the two of them to his office when he heard that Luz was new with Amberson Racing. Seated in his office were two avuncular men reminiscing about their past. When Luz walked in, they both stood up. Jeff made the introductions to the men: Billy Wojinski, a sandy-haired man with round wire-rim glasses that emphasized his hawklike eyes, and Carter Holland, who was graying at the temples and had a tall, trim physique.

"Billy has won more races here than any other living driver, and Carter was his crew chief when he drove for the Plains Oil team. Luz is an old friend and now employee of Amberson Racing," Jeff said.

"I haven't seen Clint around the speedway yet. Is he waiting for next weekend to show his ugly face around here?" Stan Green asked.

"He had a stroke a couple of weeks ago. Michelle is with him in Texas. Hopefully he'll be able to be here for the race," Luz said somberly.

"How come nobody called to tell us?!" Carter Holland exclaimed. "We'd do anything for them."

"You must be a pretty special lady for those two to ask you to come here for the month. The least we can do is be of help to you while you are here," Billy said, his eyes piercingly direct behind his glasses.

Luz sighed with relief. Someone besides Jeff and his team wanted to help her instead of challenge her authority or competency.

"I need someone to explain the qualifying process to me. It would be nice to get a clearer idea of how the teams work. I keep hearing all these new words, and I don't really understand what they mean," Luz said, trying to describe the gaps she felt as an outsider looking in. "Jeff has been great explaining things so far, but he has his own team to run."

"When do you want your first class?" asked Billy. "You gonna be around tomorrow afternoon? Would that work for you, too, Carter?"

"Fine with me. It sounds like this lady needs our help sooner rather than later."

"Tomorrow would be perfect," Luz said. "Where do we meet and when?"

"Let's meet here, right before happy hour, say around four-thirty in the afternoon. We can watch practice and go over the info you'll need to know before qualifying."

"Sounds great. See you then." Luz shook hands all around. "I'll catch up with you fellows tomorrow," she told Billy and Carter. Before she left the director's office, Luz thanked him profusely for introducing her to the two racing stars, now her new tutors.

Throughout the visit in pressroom office, Jeff watched silently while Luz conducted business on behalf of her old friends. With her candor, and without Jeff's help, she had won over two of the crustiest old buzzards at the speedway.

When they left the pressroom, it was crowded. Many reporters filed their stories at the last minute before they dashed to the cocktail parties and dinners given by the sponsors and teams working for a mention of their brand name in a story. In the stands, the cleaning crews collected trash in preparation for the next day.

As they walked back to Jeff's garage, Luz asked him again, "Why would anyone have extra numbers and backup cars too?"

"Before qualifying, different cars respond to different setups and weather conditions. A driver is looking for the best car for the track. Sometimes a team has more than one major sponsor; each one wants their livery exclusively on the car and the fire suits. A major sponsor expects to have a car in the race, so a second car acts as insurance. Once a car qualifies, it doesn't matter who the driver is for the race, but if you wreck a qualified car during practice before the race and you can't fix it by race day, then it doesn't run at all, and one of the provisional cars starts. You can't bring another car in as a replacement. Only qualified cars can race on race day. Complying with sponsorship contracts sometimes requires getting more than one car qualified to run the race."

"But it says here on the list that Harwood only has one car. What happens if it's wrecked in practice?" Luz asked him before they walked into the garage space.

"Unless I can put it back together, I'm out of luck. But I don't want to think about that now. There is a saying in racing: To finish first, first you must finish. It's very simple. Right now, we are working on qualifying, and getting everything together so we can race."

Jeff opened the door to the garage, where the crew compared notes, looked over the tires, and talked to the drivers.

Jeff turned to Luz. "Look, I really appreciate your help today. Usually I stay here till the garage area closes at eight. Would you meet me at the Union Jack for dinner around eight-thirty?"

He opened the clipboard he'd taken out of her hands and scanned the numbers.

"Looks like I can read what you wrote here. We normally have a team meeting about this time, so I'm going to have to ask you to leave. The cars are at the point where it wouldn't be right for you to be here for this meeting. I hope you understand."

Luz's face had gone from elation to confusion in a single moment, but she did understand. "Yes, I know, I'm with the other guys. Let me get my pack and then I'll be on my way. Oh, wait," she said apologetically, "I need a ride home."

"Right, your rental car is in the Red Lot right outside, I forgot all about it." Jeff pulled a set of car keys from his pants pocket. "It's a red Mustang in the parking spot under the light post, should be easy to find."

Taking the shortcut between the buildings, Luz slipped into the Amberson garage and found Roger Schneider, who was in his partitioned cubbyhole. She walked in and sat down in the chair next to his desk. He was on the phone, talking loud enough for everyone in the garage to hear, so Luz figured it wasn't much of a private conversation. When she sat down he glared at her, lowered his voice, and swiveled his chair so his back was to her.

Lowering his voice practically to a whisper and cupping his hand around the phone's mouthpiece, Roger Schneider said to the receiver, "I've got company."

Luz heard a low male voice purring on the other end of the line: "Roger, just give me a second."

"Is everything set up?" Schneider asked, looking furtively at Luz. "Sorry I couldn't talk to you when you called earlier. It's been busy at the track."

"Yes, I know. All the accounts are ready at Emerson York in the names of the offshore companies I gave you earlier," said the man on the phone, his Spanish accent now clear.

"How did you do that so fast?" Schneider sounded surprised.

"I've got connections from long ago," he said, his tenor vibrating with assurance, "people who trusted me once and don't suspect a thing."

"Good. Let's keep it that way. I've got a few personnel problems here I have to take care of and I don't have time to mess with anything else. I've got to go now, and hey, I'll call you if I need anything, okay?" Schneider hung up the phone and glared at Luz as she sat in the chair looking bored.

While Schneider had his back to her, Luz had glanced over his desk, looking over different forms and letters that looked like they had been tossed there. After years of working with clients, visiting them in their homes and offices, Luz was fairly competent at reading upside down and backwards. It had paid off a few times to know what a proposal from the competition had said, or what the latest brokerage statement from another firm listed. If it was on the desk, out in the open, it was fair game.

One letter, addressed to Blackbird Racing, was from a corporate sponsor interested in their logo appearing on Blackbird's car. Another document was a copy of the car entry form, with Blackbird as the entrant. A catalogue from Simpson's was open to the page showing fire suits of different colors and design. There were pink message slips from various people, including Michelle.

On the bulletin board behind the desk, Luz saw sketches of different livery designs, all with the Blackbird Racing logo on them. A garage list posted on the board showed phone numbers, team names, and car entrant names. Amberson was at the top of the list, highlighted, with Roger Schneider's name next to it, as crew chief. Below that was Blackbird; Schneider's name was listed there too. Luz skimmed that list until she found Harwood Racing, where both Jeff Harwood and Joe Kerr were listed as contacts for the team. Out of the corner of her eye, Luz saw Schneider start to turn around as he hung up the phone. She quickly shifted her focus to him, acting bored.

"Now what brings you here?" asked Schneider icily.

"I wanted the combination for this garage, so I can come in when you and the team have your hands full," Luz said as sweetly as she could. "Also, I'd like the phone number for the shop and this garage. That way I can stay in touch." Luz smiled, doing her best imitation of a southern belle.

Schneider gave her the phone numbers and the combination to the door.

"Would you show me how the door code works, so I can make sure I know how to do it?" Luz asked. Schneider walked her outside and showed her. Luz tried it once to make sure she had the right numbers, even though she knew it could be changed at any time. Hopefully he wouldn't try a dirty trick like that, but if he did, it would tell her a lot.

"Thank you for your help, Roger. What time should I be in tomorrow?" Luz asked innocently.

"I don't care when you come in, or if you come in at all. Why they sent you here at all is unfathomable." Roger made no attempt to hide his disgust.

"Roger, I'm glad to know where I stand with you. I'll see you tomorrow. Have a good evening." Luz turned to walk out to the parking lot and drive back to her home away from home.

CHAPTER 12

That evening she left the car windows down during the short drive from her townhouse to the Union Jack, hoping the cool wind would stimulate her brain. After she went through the papers given to her by Gena Newman, Luz pondered all the possibilities. Had Roger Schneider planned to use Clint all along? Or did his team owner's illness provide an unexpected, lucrative opportunity too irresistible to ignore? Was it just the team he was using, parts and equipment, or was there money involved? Spending the evening with Jeff would be a welcome break from her intense first day at the speedway.

Turning in to the parking lot, Luz saw the restaurant jammed with customers. Racing fever spread from the speedway: everywhere she went she saw some sponsor's name and logo emblazoned on a jacket, T-shirt, or cap. When Luz walked in the door, she found a crowd waiting for tables.

Most everyone who waited had a drink in hand, creating a

party atmosphere in the waiting area. In the display case to the left of the fireplace was another show car, a purple one plastered with Hillman's Racing and Modern Faucet decals. Jeff waved to her from a booth in the elevated seating area to the right of the fireplace. Luz passed through the crowds, smiling at the few faces she recognized from the garage area. Most of the team members still wore their uniforms from the day, so the bar looked like it was scattered with confetti as everyone there laughed and chatted, letting go of the day's tension.

Jeff was kibitzing with men who worked for Simpson, sharing a joke he'd heard earlier that day. He motioned for Luz to sit down opposite him, where she could watch all the action in the bar.

Starved, Luz ordered potato skins with all the toppings and a side salad of mixed greens. She was thrilled she had survived the first day of her new adventure and ordered a celebratory margarita. Jeff had a light beer, and a burger with cheddar cheese and extra-crispy French fries.

As if he had been reading her mind, Jeff asked her, "How did you like your first day at the speedway?"

"Thanks to you I learned an incredible amount about physics, tire stagger, suspension, and how hard it is to win this race; so many factors have to come together in the right way. The only bad part of the day was Roger Schneider. He really is a chauvinist pig!"

"Enough about him—let's have a good time tonight. Remember, a race is a party," Jeff said with a grin.

Checking out the room, Luz saw the party all around her. These racers were impassioned people, full of energy, intelligence, and enthusiasm. Very much alive, very much involved in the moment. She wondered if it was the danger, the risk of death or injury, that haunted the teams, released them to laugh, joke, and take pleasure in their everyday lives.

The waitress interrupted her thoughts as she set their plates down before them. "Potato skins for the lady, and a cheeseburger for the man. Here's ketchup for those French fries. How 'bout another beer and margarita to go along with your meal?" she asked cheerfully.

Luz looked at her half-full glass and at Jeff's empty one and asked, "What time do we have to start tomorrow?" They all laughed.

"I think you can have another one. But the morning starts early tomorrow. Go ahead; bring us another beer and margarita. This is the last chance to party before qualifying." When the waitress left, they began eating in silence: neither of them had eaten since midday.

Once the edge was off her hunger, Luz asked, "So how did you get started in this business?"

"Oh, since I was a kid, I've loved everything with wheels. Rode all over Houston on my bike when I was a kid. I made my first go-cart from the engine of the family lawn mower. Rode dirt bikes when I was in college. Raced at the Austin Aquafest after I'd been to Bondurant. I just love grease under my fingernails."

He grinned at her happily and took a big bite of his burger. Luz looked down at Jeff's hands cradling the cheeseburger he was munching on, noting that his nails looked clean and manicured.

"How did you get to know Clint?" Luz took a huge bite of one of the cheesy potato skins topped with real bacon.

"One summer I was looking for work—needed tire money so I could race. He'd just started his own oil company after all those years of working for a big one, and he was looking for some young, strong guys to be roustabouts. A friend of a friend put us together, and we got along great."

"Then why aren't you running his team instead of Roger Schneider?"

"There's that name again. If I didn't know better, I'd think you had a thing for him," Jeff said. Luz scowled at him, her mouth full.

"Remember, I did work for Clint, when I met you the first time in Orlando. I was a mechanic for him then. But I didn't have the experience. Roger actually hired me. He didn't know that I had worked for Clint before in another business. Was he surprised the first time Clint came by and patted me on the back and acted so glad to see me!"

"Why your own team?" Luz asked, her shyness slowly disappearing.

"It just happened. I had a great opportunity to buy some used pit equipment, a rigged-out trailer, and a test car. After being around the garage area, I knew who could do their job and who couldn't, and I knew who would stick with me if times got tough. I even talked to Clint about it, and he helped me find my first sponsor. It all came together at the right time for me."

Luz pushed her plate to one side and sipped her margarita. Jeff dipped a long, crispy fry into the pool of ketchup on his plate. He looked at the check the waitress slipped under his plate, then he fished a couple of twenties out of his pocket. Luz grabbed her purse, opened her wallet, and took out a few bills to cover her share, but he reached across the table and put a hand on hers. "I know you can pay your own way. But I'd feel better if I took you out to dinner tonight. I like you, Luz. You've got balls. There aren't many women who could hold their own at a place like Indy. You're a team player and you're smart. I'd like to see more of you."

Their eyes met. Luz could tell he was serious. She looked down, like she was looking for something in her purse. Then she looked up to see him grinning at her.

"Can't take it, can you? Doesn't anyone say anything nice to you? Ever? If you're going to hang around me, you'll just have to get used to it. C'mon, are you ready? Let's go."

He took her hand, pulled her up out of the booth, wrapped his arm around her waist, and guided her through the crowd, out the door, and into the parking lot.

"Where's your car?" he asked. Luz pointed to a spot on the far side of the lot, under the light.

"Good. I'm glad to see you had the sense to park there under a light. It's a lot safer that way. Let's go."

With his arm around her, they walked in step across the parking lot. She pressed the button on the key fob, and the car answered with a reassuring chirp. When they reached the car, he leaned up against the driver's door, pulling her close to him. One hand at the base of her neck, he kissed her on the lips, slowly and gently. As this languid, lingering kiss ended, they parted slightly and gave each other a searching look. Then Luz leaned forward and pressed her lips to his again, her tongue searching for his. She could feel him grow hard against her as their embrace tightened. It seemed to last forever. When they parted again, both gasping for breath, Jeff said, "I could do that all night, but not tonight. I wish, but not tonight."

He opened the door for her and helped her into the little coupe. Once she was inside, he closed the door. She rolled down the window and asked, "Could I have one more kiss to go?"

"Okay. It won't be the same, but it will be something to keep me going."

He leaned his head into the car, and gave her another slow, sensual kiss. Both of them were light-headed as their lips parted.

"I'll follow you home to make sure you get in okay," he said, grasping her hand for another moment or two. He let go reluctantly, then walked towards his car.

Luz drove slowly out of the lot and down the dark streets, paying special attention to the lights and stop signs. Jeff was right behind her. When she reached her apartment complex and parked her car, he stopped behind her. She ran up to his window and gave him one last kiss before walking to her doorway. After she opened the door, Luz blew him a kiss and went inside. He sped off after she closed the door behind her.

CHAPTER 13

The next morning Luz woke early and went downstairs. While she waited for coffee to brew, she pushed the curtains aside and peeked out the sliding glass doors to the patio overlooking the retaining pond. Clouds covered the sky, and the shrubs around the patio leaned with the north wind. She put her hand against the glass and found it cold to the touch. After pouring a cup of coffee and spreading jam on her muffin, Luz carried them upstairs: she could have breakfast while she dressed for the day.

Last night, before she went to sleep, she tried to put it all together, but she was missing something. When she visited Clint in the hospital, what upset him was the article about the Blackbird Racing team. The comments she heard at Loctite were about Roger Schneider fielding his own team. The list of entrants, which she had looked at again last night before going to bed, showed Blackbird Racing and Amberson Racing sharing the same team manager and crew chief. Was Roger Schneider fielding his own team? Where did he get the money and the equipment? Or was he using the Amberson equipment, men, and money because Clint and Michelle weren't at Indy this year to keep him honest?

As she drove to the speedway, Luz realized she needed more information about standard operating procedure for a team. It seemed unusual that the Amberson team was working on the Blackbird car. Gena Newman had given her pages of information, but Luz needed an explanation about how it related to Roger Schneider, Amberson Racing, and the Blackbird team.

The turn into the speedway jolted Luz out of her ruminations. She flashed her badge twice—once at the entrance, where the Yellow Shirt recognized her from the day before, and then again, at the Red Lot, where a surprised Yellow Shirt waved her in after seeing the parking tag on the dashboard. Careful not to park near Schneider's dirty black truck, Luz left her car beneath one of the light posts not knowing whether she would leaving late again.

As she opened the door of her car, she saw Christi Cole walking off the golf course in sweats and running shoes. Christi stretched every few steps as she walked. On seeing her, Luz shouted out, "Good morning! Have a good run?"

"Yeah, about twenty minutes. It wakes me up and this helps me develop stamina. Racing is an endurance sport. You're welcome to join me anytime," Christi said. "Every week I take one really long run, and every other day I lift weights."

The two women walked into the garage area and flashed

their badges, while the Yellow Shirts admired them. They might not have been sexily clad knight fighters, but they were among the few women around, and each of them was pretty in her way.

"Will I be seeing you at the Harwood garage today?" Christi asked.

"No, I'm working at Amberson today. Hope to see you later."

After walking to the garage in building 3, Luz punched in the key code to open the door. Thankfully, it worked; at least Schneider hadn't changed it yet. It occurred to her that the same code might open the Blackbird garage if the two garages were separate; that was something she could check into on her own.

A few of the mechanics stood around doing nothing. Roger Schneider was not there. Two golf carts with the Amberson logo on them were parked outside. Luz figured she could take one, but neither had keys in the ignition, so she'd have to ask for them. Sid Fury, one of the team members who responded politely to her the day before, sipped coffee while he leaned against his toolbox.

"Sid, I'll be taking one of the golf carts outside to the credentials office. Where are the keys?" Luz asked in the most congenial voice she could muster.

"Upper drawer of the desk. I'll let Roger know," Sid said as he walked behind the partition separating Roger's desk from the rest of the garage area, opened the top left-hand drawer, and fished out a set of keys. He tossed them to her and she caught them.

Outside she found the cart that matched the set of keys she had in her hand. Remembering the route from the previous day, Luz drove out of the garage area, through the trailer lot, under the track, and beneath the stands.

At the credentials office Luz walked in the side door, held open for her by Buck Marshall, the Yellow Shirt she met the day before. "Thank you," she said.

No one was waiting in line. Most of the staffers were working at their desks. Luz walked up to the window for team credentials and waited until someone noticed she was there.

"May I help you?" asked a smiling, gray-haired woman with glasses.

"I'm looking for Gena Newman. May I speak with her, please?"

"She's back in her office—let me get her. You look more pleasant than most of the characters who come in here."

The older woman walked to the back, where several private offices were lined up next to a conference room. Gena Newman came out of her office and strolled to the front window to meet Luz. She looked at Luz expectantly. "I understand you wanted to see me?"

"Thank you for being so nice to me yesterday. I went through the papers you gave me, and there are some things I don't understand," Luz said cautiously. She continued, "Clint and Michelle are old friends of mine. I've managed their money for years, and they asked me to help them to oversee the team. I told them I don't have a clue about this business, but I didn't want to let them down, either. So if you could spend a little time with me and let me ask you a few questions, maybe you can fill in the blanks for me. Would now be a good time for you?"

When she finished, Luz realized that she was clenching her fists. Close to losing patience with her new surroundings she was acutely aware of her own feelings of frustration about her inadequacies on the job. But she wasn't a quitter, and she didn't give up easily.Gena Newman listened closely to Luz and could hear the intensity of her frustration. She found that this was someone she wanted to help, someone who was in way over her head simply because she was coming to the aid of an old friend. "I'd like to take a little break from this place. We're not busy right now. It's early yet, and everyone here can handle anything that comes up in the next hour. How did you get here?" Gena asked.

"Golf cart," Luz chirped.

"Good. I haven't been trackside so far this year. Let's get a cup of coffee and something to eat."

"Thanks. Coffee would be good right now," Luz said gratefully, adding, "My cart is right outside."

Luz passed through the double doors of the credentials office, and then went out to the parking area to start the cart. Gena slid out the back door of her office and perched on the seat. She said, "They have pretty decent coffee at Loctite, but I don't want to be overheard. Let's go to the concession stand. They have tables there, or we can drive around and talk. I don't usually get out much during race weeks. Handling all those foreign press credentials keeps me at the office most of the time."

Luz drove over to the concession stand behind the Tower

Terrace suites, next to the entrance to Gasoline Alley. She parked the cart out of the way and remembered to take the keys, so it wouldn't disappear. Since it was a bit chilly, they moved to one of the small tables inside, sitting away from most of the crowd. Luz nibbled on a chocolate chip cookie, while Gena had a cinnamon roll. Each sipped coffee while the other talked.

Gena began, "Clint having a stroke is a shame. We all thought this would be Clint's year to win. It's turned out to be the worst situation possible for that outcome. It's been an opportunity for someone to take advantage of his absence," Gena said, then took a bite of her cinnamon roll.

"What do you mean by that?" Luz asked tentatively.

"All I can tell you is what I see in my office. Some very strange things have been going on regarding credentials. Most of the Amberson team has credentials for Blackbird Racing. And that isn't normally done. Team members usually belong to one team; that way setup secrets and tire stagger data stays within the team. Occasionally someone will get mad and move from one team to another. When there are two or three cars fielded, you might find crossover on the part of the engineers, or chief mechanics, but they are still considered part of one team."

"What can I do about it?"

"I don't know that there are any rules against it, but what I'm afraid of is that Blackbird Racing, which is Roger Schneider, is using Clint Amberson. Roger puts on an innocent look, and he has a lot of friends here from the years he's worked for Clint," Gena said. "Did you look at that envelope I gave you yesterday?"

Luz nodded, but her face was puzzled. "I looked through the papers, but I really didn't understand why you wanted me to have them. Could we go through them now? I have them right here." She pulled an envelope out of her backpack.

"I didn't realize that you'd never been here before, that it's your first time, that you're a virgin at the speedway," Gena said, surprise reflected in her face. "Yes, let's look at them now."

Gena looked behind her to make sure no one was sitting too close. She took the envelope from Luz and pulled out the documents.

"You can keep these copies. Here is the list of the Amberson team, and here is the one for the Blackbird team. They're more or less identical. This document shows that Roger Schneider owns Blackbird Racing and claims he is the car owner too. Roger picked up the sponsors credentials and signature sheets for both teams; that's indicated by his signature here," Gena said, pointing. "Each team gets twenty-five credentials permitting guests or sponsors to access the pit road and the garage area. Make sure you have those for the sponsors who will be coming during the qualifying weekends. I normally give the sponsor credentials to Michelle. But since Roger asked for them, I assumed he was authorized to take them."

"Who knows? I don't know why Michelle didn't tell me more," Luz said, frustrated.

"How could she have known what would happen? Maybe there's some agreement between Roger and Clint. Schneider has been a trusted member of the Amberson team for years. Maybe he was going to quit, and because of Clint's stroke decided not to, decided he should stay on anyway. The entries had to be in by the first of April for the race."

"The deadline was April first? It seems a bit irregular, Schneider entering his own team, no sponsorship," Luz said. "It really looks suspicious, but I don't have any proof, except these copies you've given me. Thanks."

"I don't know that you have anything to thank me for yet. Read the rule book—you may find an answer there. It's hard to believe anyone would want to take advantage of Clint Amberson. He has a heart of gold." Gena smiled, putting the copies back into the envelope she handed to Luz. She stood up, wadded up her napkin, stuffed it into her coffee cup, and tossed it into the trash. "It's a shame this happened this year, this time. It's a real shame. I've got to get back. Let's go."

They got into the cart, and Luz made her way to the other side without incident, safely delivering Gena to her office door.

"Thanks for your advice and your help. I could tell something seemed 'off,' but I wasn't sure what it was. You helped me see everything more clearly, and I appreciate it."

"Call me anytime, or leave me a note, and I'll call you back after hours. Good luck. Clint and Michelle are lucky to have you on their team," Gena said as she walked back into the building. When she reached the door she waved goodbye.

Luz drove the cart to the motor home parking next to the garage area where the recreational vehicles were lined up, each parked in its numbered space. Teams served elegant meals from the tented areas off to one side of each coach, part of the sponsorship agreements that kept the race team finances in the black. Luz saw the bright red Amberson motor home, a tent to one side and racing flags flying. As she drove by, she observed that team members in both Amberson and Blackbird livery, seated at round tables, were eating fried chicken from the buffet. She drove up and down the motor home paths to look for a separate reserved spot belonging to Blackbird Racing, but she couldn't find one, so she returned to the garage area to prepare for her qualifying lessons with Billy Wojinski and Carter Holland.

CHAPTER 14

Luz grabbed her backpack from her locker and walked to the pressroom to look for a quiet place to study the rule book. She spied a space in the back where she could read while she waited for her appointment. The rule book was dry reading, and the chatter of the press corps easily distracted her. Occasionally she heard an announcement about a wreck on the track or a new sponsor for another team. Luz found herself daydreaming and thinking about the events of the day.

"Luz. Hey, Luz!"

She heard a voice saying her name. Looking up, she saw Billy Wojinski. "Hi, Billy. I must have been daydreaming."

"I think you fell asleep. What are you reading?" He turned over the rule book, open to the section on qualifying.

"Oh, no wonder. That book will put anyone to sleep. I've got to admire you, though. Few people read it, but those who do are way ahead of everyone else. Are you ready to go?"

"Yes, I'm looking forward to it," Luz said, returning the rule book to her pack. "This was duller than the material I studied for the securities exam."

"Oh, sometime I'd love to hear what you think about my little portfolio. Another time. By the end of today I want you to feel you have a strong understanding of how qualifying works. This week leading up to it can be tense for the teams and the drivers. Is your cart outside?" They walked out the door.

"Yes. Is Carter joining us?"

"Yes, he's looking over some of the run sheets so we can identify all the cars and drivers from across the track. We think the covered stands opposite the pit road are the best place to see the last hour of practice," Billy said as he spotted Carter Holland, who waited for them outside, a folder under his arms.

Carter smiled eagerly at the pair and stepped forward to shake Luz's hand.

"Good to see you again. Been busy this afternoon?"

"I caught her napping in the pressroom while reading the rule book," Billy chortled.

"The rule book! You really are serious about learning everything you can about this sport."

"Let's go—we're burning daylight," Billy said. "Luz, do you mind if I drive? We might get there faster."

"Sure. Okay with you, Carter?" she asked, giving him a wink.

"Fine with me. But I get to drive on the way back." They all laughed.

Billy drove the cart like the championship driver he was,

taking the turns as fast as he could, whipping down the path-way under the track, and swinging into a good parking place under the Paddock grandstand.

"Here we are. Let's climb about halfway up the stands for the best view of the pits, and then we'll review the qualifying rules so next weekend you'll understand everything when it starts," Billy said as he handed Luz the cart keys, just like a kid would hand them back to his mom—reluctantly but obedient-ly, not waiting to be asked.

Billy led the way to the seats that were covered and shaded from the afternoon sun. Directly across from the opening for Gasoline Alley, they sat three abreast, with Luz in the middle. As they watched the activity in the pits intently, Luz opened her pack to bring out the rule book and found the section on qualifying.

"Most of the teams are still searching for more speed for qualifying," said Carter. "From the looks of things, they are simulating what qualifying will be like, using this opportunity to test their setup."

"The chassis is qualified, not the driver or the team," Billy added. "Amberson normally enters four chassis so two drivers can race one car each, with a backup car. Never know when there might be a wreck in practice. I remember the first time I qualified here at Indy. I was nervous, biting my nails. You drive two warm-up laps, and then four qualifying laps. During the first two laps I relaxed, focused on driving the car gradually to speed. Then I'd push down on the throttle with my right foot and hold onto the edges, hoping to make it all the way around the track faster than anyone else. The hardest part of qualifying is watching for the flags on the front straightaway," he said wistfully.

Carter chimed in. "Normally the car owner and the crew chief are at the leading end of the front straightaway in the gutter between pit road and the track. Each one times the warm-up laps with a stopwatch, checking the car as it speeds up in preparation for the four timed qualifying laps. If the car isn't fast enough by the second warm-up lap, the crew waves a yellow flag to signal the driver to abort the attempt to qualify, or a green flag to tell him to go ahead and make his best attempt."

"Yeah, but by the time you see the yellow flag," Billy said, "you still need those remaining laps to slow down and make it into the pit lane. One time I was coming off the track and they had signaled another car to start their qualifying run. We almost collided as he was coming out and I was going in!"

Carter resumed: "Before a car can even begin its run on the track, it has to pass tech inspection. They measure the height, the weight, and the distance between the undercarriage and the track, and then verify the car specs meet the guidelines outlined in the rule book." He picked the rule book up from the grandstand seat and thumbed through it to find the specific section, then marked the page by turning down the corner.

"Your crew chief knows all that, but it won't hurt for you to be aware of it too," Billy said.

On either side of the opening to pit road, teams waited for the track to go green. More than twenty teams were taking advantage of the favorable weather. Most collected data during practice to determine the correct setup. The confident few ran full tank tests to determine how the car handled with their race setup, hoping the car performed as well at the beginning of the race as it would later with very little fuel to weigh it down. Every driver took into account the effect of centrifugal force on the liquid methanol that filled the fuel tank. The more minutes they practiced under different conditions, the better the results would be on race day.

Some teams tried to find the right setup for qualifying. They ran four to six laps and then came in. The team members swarmed over the car, checked tire temperatures, plugged in computers, and hoped to find a little more speed somewhere. Adjustments were made to the front wing or maybe the back wing to give it more downforce. After the tweaking and tuning, the driver sped onto the track again. Each lap was carefully timed.

Luz looked for the Amberson pits and found them three spaces to the right of the pit opening. Farther to the right, about ten pit boxes away, was the Blackbird Racing equipment, with tires stacked on the pit cart, but no team members around. The car was in the pit box, but only the driver leaned against the wall. From where she sat, Luz could not identify the person in the yellow fire suit.

"Let me look at the driver roster," she asked Carter. He handed her a sheet of paper listing the car numbers, sponsors, car owners, crew chiefs, and drivers. Luz scanned the list and found Blackbird Racing, but no driver name.

"Does it matter who the driver is?" Luz asked.

"Hell, yes! Of course it matters!" Billy laughed. "Some drivers are better than others. Some tubs are harder to drive than others. One driver might qualify a car that another driver couldn't."

"I mean, can one person qualify a car and another person drive it in the race?"

"Sure. It happens if a driver is hurt in practice. Can't remember a time it was planned that way. So many drivers are looking for rides—you wouldn't need to use someone else," Carter said thoughtfully.

Luz noticed some movement in the Blackbird pit box and watched closely while half the Amberson team walked to that pit and worked on the car. The engineer carried his laptop computer and plugged it into the chassis, while the tire guy checked his notebook, comparing his data with the readings on the Blackbird chassis. At one point the Amberson pit cart loaded with spare parts was in the Blackbird pit stall. Luz was flabbergasted.

"How about some pictures?" she said. "My friends in San Antonio aren't going to believe I met you two. They are going to be so jealous. And I really have to have some scenic shots too. This is probably the only time I'll have this opportunity."

Luz grabbed her camera out of her pack and began to shoot pictures as Billy and Carter posed for her. She snapped away, capturing images of the car, the crew members, and the pit cart. Luz carefully focused the telephoto shots on first the Blackbird pit box and then the Amberson pit box.

With only fifteen minutes left till happy hour, Luz was afraid she might have missed some important detail about qualifying. Thinking about what she'd heard so far, there was still more she wanted to know.

"Can you give me a quick summary of what happens between now and qualifying?"

"Track opens for practice on Wednesday. Early Friday evening is the drawing for qualifying order, which is more like a fifty-yard dash at a company picnic. It's first come, first served to draw the numbers determining that order," Carter answered. "Some guys think it is a big deal to draw the first number; others don't care one way or the other. Most teams want a chance to qualify on the first day, to have a shot at the pole."

"Normally the first to qualify gets a lot of media attention," Billy added. "And if you have a decent run, you might stay on the pole awhile. Seeing your car number in the pole position is a good feeling."

"Coming from a three-time polesitter, that's really funny." Carter chuckled. "I remember the year you were the first qualifier, and each time a car attempted to knock you off the pole position, you stayed there, nobody could beat you." Carter smiled as he told this story about his good friend and fellow competitor. "Every time a car sped out on the track you held your breath, afraid the next guy would have a faster time than you. At the end of the day you were so exhausted from worry you didn't enjoy the celebration afterward."

Billy explained, "After the drawing Friday afternoon, the teams make their final preparations for the next day. Saturday morning team members arrive around six in the morning, with qualifying starting around eleven. The teams line up for tech inspection, their pit carts loaded with spare tires and rims, toolboxes, parts, whatever they might need to be sure the car makes it off the qualifying line. It looks like a wagon train making its way across the prairie going west to the Promised Land."

Luz laughed at this description. She wondered if the Amberson team members felt like pioneers as they moved up and down pit road that day hauling equipment and supplies.

Carter continued the lesson. "If a car passes inspection, then the team readies for the qualifying run: getting the starter equipment cart ready, making sure the driver is settled in the car. A golf cart driven by a sanctioning body official takes the owner and the crew chief to the leading end of the gutter between pit road and the track. There they decide whether to take the run or not." He added, "When the run is successful, the cart returns to the opposite end of pit road, where the camera crews are waiting to take the qualifying pictures with the different sponsors who are present. That's where they do the hat dance: changing hats for each sponsor to have their own personalized qualifying photo."

"Afterward another technical inspection recertifies the car as eligible to race and the tires are impounded to be used for the first laps on race day," Billy said. "Most teams take a day off after qualifying. They celebrate that night and hope no one bumps them out of the lineup. Then they come back, take the car apart, clean it up and test the parts, put it back together, and go out for one last practice before the race."

"To give a driver more practice, teams use the backup car," Carter added. "If there is a wreck where the chassis is damaged, there is still a qualified car for race day."

As Luz sat between the two men listening to them talk, it felt like a tennis match, a verbal volley. She had no better sources; they answered most of her questions, and provided other information as well.

As the last few cars came in off the track, the lights on the "Christmas trees" that rimmed the track turned red, signaling that practice was over and the track was closed for the day. Luz packed her gear before she walked down the stairs. Billy led the way again, while Carter brought up the rear. When they reached the cart, Luz handed Carter the keys.

"It's your turn. Home, to the Amberson garage." She hopped in the back seat.

Carter, a more sedate driver than Billy, eased the cart out of the parking spot, swept right into the tunnel under the track, and deftly maneuvered around pedestrian traffic and the big semis outside the garage area, to bring them right to the Amberson garage. Roger Schneider snarled at them as they drove up.

"What do you think you're doing with my cart?" he yelled, looking straight at Carter. "Just because you've had more wins here as a crew chief than anyone else doesn't give you license to take my equipment. I've been looking for this cart all day long. Just who do you think you are?"

At this point Roger was roaring. Passersby moved to the other side of the garages, shrinking from his anger. Carter got out of the cart, standing tall at his full six foot three, and turned around to give Luz his hand, helping her hop off the cart. Totally ignoring Roger Schneider, he said, "Thank you for the lovely afternoon and for the ride in your chariot. Does this lout always act like he's Brando in *Streetcar*?"

Luz couldn't help laughing. Then she walked towards Roger Schneider and stopped within six inches of him.

"Excuse me," she said. "I had the cart all day. When I came in this morning at seven, you weren't here yet. I had business to take care of today. I took the cart. I will take the cart tomorrow too, and the next day, and every day after that while I am here. Please make plans accordingly, Roger. Goodbye—I'll see you tomorrow."

She pocketed the keys and turned to walk away, arm in arm, with Billy and Carter.

CHAPTER 15

Before she left the track, Luz stopped by the Harwood garage to see Jeff. With both garage doors opened to the cool evening breeze, the mechanics worked on the gearbox, the car propped up on jack stands.

The murmur of hellos followed Luz as she wound her way to the back of the garage, where Jeff talked to the engineer, both of them bent over the display on a laptop computer. She sat down in one of the plastic laminate chairs kept nearby and watched the team perform.

Luz marveled at how intently each of the men toiled. At the nose of the car, mechanics adjusted the huge suspension coils. Others removed bolts that held the car chassis and engine together. Once these were removed on one end, Joe Kerr, the crew chief, yelled, "Hey guys, everyone over here, it's time to take this cow of an engine out."

Like a wave rushing to the beach, all ten men moved together in unison, lifted the back of the car up and off the jack stands and then placed it back. While four of them balanced the front of the car on stands, the others cradled the engine in their arms grasping, it from both sides. Clasped together like a sling, they carefully moved the motor to the shipping crate to return it to the manufacturer for refurbishment. When it was all over, the team members whooped, cheered, and slapped each other on the back.

"That was great, guys! Thanks for not dropping that sucker. They'll come pick it up tomorrow," Jeff said, wiping the sweat off his face with a shop rag. As he wiped his neck, he spied Luz still sitting in the corner quietly.

"When did you sneak in here?"

"A while ago," Luz said. "That was impressive."

"That was stupid. If we'd dropped the engine, it would have been $500,000 we'd owe the manufacturer. We can't afford an engine lift, so that's our only alternative. Wait till you see our next trick—we're going to put a new engine in. That makes me really nervous."

"I was hoping you might have time for a bite to eat."

"Can't. Not tonight. Got to get this engine in so we can work on the setup and be ready for Thursday practice."

"Oh. Sorry," Luz said.

"But you could do me a favor."

Luz brightened up.

"Could you go to the hamburger place right across from the speedway on Sixteenth and pick up dinner for me and the boys? I'll give you the money," he said, reaching into his pocket.

"Sure, I'll be happy to, if you'll let me stay here and watch while you change out the engine. I've never seen anything like it," Luz replied.

"It's a deal. I don't think you will learn any secrets that would matter to any other team." Jeff peeled off a hundred-dollar bill and handed it to her.

Luz grabbed her pack, headed for the door, and said, "Don't change the engine until I get back. I really want to see that."

As she walked through the garage area, Luz felt the vibration of her cell phone. Pulling it out of her pocket, she glanced at the screen. Not recognizing the number, she hesitated to answer, wondering whether she'd be able to hear with all the engine sounds surrounding her. Thinking it might be Jeff with an additional food order, Luz accepted the call. "Hello?"

"*Preciosa, donde estás, mi amor*? Precious, where are you my love?" she heard Mauricio's purring tenor above the cacophony. "Are you getting your car repaired? It sounds like you are at a garage. Is your little red car *descompuesto*, broken?"

Annoyed with herself for answering the phone, Luz thought about how much she did not want to say and how she was going to end the conversation.

"Mauricio, yes, I am at a garage. It is very noisy here and I can barely hear you. Let's talk later. Bye," she said, hanging up abruptly.

Immediately she input his information into her phone so that if he called again she could send it directly to voicemail. As she was stowing her phone in her pocket, it vibrated again, and now his name appeared. She ignored the call and went on her way.

By the time Luz drove out of the parking lot onto the infield loop, most of the fans had left the speedway. She made a right turn onto Sixteenth Street and then a left into the drive-through lane, where she studied the menu and figured up the total for the crew's huge order. Fortunately, her wait was short: there was only one other car ahead of her in the drive-through line. Returning to the speedway was easy enough too.

Finding her way from one area of the track to another was simple now. She felt as if racing had been her life forever, with most of it spent at the Indianapolis Speedway. Walking in the same gate she had walked out of, the Yellow Shirts didn't bother to ask for credentials. They recognized her, and they smiled as they waved her through.

"Any of that for us?" she heard as she passed by.

"Not tonight. Maybe next time," Luz said, as she made a mental note to buy a few extra burgers the next time so she'd be able to share with these fellows.

As she passed a group of mechanics from another team on their way out for the evening, one playfully grabbed at one of the bags in her arms. She leaned away in time to dodge him, laughing, only to look up to see a pit cart speeding straight towards her. With quick footwork on her part, she twirled into another mechanic, who grabbed her by the shoulders, helping her stop.

Shaken by the near miss, Luz looked behind her to see who was driving the cart, but it had vanished around a corner by the time she thought to look for it. Holding her bags of burgers, she started back to the Harwood garage. She found her path blocked by a man wearing a Speedway official's uniform.

"Hey, you okay? That cart almost ran you down. It was going pretty fast. Let me help you carry these," he said as he took the bags from her arms. "I'm Bart Soules, with Speedway security. I thought for sure they were going to hit you."

Visibly shaken, Luz hunched over, her hands resting on her knees. She breathed slowly and deeply, trying to clear the dizziness from her brain. When she stood up, Luz looked wide-eyed at Bart. She tried to talk, but no sound came out of her open mouth.

"You did a good job taking care of yourself. I saw that fancy maneuver—looked like you were a contestant on *Dancing with the Stars*. Where are you going with all that food?"

She pointed to the left, between the B and C buildings. "Harwood garage. The door should be open."

Saying as little as possible, Luz still had not caught her breath. With the pit cart moving so fast, Luz wondered if she had imagined the Amberson decals on the sides. Still, she had been asking a lot of questions about Roger Schneider and Blackbird Racing. Maybe she'd need to be a little more careful with the questions she asked and who she was with when she asked them.

"I thought you were with Amberson Racing," Bart said, mystified.

"I am, but they don't like me to hang out with them. Clint and Michelle introduced me to Jeff at the Disney Two Hundred, and he's been nice enough to show me the ropes here at Indy." Luz took another deep breath to regain her composure before they entered the Harwood space.

As they walked in with bags of burgers, the mechanics were

drawn to them like metal shavings to a magnet. Luz handed out the burgers and fries, and Bart gave out the drinks. Jeff walked up to them and asked, "Luz, haven't you learned not to pick up stray animals?" Then he turned to her new friend: "Bart, you moocher. I can't believe it. You always come for the good stuff—steak burgers, not baloney sandwiches. What happens, you just smell the food and your feet take care of the travel arrangements?" Jeff patted Bart on the shoulder.

"He practically saved my life," Luz told him, her voice shaking. Jeff frowned. "This runaway pit cart came barreling towards me out of nowhere," she continued, her face red with anger.

"She dodged one attempt on the life of your burgers, and then ended up in the path of the cart," Bart said. "Her fancy footwork getting out of the way spun her out of control, so I grabbed her to pull her out of the way. I saw the whole thing."

"And here's your reward." Luz handed him her burger and drink and gave him a peck on the cheek.

"Wow," Bart said. "I'll save your life anytime!"

"And just what are you going to eat?" Jeff asked Luz.

"I'm not really hungry now. That was more excitement than I've had in a while. But some water would be good."

"I'll save you a bite of my burger. After you calm down, you'll be ravenous. It happens to us out in the pits when adrenaline hits."

"Yeah," said Bart. "You remember that time during practice when we were in the very last pit stall closest to the opening to pit road, and a car was way loose in turn 4, hit the outside wall, and then ricocheted into the pit road and hit the car we had waiting to go out? What a fireball! We were doing full tank testing. Lucky no one was in the car or next to it when it happened. It could have been ugly. I couldn't eat for hours."

"I never thought about it being dangerous out there," Luz said, horrified. "What do you do when that kind of thing happens?"

"You kiss the inside of the pit wall, where it meets the floor. And you pray a lot," Bart said.

"It's over in no time," added Joe Kerr, the crew chief. "Gotta be careful, though, 'cause methanol is invisible when it is burning, so if you feel heat, keep rolling to put out the fire. Or get someone to throw water on you."

Luz sipped her water thoughtfully. She'd never realized how dangerous the pit area was before. Everyone was so focused on their work and so keyed up about how the car and driver were performing, without any thought for their personal safety, but the undercurrent of danger was always there.

Now that the burgers were gone and the drinks consumed, the mechanics set about replacing the engine with the one in the crate. Again, forming a human sling around the engine, half the team lifted it into place, while the others rapidly bolted it onto the front of the tub and settled jack stands beneath it. Fuel lines and oil lines, as well as the headers and the gearbox, had yet to be connected. The engine was ready for the essential elements to bring it to life.

Luz watched carefully as the work was done. Occasionally her mind wandered to her near miss with the pit cart earlier in the evening. She dozed off for a few minutes, until Jeff woke her up by jostling her shoulder.

"Hey, sleepyhead. We've got to clear out of here in five minutes. Get your stuff together, and I'll walk you out," he said gently.

"Hmmm. Oh, five minutes." Luz sounded sleepy. She looked around for her pack, then realized she'd left it in the car. Digging her hands into her pants pockets, she found her keys. Jeff turned out the lights as she slowly walked to the door.

They ambled silently to the exit gate and mumbled good-night to the Yellow Shirts. Luz yawned, covered her mouth, and waved goodbye. As they approached her car, Jeff said very loudly, "I'll be following you home, Luz. See you there!"

He opened her car door at the sound of the reassuring chirp, held it open for her, and closed it once she was inside. He pointed to the locking mechanism and said, "Lock your doors."

At first, in her sleepy stupor, she didn't understand, but the second time she nodded and pushed the door lock button. While she adjusted her seat belt and opened the window to let some of the cool evening air into the cabin, Jeff found his way to his car and pulled up next to her, signaling her to lead the way to her apartment.

The drive home was uneventful, thankfully. At the apartment Jeff walked her to the door, opened it with her key, turned on every light, and walked through the apartment checking every closet and cubbyhole. He made sure the locks on the sliding doors were secured, and then satisfied she would be safe and alone for the night, he took her in his arms and gave her a long, lingering kiss.

Still holding her, he touched her nose with his and said in a low voice, almost a growl, "I want to see you tomorrow morning. Fix extra coffee—I'll be by around six. We need to talk. Goodnight. Sleep well. I'll see you then. Lock the door. I'll call to check on you when I get home."

She watched him get into his truck, then closed and locked the door. She sighed, glad to have a friend who'd already experienced the month of May at the speedway.

CHAPTER 16

As the first light seeped through the blinds, Luz stretched, now aware that she had been half-awake for a while. Over and over, her mind ran the image of the pit cart speeding towards her. It was lucky her quick footwork had gotten her out of the way. The memory of Bart as the safe harbor that stopped her from spinning out of control gave her comfort.

Luz could not remember meeting Bart Soules before, although he and Jeff seemed pretty chummy. He wasn't wearing a team shirt she recognized, yet he seemed to belong at the speedway. Maybe she'd learn more about him when she and Jeff had their talk that morning.

Luz slowly crawled out of bed, feeling the soreness in her muscles, most likely from her fancy footwork of the night before. Her mind wandered while she showered. It was Monday, a brand-new work day with a completely new routine.

Luz found that most of her clients preferred to be called

in the morning, leaving her afternoon free. If someone needed something that afternoon, her assistant could enter orders. Her clients were excited to know an insider at the Indy 500. Most of them had grown up with the Indy 500 as the highlight of their Memorial Day weekend, with family get-togethers planned around watching the big race. The clients from Mexico were thrilled, as they were big race fans, enjoying Formula One events and other open wheel competitions.

As she met more and more people at the racetrack, Luz realized that many of these very high-powered, influential people from different industries were potential clients. At the end of the month she'd have more opportunities for business than ever before.

Toweling off after her shower, she patted her face dry, looked into the mirror, and thought about how frightened she felt. If she'd moved the wrong way, whoever was driving the cart would have hit her, and now she would be in a hospital bed, paralyzed or dead, not taking a shower and putting on makeup.

With only about fifteen minutes before Jeff planned to arrive, Luz pulled her wet hair back into a twist. She had work to do for her clients, and for Clint and Michelle. Whoever had been driving that cart meant to scare her back to Texas. Big money and big prestige were at stake at Indy. It was obvious to her now: some people would do anything to finish well.

The doorbell rang as she slipped on her shoes. She ran down the stairs, looked through the peephole, saw Jeff standing there, and opened the door. "I haven't made the coffee yet. I've been a bit distracted this morning."

He walked in and took a look at her. "I like your hair pulled back that way. Looks really good."

He handed her the bag of muffins he'd brought, kissed her forehead, and moved on to the kitchen.

"The coffee's in the freezer," Luz said as she followed him through the apartment.

With smooth, precise moves, Jeff found the coffee and set the machine to brew eight cups. Luz pulled two mugs out of the cupboard, along with sugar, and cinnamon creamer, then grabbed the milk from the fridge.

While Jeff was waiting for the coffee to brew, he opened the curtains to the sliding glass door, where they could both see the sun slipping between the clouds as the morning began. The sky was reflected in the mirror finish of the reflecting pond. Two ducks began their morning swim, sending ripples along the surface. A slight breeze ruffled the leaves in the young trees outside the door. If the day turned out anything like these few moments, it would be a beautiful one.

"You need to watch your step, Luz," Jeff said, looking out the window. He turned to look directly at her.

She looked away from his piercing eyes, knowing what he was telling her.

He grabbed her hands, holding them with his fingertips. "Look at me, Luz. So many things can go wrong at a racetrack. It would be easy to make anything look like an accident. And it would be hard to prove otherwise."

Taking a deep breath to calm down, Luz squeezed Jeff's hands. Working so hard to control herself, she did a few shoulder rolls, and let go of his hands, making every effort not to reveal her discomfort. Her body shook, but the slow breathing helped.

"Sit down. I'll get you some coffee. You like the cinnamon creamer in it, right?" Luz nodded. He pulled out a chair for her at the breakfast table, giving her the view of the ducks in the pond. She sat down, taking the cup from his hands once he'd filled it for her. The first warm, creamy sip soothed her. Jeff handed her a muffin on a small plate and placed a handful of napkins in the center of the table.

Pulling a chair around to the side of the table, where he could see both the pond and Luz's face, Jeff sipped his coffee and started eating a blueberry muffin. He took a deep breath. "I talked to Bart after I got home. He works for the racing league. He knows everybody. He couldn't tell me who drove the cart, but he told me they meant to run you down. What have you been doing these last two days? You've pissed someone off, and I need to know who."

"Oh, Jeff, I know you promised Clint and Michelle to take care of me. But you can't take responsibility for what happened."

"To hell with Clint and Michelle. I don't want anything to happen to you, Luz. I like you. I'd like to see more of you, and not in the hospital."

Luz felt stunned and uncertain. She'd gotten to know Jeff only recently, but he was a likeable guy, and he had known Clint for years. Maybe she did need to share what she knew with someone she thought she could trust.

"Come on. Tell me, Luz. Whatever it is, somebody thinks it's important."

"Okay, Jeff. But I don't think I have enough proof."

"Proof? Wasn't last night proof enough for you that whatever you are sticking your nose into is none of your business? Tell me what you know or what you think you know."

"I think Roger Schneider, as Blackbird Racing, is stealing money and equipment from Amberson Racing, from Clint and Michelle."

"Okay. Keep going."

"Ever since I got here, Roger has been really snotty to me. At first I thought it was because I'm not a man, but the more I've learned, the more I think it is because he thought he would have this May all to himself, without anyone looking over his shoulder. According to what I've learned, Roger entered his own car in the race by the April first deadline, at the same time he entered Clint's cars. That was before Clint's stroke. I think all along he planned to field his own car and quit Amberson Racing."

Jeff motioned for her to keep talking as he finished his muffin and sipped his coffee.

"Roger had trouble finding sponsorship. So maybe when Clint had his stroke, Roger figured he could use manpower, parts and equipment from Amberson Racing and no one would know the difference. From what I could tell from talking to Michelle, Gena Newman, Carter Holland, Billy Wojinski, and the guy at Loctite, everyone thought this would be the year the Amberson team would win the 500. If so, who would notice a little more spent here and there on parts and equipment? But also, what an advantage for Roger to be able to run his team on a shoestring and have access to all of the fine equipment, employees, and contacts Amberson has built up."

Luz sipped her coffee and started to nibble on the muffin, then said, "When I watched happy hour yesterday, I took pictures of all the Amberson team members working on the Blackbird car. I even have some photos with the equipment from the Amberson stable surrounding the Blackbird car. And there are copies of the team rosters from both teams, and with a few exceptions, like my name, the list of names are virtually identical."

Luz stared hollow-eyed out the window.

"My job here is to watch out for Clint and Michelle's interests," she continued. "I don't believe there is an agreement between Amberson and Blackbird to share team members and equipment, but I am going to find out. All the insiders know what is going on, and no one is saying anything about it. Nice friends Clint and Michelle have here. I think it is disgusting. So if someone is pissed off, it means I'm on the right trail, and I need to keep going until I blow the whole thing open."

"And what if it blows you open?" Jeff asked softly.

"I don't think it will. Last night someone meant to scare me away, to scare me back to Texas. I don't scare easily. I've been treated worse in the business I'm in. But I cannot afford to be careless or unaware of my surroundings, like I was last night."

Jeff looked at her with surprise. He hadn't realized how spunky she was. "So what is your plan for today?"

"I have to work here for a few hours taking care of my brokerage clients. I thought that might give whoever tried to run me down the idea I'd been scared off. In fact, if anyone asks, it wouldn't hurt to start a rumor that I've gone back to San Antonio. I'd like to lay low for a few days, and let them think I'm not here anymore."

"So you're not going to go out at all?"

"Oh, no. This afternoon I plan to pay a visit to the Amberson shop. No one knows me there. Everyone from that team who's met me is at the track. After all, I'm supposed to be watching over things, so maybe it's time for a surprise visit."

"Remember, Roger is part of the good-old-boys club here. He has support from high up in the league. They may not be happy about you smearing mud on the reputation of one of their fair-haired boys."

"I realize that, Jeff. But I also realize this is big business— hundreds of millions of dollars' worth of business. Sponsors pay money to teams to race with their logos emblazoned on their cars. They want the best outcome for their money. They want to sponsor the winning car. They want to sell T-shirts, caps, and toys with their logos on them. If some of that money is going somewhere else to someone else, or if some of the team members are so exhausted because they are working on more cars than they should be, then the sponsors are being cheated, and if the sponsors are being cheated, that's bad for the sport, both now and in the future. I believe the good old boys will understand that concept," Luz said, her voice growing more and more heated.

"Okay, okay. Cool off. I just wanted you to know who's who." Jeff held up his hands as if surrendering to her.

"I'm sorry. I was way off the chart there. It burns me up that Roger would take advantage of someone who has been so generous to him, who has given him so many great opportunities. As crew chief of Amberson Racing, if he won the race this year, he could name his price and he'd have no trouble finding sponsorship. But he's greedy, and selfish, and a thief. I have no respect for him and no sympathy for whatever happens to him."

"Remind me never to be on the opposite side of the table from you in an argument," Jeff said with a grin. "How about dinner tonight, and you can let me know what else you've learned?"

"Sounds great. Call me when you're finished at the garage, and we'll figure out where to go from there."

Jeff got up to leave, taking his cup to the sink. Luz gave him a big hug when he turned around to head for the door.

"Thanks for listening. It was great to get that off my chest. You're a good friend."

"I want to be more than a good friend. But we'll talk about that some more tonight." Jeff kissed her on the forehead, then he turned to open the door. "Have a good day. Be careful. Good luck."

Luz watched him walk to his truck, and waved as he drove away. She felt like she'd had a full day already, and it was just beginning. Time now to call the office and see how things were going.

CHAPTER 17

The morning flew by as Luz made calls and reviewed portfolios with her clients. She talked to ten people between nine and noon. All of them were impressed she had called them while she was in Indianapolis; all of them were pleased she was their adviser. Luz made herself a grilled cheese sandwich for lunch, then called her assistant, Anita Cruz, to tell her she would be on her cell phone for the rest of the day.

As she neared the Amberson Racing shop, Luz called Michelle, hoping she could arrange a better reception for her there than she had experienced at the garage area. Michelle answered on the second ring, just after Luz arrived at the Amberson compound. While Luz talked she looked at the parked cars to see if Roger Schneider's black truck was in the lot.

"Michelle? It's Luz. How are you?"

"I'm fine, Luz. It's good to hear your voice. The army of doctors, nurses, and therapists are working miracles with Clint. He plans to make the race."

"Great! So many people will look forward to seeing him. Billy Wojinski and Carter Holland say hello!"

"Super. I'll pass that on to him. He'll be happy to know he's missed," Michelle said. "Luz, I talked to Jeff Harwood this morning."

"Oh, you did?"

"Don't act innocent with me. He mentioned the incident involving the pit cart. I realize I should have told you."

"Told me what?"

"To be careful. I've been here poring over the financials and contracts with the accountant and attorney. I suspected something was amiss shortly before Clint's stroke, but I couldn't prove anything. Now the accountants have confirmed it. It sounds like you know too."

"Actually, I guessed," Luz said. "It's always about the money, Michelle."

"Well, then, you know why I asked you to go. I thought if I sent you, someone we could trust, someone smart, someone who had never been up there, we'd be able to learn more."

"Gena Newman called me a virgin. I wasn't sure if it was a compliment or an insult. Go on." Luz knew she sounded terse at this point, and a bit angry.

"I had to do it, Luz. Shortly after the entry deadline, Clint was told Roger had submitted his own entry. But we ignored it, assuming he merely needed more garage space for a setup pad. But then I heard other whispers about things, and we started to lose equipment at the shop. At first it was little things that could easily be misplaced at a test, or left behind, or even taken by a disgruntled employee. Then large pieces of equipment started to need repairs—expensive repairs, in some cases repairs so expensive it was cheaper to replace the stuff than to repair it," Michelle explained.

"Okay. I'm taking notes," said Luz, pulling a small memo pad from her pack and starting to scribble.

"We pieced together all of these coincidences when Clint had his stroke. To prove employee theft and fraud takes a great deal of detail work. I didn't tell you everything because the attorneys wanted more time, and we wanted Schneider to discount you, as we thought he would. We hoped he'd slip up somehow. We didn't think anyone would try to hurt you."

Luz could hear the sadness in Michelle's voice. And Luz could tell she was tired. Going over all the numbers and paperwork would be a tedious and time-consuming process. Looking at all the receipts and work orders while comparing them to the list of equipment and parts would be a staggering feat. Fortunately, each part and piece of equipment was numbered and then aged, with the replacement date noted on the computer system at the predetermined intervals recommended by the manufacturer. With the lives of team members at stake, Clint Amberson made sure there would never be a question of whether safety procedures were followed. He made sure every part on his cars was in the best possible shape to ensure the safety of the drivers and team members.

"Michelle, is it possible that the new equipment went to Blackbird Racing while the old parts and equipment remained at Amberson?" Luz asked.

"Luz, we aren't sure. And that's what is making us crazy now. To do an audit of all the equipment during the month of May would be insane. It would disrupt the team, and of course the timing couldn't be worse. Besides, Roger is a bit touchy to begin with, and he'd quit before he'd get caught. So to catch him, we have to keep working here and hope to find something."

"I'm here to help you on this end," Luz told her.

"According to Jeff you are in danger. We can't have anything happen to you," Michelle stated bluntly. "By the way, Jeff said you took photographs during practice. But I really didn't understand their significance."

"I took photos of team members in Amberson uniforms, working on the Blackbird Racing car yesterday. Also, they were driving equipment with the Amberson logos on it to the Blackbird pits."

"Good. Please email me the most important ones today and then send me one set of prints, and make another set for yourself. And Luz, if I send you a list of equipment to photograph, could you do that for us?"

"Sure, I'd be happy to do that. Email me the list. I'm at the shop now, so I can send you the pictures right away."

"Do it as inconspicuously as possible. Afterward, compare the serial numbers of the equipment to the list I send you."

"Okay. Most of the serial numbers are easy to see, on placards or stickers positioned for easy reading. I've noticed some of them when I've been around the garage. Hopefully I can get a few good images of them for you."

"We suspect they have two sets of books. If their guard is

down, you may be able to find out even more than we hoped."

"I'll do what I can, Michelle. Send me the list of equipment, with the serial numbers, and also a brief description of the where the equipment is kept and how it's used. That way it will be easier for me to check everything."

"Please be careful, Luz. We didn't realize the extent of the corruption. There are others besides Roger who are involved in this betrayal. Be careful whom you trust. Jeff obviously cares for you and is interested in your well-being, but anyone else, who knows? Even old friends at the speedway are looking the other way. It's a shame, really, but they have closed ranks." Michelle sounded disillusioned.

"I'll do my best. Most weekdays I'll be at the apartment in the morning and then at the track in the afternoon. Right now I'm outside the Amberson shop, and I'll be going inside after we finish. Maybe I can make a difference today," Luz said brightly.

"Take care of yourself. Clint and I are very grateful to you for watching out for our interests. We're lucky to have you working with us. We'll talk tomorrow, Luz. Bye."

As she hung up the phone, Michelle Amberson looked worried. In her right hand was a sheaf of papers, spreadsheets given to her by the accountant and attorney, who were seated across the desk from her.

"So what these tell me is that money went to offshore accounts, and some of the wire transfers went to a parts company that doesn't really exist. Can we contact the bank about the funds and find out who the corporate officers are? Surely there is some way to catch these people," she said angrily, throwing the papers onto the desk. "We trusted Roger. We never thought he'd cheat us or embezzle from us, or take advantage of us in any way. And now I find these things out and I feel sick to my stomach. It makes me question everyone and everything they say and do."

"We're contacting all the appropriate federal agencies to get their cooperation, Mrs. Amberson," the attorney told her. "Please believe we are doing all we can to help you."

"Luz Dane is at the shop now to obtain evidence regarding the equipment and parts. She's quite a woman—lots of courage and spunk, but if something happens to her because we didn't act fast enough, I don't know what I'll do. I can only hope that with your firms working the numbers on this end and preparing the documents we need to file in court, we can act before somebody gets killed!"

"We have staff working round the clock. We're all doing what we can to wrap this up without giving Roger a clue that we are on to him. We should get an arrest before month is out."

"I hope so. It would break Clint's heart for someone he trusted to get the better of him. It wouldn't be right," Michelle said. "Let's hope we can take care of it soon. I really don't want to see Roger Schneider win the 500 with my money and my equipment."

CHAPTER 18

After her talk with Michelle, Luz thought about how to approach the staff at the Amberson shop. Most of the team was at the speedway, but there certainly had to be some comings and goings during the day. Obviously there would be a receptionist and the bookkeeping staff. Luz wondered if the Blackbird shop was at Amberson, since there was no one around who would notice.

Luz felt her cell phone vibrate. It was her assistant at Emerson York. "Hi, Anita! What's up?"

"I wouldn't have bothered you, but Mr. Barstow called me earlier this morning really agitated about something, and he just called back again. I knew we were scheduled to talk in about an hour, but I think he would feel better if you could call him immediately. I've texted you his number, you should be getting it right now."

Luz felt her phone vibrate again and saw the text with the

phone number.

"Got it," she said. "Talk to you in a little while."

She sat in her car, watching the entrance to the Amberson Racing shop as she dialed the number for Mr. Barstow, a client she'd known for over ten years. When he answered and she heard his gravelly voice, she said, "Hi, Mr. Barstow, it's Luz Dane. Anita tells me you have some concerns today."

"Luz, I'm glad you called. I'm not bothered by the market, but I did want to take care of a charitable gift I'd forgotten about, and my pledge is due, and I'm not sure how to go about making this happen. Can you help me?"

Luz smiled as she answered his question, recommending a stock she knew was a large position in his account. It had tripled in value since he bought it, so it was a perfect candidate to give to the university awaiting his contribution.

"That stock is about $75 a share, and your pledge is for $5,000 this year, so it looks like you need to give about seventy shares to cover your gift and any transaction costs for the charity. I remember you gave them stock last year too, so I bet we have a copy of the letter authorizing the transfer to them. We can just prepare a new one for you to sign and then everything will be taken care of for you. Let me check with Anita, and then I'll call you right back."

Luz called Anita and asked, "Would you look in Mr. Barstow's file and see if we have a copy of the letter making a transfer to the university last year, so we can prepare one just like it for this year for him to sign?"

While she was on hold, Luz mentally reviewed the other things she wanted to go over with Anita so that clients could be contacted that afternoon regarding items pending in their accounts.

"I have it right here, Luz. I'll call them to verify that the brokerage account information is still correct, and then we'll type up a new one. Is he coming in to sign it or am I faxing it to him?"

"He said he would come in when it is ready, if you would call him and let him know."

"Okay. And John Sanders called about setting up an appointment to talk about his rollover on his 401(k). And, um, Mauricio called." Now Anita sounded hesitant.

"Ask John what morning works best for me to call him, and then email me the time and the best contact number for him for that appointment, please. As for Mauricio, I don't know what to think. He's been calling my cell phone. How did he get that number?"

"He pulled a fast one. I wouldn't give it to him, so he called Mark Sloan, his old buddy, and they got reacquainted."

"I wish Sloan would stay out of my personal life. Under no circumstances do I want to have any kind of relationship with Mauricio, personal or professional, so tell Sloan he can take care of him however he sees fit," Luz said. "I thought I'd gotten him out of my life years ago, and now he's trying to crawl back in."

"Maybe you'd better tell Sloan that yourself. He's been skulking around your desk and mine, wanting to know how it's going for you at Indy."

"Okay, I'll call him today and get it over with. I hope I have a job when I get back," Luz said. "Thanks, Anita. Sorry I get so frustrated and share it all with you."

"It's okay. Mauricio hurt you really bad and took advantage of you, and you are just now putting yourself back together again. He's trying to weasel his way back into your life, and you and I both know he's no good. Got another call. Bye!" Anita hung up.

While she'd been on hold, Luz had had an idea about the easiest way to gain entry to Amberson Racing under the radar. All she had to do was identify herself as the representative of a potential sponsor: Emerson York was a large corporation, and Indy car sponsorship might be an appropriate consideration. As long as she acted to suit the part, there would be no one questioning her behavior or her inquiries. Roger Schneider wouldn't care, since he had discounted her once before. And today she looked the part: she was wearing a dark navy business suit, pumps, a white blouse, and pearls, and carried a small leather bag with side pockets where she could stash her smartphone and sunglasses.

Luz surveyed the entrance to the shop. Floor-to-ceiling glass windows faced the parking lot. An Indy car was featured in the center of the building's lobby. Off to the left was a reception desk, and on either side of the car were two leather couches with a low sofa table between them.

When she walked in the door, the receptionist was deep in conversation with someone, talking in a low tone of voice. She barely looked up when Luz approached the desk and slowly wrote "L. M. Dane" and "Visitor" on the sign-in sheet. Luz quickly skimmed the sheet as she signed in.

It seemed as if everyone from every company was there to

see Don, so Luz decided to visit Don, too. After signing in, she sat down on one of the sleek Italian leather sofas and picked up one of the many auto magazines on the table in front of her. Soon the receptionist finished her phone conversation, looked at the list, and made an intercom call to Don. She then stood up and walked over to Luz, bending slightly to speak with her.

"Ms. Dane?"

Luz nodded in acknowledgment, then said politely, "Yes," looking up from her magazine.

"Don will be down in just a moment to see you. We didn't realize that Emerson York was interested in auto racing. We think our team is a great opportunity for your company. Don will tell you all about it."

Luz watched her make direct eye contact and sincerely state her pitch.

A short squatty man wearing khaki pants and a white polo shirt with the team logo on the breast pocket came towards her. He stopped next to the receptionist, who introduced him.

"Ms. Dane, this is Don Osborne. As I mentioned to you a moment ago, Don, Ms. Dane is with Emerson York, the international investment firm. Don will show you around the shop, tell you about our programs, and then go over the sponsorship opportunities that are available. We hope you enjoy your tour."

They shook hands and Don motioned Luz over towards a locked steel door fitted with the same kind of lock as each of the garage doors at Indy. As he was opening the door, she asked, "Do you mind if I take some pictures as we stroll through your shop?"

"No, of course not. We don't have any secrets here. All our

secrets are at the garages at the speedway now. If you decide you want a tour there while you are in town, please let me know and I'll arrange it for you."

"Thank you—I'll think about it. Today's tour will be a good start."

Don Osborne walked Luz Dane through the cavernous shop, starting the tour where they parked and loaded the huge transporters that carried the cars from race to race. With a roof about three stories tall, the structure dwarfed the big trucks, which looked like children's toys by comparison. As she walked around the trucks she noticed offices on the second and third floors overlooking the open area where the team members worked on assembling the chassis after painting. The only Amberson transporter parked inside was being loaded with parts and equipment as they walked by. Luz snapped a few photos, smiling at Don each time she did it, doing her best to look star-struck by all that was going on around her.

Inside the paint booth, the car parts suspended in air resembled a mobile by Alexander Calder. The dyno room, where engines were mounted and connected by the various fuel lines and exhaust ports to sensitive evaluative computer equipment, was next on the tour. A few feet away, resting on a setup pad, was a chassis with the logo of Blackbird Racing emblazoned on its side pod. Luz snapped a picture, capturing both the chassis and the Amberson logo on the back wall behind it. Over to one side were several engine crates stenciled with the name Blackbird Racing.

"Now that you've seen most of our work area, let me show

you our corporate offices, where we can talk about the sponsorship opportunities we have available," Don said.

Luz was afraid she might not be able to get pictures of those crates once she went upstairs. Seeing the signs for the restrooms, she asked, "Would you mind if I took a quick break?"

"Not at all. After you pass the crates take a left, then a right. I'll wait for you here."

Luz followed the directions, walking slowly. As soon as she was out of sight, she captured the crates in the foreground along with the big Amberson sign in the background.

Lining the hall were employee lockers. Some had Blackbird decals on the outside. Luz recognized the names of team members she had met a few days before. While she captured evidence, she wondered how many team members were in on the Blackbird/Amberson deception that took advantage of Clint and Michelle Amberson.

When she returned from the restroom Don motioned her up the stairs. She turned around once to survey the shop's entire work area and snapped two more photos establishing the fact that the Amberson shop was used by two teams, not just one.

They walked through the bookkeeping department, with all its computers; the impressive conference room, decorated with photos of the different podium finishes of the Amberson team; and finally the marketing department. Two six-foot-square marker boards covered the back wall of the marketing department. One was labeled Blackbird Racing, the other Amberson Racing. A running tally on each listed a company name, the contact person, their phone number, an amount of money, and a closing date. Luz noted that the two names she had given them, L. M. Dane and Emerson York, appeared on both boards, hastily scribbled by someone after she arrived. She knew she needed a photo of those two boards.

Once in his private office, Don offered her a seat at the front of his desk. Two folders had been carefully placed there, one with the Amberson logo, the other with the Blackbird logo. Luz carried a small digital recorder in her purse, and she was ready to use it.

"I'd like to take notes. Let's see, where are my pen and pad?" She fumbled around in her purse, took almost everything out of it, and set it on the chair beside her. Inside the purse she switched the recorder to voice activation, replacing everything in her bag to allow the recorder to stay on top. She left the bag unzipped, hoping for a clear recording of her conversation with Don Osborne. At the very least, she would be able to take both folders with her. That alone would give her a lot of the information she needed.

As he waited for Luz, Don adjusted his posture, sitting up straight and taking a deep breath. Luz knew from experience that he was preparing to deliver a well-rehearsed sales pitch.

"Ms. Dane, this year provides a special opportunity for companies like Emerson York to get in on the ground floor of a new race team. Roger Schneider, who engineered successful wins for Amberson Racing for years, formed his own team under the name Blackbird Racing and is entered in this year's race. As it is the inaugural year at Indy for Blackbird, we have many sponsorship packages available to you. Some even provide the opportunity for minor sponsorship on the Amberson car as well. With many teams these days fielding more than one car, companies are looking to gain more exposure by sponsoring more than one team. Let me go through material in front of you to explain what we have to offer."

Don explained every detail of the sponsorship packages. He and his colleagues clearly used the Amberson name and reputation as a draw, then converted potential sponsors to Blackbird Racing. Roger Schneider would go on to a life of fame and fortune, leaving his trusting old boss with nothing. Had this been the plan all along, or had Roger taken advantage of Clint's infirmity? Had Clint treated Roger so badly that he deserved such dishonesty?

When Don finished his presentation, Luz gathered up the folders and looked at her watch. "You have explained everything clearly, Mr. Osborne. Thanks again for all your time and the courtesy you have shown me."

As she walked out of the marketing office, Luz saw one of the assistants making notes on the board next to L. M. Dane's name. No one had bothered to ask for any of her contact information, neither a phone number nor an email address. Don directed her to the exit, where she thanked the receptionist as she left. Luz practically skipped to her car, realizing that without a phone number, no one would be able to find L. M. Dane or the proper contact at Emerson York. Only Roger Schneider would know how to find her, but by the time he realized what had happened, it would be too late to do anything to prevent her from sharing the truth about Blackbird Racing leading sponsors away from Amberson Racing. Even with the sincere and practiced sales pitch, without contact information on a lead, the Blackbird team had no chance to acquire new sponsorship; the only way was to steal it. As soon as she was in her car, she stowed the brochures in her briefcase, then drove to the nearest drug store to have the sets of prints made. She would be able to pick them up later that evening.

CHAPTER 19

Luz stopped by the apartment to pick up the documents she would be sending to Michelle that evening. At the shopping center where she dropped off the flash drive of photos to be printed, Luz purchased every auto magazine she could find, along with a special newspaper publication of the Star about qualifying weekend.

She skimmed the different magazines, and looked for any reference to Blackbird Racing. She found nothing in any of the national magazines about Roger Schneider or Blackbird Racing. The local paper, however, devoted an entire page to his story and his exciting new venture. This special feature was titled "Roger Schneider: The Hometown Boy Who Made Good." Not a word in the story mentioned his present employment, other than one line that read "Roger Schneider got his start at Amberson Racing."

Obviously Roger had forgotten who signed his paycheck.

Irritated, Luz promised herself she'd do everything in her power to end his Indy car career. She placed all the magazine articles, the run sheets, and the newspaper features into a large envelope, leaving room for the photos from earlier in the day. Stowing that envelope in her briefcase for her afternoon meeting, she left for the speedway for her appointment with Jonathan Barrow, chief of security, someone the Amberson attorneys wanted involved in the case.

Parking in the beautifully landscaped parking lot in front of the speedway headquarters building, Luz was grateful to find a spot open. With so many media and industry leaders securing their credentials, the lot was so full that cars circulated slowly while waiting for a parking spot.

Just as she was about to get out of the car, her phone rang. Luz looked at the screen and saw Mauricio's name, and immediately she sent it to voicemail. Sooner or later, Luz would have to call her manager, Mark Sloan, and clear the air. Now was as good a time as any time, so she punched in the number, put a smile on her face, and took a deep breath. Fortunately she was still in her car and had privacy while she waited for the phone to answer.

"Mark Sloan." He answered his own phone whenever possible.

"Hi, Mark, it's Luz Dane checking in from Indy. Things are good here and my clients are pretty happy, and business has been good too." Luz cleared her throat, waiting to hear about his latest issue.

"I'm glad you called. You remember that guy you used to date—nice guy—Mauricio, what's his name?"

"Yes, I remember him." Luz tried not to sound too annoyed.

"Well, he called me, and oh, I hope you don't mind, I gave him your cell number. Said he didn't have it. Anyway, he wanted to set up a few more accounts, so I took care of that for him. Do you want them under your number or shall I handle them for him?" Sloan feigned a nonchalant tone.

"Mark, I wish you hadn't helped him do that. You do what you think is best. If you want to handle his accounts, great. We are no longer an item, and I think it is better for me if I don't have contact with him anymore. He's all yours!" Luz said emphatically.

"Okay, well, it sounds like you are doing all right with this double duty. I might have been wrong about trying to keep you from going, Luz. Glad we can support you here."

"Thank you. I'm grateful for the opportunity to help the Ambersons and get the support I need from you. Anita and I talk every day, so you can let her know if there is something I can do for you. Gotta go!" Luz pushed the button to end the call.

Luz walked into the building through the front door for the first time. It felt different than coming in the side door by credentials, a little more formal, a bit more businesslike. She signed in at the desk, noting the time and Jonathan Barrow's name. Still dressed in her suit, she waited in the lobby, amused by the passing by of so many team members she knew who didn't recognize her in formal business attire.

She heard a deep voice say, "Ms. Dane, I believe." Jonathan Barrow walked towards her from his stop at the reception desk. A tall, stocky man, his black hair slicked back with gel and his temples graying, Barrow had a former pro–football player demeanor, combined with a stature that reflected military discipline.

Luz stood up, smiling, and shook his hand.

"My office is this way," he said, "towards the credentials office."

Luz followed him as he rambled left down a long hallway that led to a private office with its own reception area. Solid glass windows lined three corners of the enclave, offering spectacular views of the front straightaway, the infield of the speedway, and the front parking lot.

"Please sit down, Ms. Dane," Chief Barrow said. "Shortly after Clint had his stroke, the Amberson attorneys informed me of their suspicions. Apparently you are quite the detective, but it has put you in some danger, I hear."

Luz looked surprised, yet realized that if anyone should know what she had been up to, it was the chief of security.

"It's a pleasure to meet you. Bart Soules told me what happened in the garage area. He's our undercover man, yet I'm afraid he can't be everywhere. I heard you have some information for me. Perhaps we can share what we know with one another. Two heads are better than one, I've found." He touched his temple with his forefinger.

Luz opened her briefcase and removed the pertinent papers, feeling sheepishly amateurish in front of a man who obviously knew many important people from the looks of the autographed photos displayed on the hallway going to his office. He'd obviously handled security for royalty, professional athletes, politicians and captains of industry, so he knew what he was doing—more so than she did, she thought. Taking a deep breath, Luz made her presentation, adding all of the information Michelle had shared with her earlier. When she finished, she took a deep breath and sipped from the glass of water he had kindly provided.

Jonathan Barrow jotted down comments on the information Luz gave him. Looking down his notes, he turned to Luz to ask her one more thing. "Do you know this man?" Barrow opened a file and pulled out a photograph of a swarthy gentleman with dark hair and a carefully groomed mustache and goatee.

Luz studied the photograph carefully. After a minute she spoke. "I met someone who looks like him, but I'm not sure it's the same man. He came into the office the day Clint had his stroke—said he wanted to open an account. When I asked him the standard profiling questions, he was very evasive in answering them," she explained. "One thing I do remember is that he stormed out of the office in a rage. If I am remembering it properly, I think his name is Ricardo Delgado. What does he have to do with Amberson Racing?"

"I don't know for sure. This man is involved with some very dangerous people." Chief Barrow stood up, signaling the end of their visit. "Please be very careful, Ms. Dane. I'll call Michelle and the attorneys and let them know what we've put together. You do the job they sent you here to do: watch out for the team. Don't make accusations, and don't ask any more questions without clearing it with me first. I'll call you as I learn more."

"Thanks, Chief, for all you are doing. I'll be around if you need me."They shook hands before walking out the door.

"Watch your back. Bart can't be everywhere all the time," Chief Barrow said as he escorted her down the hallway and to the building's exit.

When she left the track, Luz was exhausted. She had to make the deadline for overnight delivery to get everything to Michelle so the attorneys could act as quickly as possible. On her way back to pick up the photo prints, Luz had a feeling she was being followed. Looking in her rearview mirror, she saw a black pickup truck, similar to the one Roger Schneider drove, sitting two cars behind her at the light. Instead of speeding away, which is what she felt like doing, Luz slowed to a crawl, hoping the vehicles behind her would pass her and give her a chance to look at the driver of the truck. Just as she reached her parking lot entrance, the black truck passed her with Roger Schneider at the wheel, his face red and his voice loud, yelling into his cell phone. He turned towards her and gestured obscenely her way. When he saw Luz looking at him, a look of surprise washed over his face, as if he had not expected to see her again after what had happened with the pit cart the night before.

Now parked in front of the shopping center, Luz breathed deeply, her own fear surprising her. It was daylight, and she was driving. He wasn't going to chase her; was that what she feared? She had a job to finish, and this was a big part of her responsibility to Clint and Michelle. She retrieved her prints from the store and got back in her car. Quickly flipping through the photos, she found great pictures that clearly showed the link between the Blackbird team and Amberson

Racing. Luz sorted the photos and placed one copy of each, along with a flash drive, into one of the photo envelopes, then added those photos to the collection of news and magazine articles, as well as the speedway entrant list and timing sheets she had compiled to send back to San Antonio. She stapled together the lap times and other run sheets, and included all of the documents from credentials too, along with the motor home parking receipt. She drove across the highway to the FedEx office to overnight Michelle the information.

Reminded of her talk with Jeff that morning and her recent sighting of Roger Schneider, Luz drove a few blocks out of the way, taking a different route to her complex to make sure no one followed her home. Once there, she parked, entered her apartment, turned on lights as she walked in, and locked the door. Luz was a bit rattled. She reminded herself that greed was a powerful motivator and a dangerous force. Now it was time to stay out of Roger Schneider's way if for no other reason than to give him enough room to show off and play his hand to the fullest.

CHAPTER 20

Rising early, Luz started her day by checking email and making phone calls. She visited with many of her clients, reviewed portfolios, summarized the financial news from overseas, and continued to contact the people who counted on her for help with their investments. Around noon Luz called Michelle and asked, "Did you get my packet?"

"We received it over an hour ago. The photos are fantastic, exactly what we needed. With the bank's help, we've traced the wired funds to an offshore corporation. The review of the books is completed. Your pictures are the icing on the cake."

"I have more! Last night Roger was on television, touting his team. I've already called a clipping service and arranged for a copy. An article in the racing section of the paper today featured an interview with Schneider about his new venture."

"Excellent. Don't send anything else. Keep everything there. I am arriving this afternoon with the attorneys. Stay away from the track, Luz. We don't want anything to happen to you."

"I'd like to meet you at the airport this afternoon. What time should I be there?"

"The plane is scheduled to land at the private hangar at four-thirty. I'm staying at the Chaucer in the usual suite."

"Okay, then. I'll see you later today."

"Good. Till then!"

With a few hours remaining before their arrival, Luz changed into her walking clothes. She donned the Harwood Racing gimme cap Jeff had given her, along with sunglasses, as it was bright and sunny out. Luz charged into the sunshine: she walked at a fast pace around the athletic course at the complex. Ducks swam on the retention ponds in the afternoon sun. She felt the wind pick up and noticed rain clouds to the north. The air was cooler than before. As she ventured onto a nearby street that led to a shopping center and deli, Luz slowed her pace considerably. Determined to make the best of this free time to herself, she thought about the last few days.

She felt lonely working by herself in the apartment. The weekend before, when she met new people, her natural curiosity served her needs. As a girl, she delighted in meeting newcomers, whom she soon converted to acquaintances and sometimes to friends. When she traveled to new cities, Luz made a home wherever she happened to be: a hotel room, an apartment, a friend's home. It was a skill she had mastered. Luz longed to explore, to see the sights, to get to know the neighborhood, and the neighbors. When she was in a new community, she rarely stayed inside for very long. She looked for the local bistro, the spot where everyone gathered after work and adopted it for a short time in whatever new place she visited.

The quirky Union Jack pub came to mind and then, naturally, Jeff. They first met in Orlando, when he worked on Clint's team, and now he had his own team. What an accomplishment! But more than that, she thought about his happy demeanor, juxtaposed with a serious attitude about his business. He was obviously competitive, but still good-natured. He joked with his team members to lighten the tension, but he was a strong leader who gave specific orders and delegated responsibility effectively.

As she daydreamed about Jeff and pondered the pros and cons of his character, she saw a sign for Trudy's Race Team, a little shop across the street on the corner. Her curiosity piqued, Luz waited at the intersection until she thought it was safe to cross.

When the light signaled to walk, Luz looked both ways and strode into the crosswalk. As she approached the other side, she heard brakes lock up and tires squeal as a beat-up sedan tore around the corner and barely missed her. It was so close she felt the air from the movement of the car slap her in the face like a whip. As it roared down the street, Luz looked for the license tag, but there was none. Stunned, she stood still in the middle of the intersection, unable to move. Inside Trudy's, the shoppers witnessed the near-accident and came outside to drag her into the store.

"Heavens to Betsy, girl, that car almost hit you."

"I saw the whole thing. If I didn't know better, I'd think it was done on purpose."

"Goodness gracious, let's get you some water. Sit down over here."

"My, my. Did anyone get the license plate? That driver should be arrested."

"I couldn't see what the driver looked like. He had a hat pulled down over his face."

"Whoever it was sure was in a dagburn hurry, like he was going to a fire."

The ladies chattered and fluttered over Luz. They brought her ice water and a cold rag for her neck. Seated in a comfortable chair, they put her feet up on a box that served as an ottoman. Luz felt she was in her Aunt Susie's gift shop in Houston, except at Trudy's everything in the store had a racing theme. There were little bears in fire suits, and bunnies wearing black-and-white-checkered poodle skirts.

"I called the police, and they are coming right over to get a report from all of us. Young lady, you are one lucky girl. You could have been killed. The nerve of that driver, running the red light, not even stopping, and then taking that turn at that speed."

Luz had not said a word; she just listened and sipped her water. Her heart raced, and it was obvious she was in shock. First her body felt too hot, then too cold, and finally clammy. She felt faint, but breathed slowly and deeply to calm herself. She wanted to memorize everything that happened in that short, brief moment, when she heard the brakes lock up and the tires squeal around the turn. From what she'd learned so far at the track, whoever it was knew what they were doing:

when to brake, when to turn, and how fast to accelerate, to get in, out and away. Luz knew deep down, that again, someone wanted to scare her away, and even more, it confirmed that she was being watched and followed.

"Are you okay, dear? You haven't said a word, since we brought you in here. Can you speak, dear?"

"If I was her, I'd have had the words scared out of me. Let her alone, Isabel, she's probably trying to pull herself together. Give her some room to breathe."

At that moment a policeman who looked very fit came into the shop, and the ladies moved aside like the parting of the Red Sea. With pad and pen in hand, he looked down at Luz as she sat in the overstuffed chair. She didn't know whether to get up or stay seated: she was frozen to the spot, looking like a small little girl who had lost her puppy.

The policeman looked around and asked, "Which one of you is Trudy?"

The heavy-set woman who had shooed Isabel away from Luz answered, "I am."

"Did you call about a serious accident on this corner?"

"Why, yes. This young lady was almost run over by a car going way too fast."

Then all the women in the shop had to add their two cents' worth to what had happened: "Had to be going at least fifty." "Ran the red light, didn't even stop or slow down." "Flew right by her like he didn't even see her." "She was shaking like a leaf, so we brought her in here." "She was crossing the street— he should have stopped or waited."

"Ladies, ladies—one at a time!" The policeman held up

his hands and raised his voice, hoping the ladies' squawking would stop.

He asked each of the ladies to step outside with him while he asked them questions. When he was finished with most of them, he turned to Luz. "Seems like someone tried to run you down. At least that's what most of these ladies think. And since half of them are grandmothers, and therefore trained observers, with a few years of experience, I'd say they might be right. So what is your story?"

Luz told him who she worked for and why she was in Indianapolis. At first he was skeptical, but the more she told him, the more he believed her story. The ladies in the store pretended to shop, but they were clearly eavesdropping.

"So two nights ago you were in the garage area and a pit cart came straight for you, and now today you're on an impromptu walk, and there's another close call with a car. Who doesn't like you?"

"It could be any number of people. I'm really tired now. In two hours I need to pick up someone at the airport. Can I go now?"

Not wanting to say too much more because she felt the ladies hovering around listening, Luz added, "If you need to know more, you are welcome to come with me to the airport, and I can answer more questions on the way there."

"I don't think that will be necessary, but in case you have any more close encounters like this one, here's my card. Call me if you need any help." With that, he extended his hand to help her up. Luz was a bit wobbly when she first stood up, but with a deep breath she steadied herself.

"Since you don't live too far away, why don't I give you a ride home?" the officer said. "I'm sure these ladies won't mind if you come back another day to shop and buy a few things. Right now I think you need to rest."

Luz nodded. She turned around to face Trudy, Isabel, and the other ladies. "Thank you all so much for looking after me. I promise I'll be back soon."

Trudy came up and gave her a quick hug. "I'm counting on that. Good luck, dear. Hope everything works out for you."

The policeman put on his hat and led the way out of the store. He opened the passenger door for her, then got in on the driver's side.

"So what's the skinny? What is it that you didn't want those old biddies to hear and gossip about?"

"We believe the team manager has committed fraud, and we hope we can catch him in the act. I'm picking up the team owner and her lawyers and accountants at the airport this afternoon. I just hope they have enough proof to stop this guy."

As he dropped her off at her apartment, the officer said, "Good luck. Watch your back. Whoever is after you may not miss next time."

Glad to be distracted by the mundane process of showering, primping, and dressing, Luz found it was a slow process, as memories of the car, the driver, and the air whipping her face interrupted her concentration. She hoped to remember some detail that might be a clue.

Careful to watch her rear-view mirror on her way, Luz drove cautiously to the airport and arrived fifteen minutes early. While she waited, she sipped on a cappuccino offered her by the friendly attendant at the fixed base operation. From the reception area's floor-to-ceiling windows, she saw the pointy-nosed jet land and taxi down the runway. Once the door opened, Michelle and two men disembarked from the plane. Luz smiled as she saw them, thankful for their arrival. At that moment she was reminded again of how alone she felt and what a big responsibility she had shouldered these last few days.

Michelle hugged her warmly when she saw her, then stepped back to look at her. "You look like you've lost weight! You have circles under your eyes, Luz. You look exhausted. Did something else happen since I talked with you?" Michelle, who always looked like she'd stepped from the pages of Vogue, had a dewy freshness about her, even after three hours on a plane.

"Oh, nothing, just a little accident today," Luz said, her voice soft, like a little girl's.

"What kind of accident? Are you hurt? Was anyone else involved?" Michelle asked, genuine concern in her voice.

"It's a long story, so I'll summarize for you." Luz regained her strength and controlled her emotions as she shared the details of her day, "I was walking. A car almost hit me as I crossed the street. Fortunately, I was in front of Trudy's shop, and all these ladies came to my rescue."

"What do you mean, someone almost hit you?" Michelle asked, slowly and deliberately. "Someone almost hit you two nights ago. How did this happen again?"

"I guess we're close to the truth. I haven't been to the track since Sunday. The policeman who took the statements from the ladies at Trudy's told me to be careful. He said it was obvious I'm being watched and followed."

"Oh, Luz, I didn't realize someone would intentionally hurt you. I thought all they wanted was money."

"Michelle, there is a lot of money at stake. Not just the prize money, but also the sponsorship money and the endorsements. Jonathan Barrow said Schneider was involved with some dangerous people, and for some people their entire life and livelihood is at stake here. They will do whatever it takes to ensure that the future they imagined happens, and they don't care who gets in the way," Luz said. "You included. We all must be careful." The attorneys who had been listening nodded, then introduced themselves to Luz.

"You've done a great job collecting the evidence we needed. Thanks for your work," one of them told her.

"Luz, I think the attorneys should take your car for the days we are in town," Michelle said. "A different car, a bit of variety, might confuse others, and be safer."

"Oh, okay. Thank you, Michelle. I'm glad you're here right now to do my thinking for me. I've been so focused on figuring out this puzzle, and so angry about how Roger Schneider is treating you and Clint, I must be too wound up to think straight."

Luz drove the two of them to the Chaucer Hotel next to Union Station, where Michelle checked into a suite and ordered room service. Luz sat on the couch and waited with her.

"How has the rest of your time been working out for you?" Michelle asked.

"Good. My clients are thrilled they know someone with an

Indy team. How were you able to leave Clint?"

"He insisted we come to take care of this mess," Michelle said, sitting down next to Luz. "He's regained a lot of his strength now. He'll be fine spending the weekend in a luxury rehab hospital watching qualifying on television."

"Since you're here, what do you want me to do?" Luz felt a bit anxious, thinking about her promise to Jeff to attend the mechanics' party.

"I want you at the track tomorrow, acting as if none of the accidents happened. Can you do that?" Michelle asked gently.

"Yes. My first Indy 500 qualifying—I don't want to miss a minute." Luz's face lighted up, then a serious look crossed it. "What is Roger going to think when he sees you at the track?"

"Since it is the first weekend of qualifying, which I always attend, he won't wonder about my being here. Anyway, we don't plan to confront Roger until Monday. We're going to give him a little time to feel uncomfortable, with the hopes he'll be contrite and ask for forgiveness."

"And how will you explain the lawyers?"

"Oh, we'll tell him they are new sponsors or prospective sponsors. He'll be so busy anyway, he won't care," Michelle said. "Luz, would you mind taking the draw for the qualifying order? Clint usually does it, but I think it would be nice for you to do it."

"What an honor!" Luz said, then she asked, "Is it better to qualify at the beginning or the end?"

"It depends on whether a team is ready. The first day is the only day a team can qualify for the pole position. If only one car is able to get out on the track to qualify, then that car wins the pole. Teams follow the qualifying draw order first, and then after that, whichever team is ready and in line for tech can qualify." Michelle added wistfully, "We've been competitive in the race for the pole for the last three years. But who knows about this year."

The room service arrived, giving them a chance to eat. Luz was hungry, having skipped lunch. Michelle ordered chicken Caesar salads for both of them, with hot crusty rolls on the side and fresh raspberries, vanilla ice cream, and chocolate cake for dessert. "I thought a little chocolate would be perfect," she said.

It was already seven, and Luz was feeling drowsy after the meal. She enjoyed a glass of chardonnay with her dinner and felt relaxed and safe for the first time that week.

"Before you leave, let's go over the paperwork you put together for us." Michelle opened the envelope and placed the contents on the table, then called the attorneys and asked them to come to her suite.

Once they arrived, Luz carefully outlined the case against Roger Schneider from all of the photographs, the financial documents, and the papers she'd received from Gena Newman in the credentials office.

"It will be hard to prove he intended to break away from Amberson Racing, even though he entered a car under the Blackbird name in April. He could argue that Clint helped smaller teams in the past or that the extra entry was for someone else. But it seems he thought of starting his own team when he sent the entry in to the speedway offices. Fraudulent use of Amberson funds is the crime we have to prove," one of the attorneys said.

"We have that evidence from both accounting and bank records," another responded.

"Yes, but we must be very discreet," Michelle said. "I want our cars to make the show. I don't want a whiff of this to be made public until we make our move."

"But what about all those sponsors he's taken away from you?" Luz asked. "Don't you want that to stop?"

"Luz, the Indy family is a very small, close community. When others discover what Roger is capable of, he won't work in auto racing for a very long time. I'm not worried about sponsors. I am worried about making the race."

"But they've been on the track every day."

"Yes, on the track, but has Roger prepared our cars, or has he been focused on his own? Luz, I don't know what the future will bring. This may be Clint's last Indy. His cars must be in the race. He's working so hard in rehab now just to be here for the 500. The only reason I came this weekend is because he wanted me to be here, to make sure we made the show. I don't care about the pole, but it's important to be on the grid on race day."

"I'll do whatever I can to help you, Michelle."

"You've already done more than I expected from you. It's very important this weekend to act like nothing is bothering you. Take the lead and everything will be fine," Michelle said, her eyes tearing up.

Luz touched her arm to comfort her. "Michelle, to maintain his reputation Roger must qualify the Amberson cars. He'll be too busy with this deceptive balancing act of his to worry about anything else. You concentrate on being the perfect hostess to all your guests, sponsors, and friends."

"Oh, Luz, you will have to work with Roger to decide on taking the qualifying run. Clint usually does that, and I—I don't think I can do it. I'm too upset right now. I need to stay as far away from Roger Schneider as I can, at least until after qualifying."

"I'll be there. Count on me," Luz said. "Goodnight, Michelle. Sleep well. I'll see you tomorrow." She gave her a hug before she left the suite. "Don't worry about a thing."

As she walked out the door, the valet handed Luz the keys to a gray sedan. "Mrs. Amberson asked that you take her car this evening."

Luz smiled at Michelle's concern. "Thank you. I will."

She turned left into the street and made her way home.

BARBIE O'CONNOR

CHAPTER 21

Luz bounded out of bed when the alarm on her clock sounded. She was excited and anxious about the mechanics' party, drawing for qualifying, and all the other new experiences coming her way that day. Feeling a bit unsure, Luz wondered if she could be fearless and open without revealing what she knew about Roger Schneider.

Fortunately, the morning was filled with phone calls to clients, portfolios to review, and investment ideas to share. She had worked hard for her clients during the week, revising portfolios for at least twenty different families. Today she would wrap up it all up. She wanted to earn this weekend off, felt she deserved time to revel in these new experiences.

Before she left for the track, she called Jeff. Fortunately he answered on the first ring. "Luz, great to hear your voice. Where are you? The rumors said you'd gone back to SA, and then Bart Soules told me about what happened yesterday in front of Trudy's." Jeff sounded stern.

"Bart Soules? How did he know?"

"Trudy is his aunt," Jeff said. "Can't keep a secret long in this town. Are you still my date for the party tonight?"

"Yes, I wouldn't miss it for the world. By the way, when and where do we go to draw the qualifying order? I'm supposed to do that for Amberson."

"Great! We can go together. It starts tonight right after happy hour, when the track closes for the day. Everyone meets in the grandstands to the left of the entrance to Gasoline Alley. There is a mad rush down the stairs to be first in line. Once all the numbers are drawn, then the party starts."

"Okay, why don't I look for you in the grandstands? You can save me a seat."

"I'll look for you there. We're going out to practice. See ya later," Jeff said, then hung up.

With her work done, and the weekend before her, Luz drove to the track. When she arrived, the Red Lot was so crowded it forced her to parallel park along the outer edge of the lot, closest to the infield loop road. From that vantage point, she saw crowds of people in the white tents set up between the golf course and the infield road. Sponsors in golf carts who were touring the facility waved to her as if they were dignitaries on a float in a parade. Luz smiled and waved back, glad they were having fun.

As she walked through the garage gates, one of the Yellow Shirts stopped her, saying, "Here's another one of those teenagers trying to sneak in when we're not lookin'. Let's see some ID," said one of the men in a Goodyear cap, winking at his partner with a Marlboro cap.

At first Luz was confused, but then she realized they were teasing her.

"You haven't been here in days. We were afraid you were sick or somethin'," the Marlboro man said.

"We hardly recognized you," Goodyear told her.

"Well, anywho, we're glad you're back, glad you're here." Both men chuckled. "Good luck today. We're rootin' for you."

As she walked into the garage area, Luz smelled the barbeque, steak, corn-on-the-cob, and hot apple pie from the hospitality tents, and it made her hungry. She walked over to the Harwood garage to invite Jeff for lunch at Loctite.

As she entered the garage past the car on display, Luz saw Beau Williams wipe his hands on a shop rag.

"Hey, Luz, where've you been? It's been three or four days since we've seen you around. Jeff made me do timing and scoring since you weren't here, and I don't write as small and neat as you do. He complained all week."

Beau's comments couldn't help but make her smile. Luz looked around the garage, and as she turned around to go out, he said, "In case you're lookin' for Jeff, he said he was going over to Simpson to get something, and then over to Loctite for a bite to eat. We don't have a fancy hospitality tent, so we're on our own around here."

"Thanks, Beau. If you see him, please let him know I'm looking for him, would you?"

Luz walked through the hallways that ran by the restrooms between the buildings. Just as she was about to walk out of the A building to go to Loctite, she stepped right in front of Roger

Schneider.

"Hey, look where you're going!" he shouted, and when he recognized her he growled, "Oh, it's you! You've made yourself scarce these last few days. I thought you'd left us," he said with a glare. "There are some things I have to talk to you about." He grabbed her arm, turned her around, and started to walk her back to the Amberson garage.

As they emerged into the sunlight between the B and C buildings, Luz shook her arm free and turned to face Schneider directly. She didn't like being touched that way, and as she started to speak her body shook with anger. "Listen! I don't appreciate the way you've treated me since I arrived here. And this manhandling is completely out of the question. I am a reasonable, professional person. I deserve a certain level of basic courtesy. Now: what do you want to talk to me about?" Luz leaned forward, her face six inches from his.

Luz kept her voice low the entire time, not wanting to create a scene in the garage area, but it was obvious from the looks on their faces that Roger Schneider and Luz Dane did not like each other.

Roger spoke slowly and distinctly, as if he was talking to a child or someone who had difficulty understanding English. "There is a drawing for qualifying order today. Ordinarily Clint Amberson draws for Amberson Racing, but since he is not with us, I thought it appropriate for me to draw for the team's two qualifying spots. Also, tomorrow when the cars qualify someone has to determine whether to take the qualifying runs. As I am more knowledgeable than you are, I think I should be the one who stands in for Clint."

Luz watched his face while he talked to her. He was so consumed with his superiority that he almost sneered. She wanted to laugh, knowing what the future had in store for him, but she promised to act as if there were no surprises ahead.

"I'm so sorry. Didn't anyone tell you?" Luz looked wide-eyed, her voice filled with pity.

"Tell me what?" he snapped.

"I'm afraid that Michelle already told the league that I'm to draw for the Amberson team when it's time."

Roger's face turned red. For a moment, Luz thought he might start yelling at her, or grab her as he had done before. "We'll see about that."

He turned to walk into the Amberson garage, and then, with a look of cold fury and a glint in his eye, he repeated, "We'll see about that."

Not sure what he really meant, but certain the day was far from over, Luz walked over to Loctite hoping to run into Jeff. As she walked into the cool darkness of the room, she heard a familiar voice say, "Hey, good lookin'."

As her eyes adjusted, she saw Bruce behind the counter, laughing with a couple of guys who ogled the tools he showed them in the catalogue spread out before them. Pouring chili on his hot dog was Jeff, with a big grin on his face.

"There you are. I thought I recognized your voice," she told Jeff, helping herself to some lunch. After grabbing a soda, Luz sat down with Jeff.

"So how are you doing?" he asked.

"My clients are pretty happy. But I haven't been doing so well here at the track."

"Oh, really?" Jeff took a bite of his chili cheese dog.

"I made Roger Schneider mad. I just left him at the garage, and his face was beet red. It looked like he was about to explode."

Jeff chuckled. "Couldn't happen to a nicer guy."

"He wants to draw for the team and be the one who throws the flag, but Michelle asked me to do it. He's being a baby. And he's got his own team. Why does he care? Oops. I wasn't supposed to say that," Luz said, putting her chin down so Jeff couldn't see her face.

"What weren't you supposed to say?" Jeff asked, bending his head so he could look at her. "Luz, have you been sticking your nose where it doesn't belong? You promised me and Jonathan Barrow and Michelle you'd behave. What have you done now?"

"Nothing—forget about it. So, six o'clock is the drawing, followed by the party?" Luz asked cheerfully. She grabbed her napkin and wiped her hands, then her lips.

Jeff gave her a direct, quizzical look, but he could see she was eager to change the subject.

"I'm looking forward to it," Luz said.

"Have you checked on the contingency money?"

"What are you talking about?"

"You know all those stickers on the sides of the cars that you see in the photos and on the models?"

"Yes. Aren't those sponsors?"

"Sort of. Certain companies award certain prizes after the race, and sometimes after qualifying if your car displays their sticker."

"Like what kind of prizes?"

"Sometimes it's an extra $10,000 if your car finishes in the top five. Sometimes it's an extra five grand if the car leads on a certain lap number. One time it added about a hundred grand to the prize money just 'cause we had the right stickers on the car."

"Then of course I want to look at the list," Luz said, wiping ketchup off her chin. "What else should I be doing?"

"You might verify that your sponsors' logos are displayed in the location designated by the contract."

"Oh, that is a good idea." Luz started writing herself a checklist.

"And one more thing, Luz. The hat dance and the qualifying picture."

"The hat dance?" she asked, puzzled.

"When the car qualifies, the crew, the team owner, and any sponsors all crowd around the car for pictures. If your sponsor wants a picture with the crew and driver wearing his hat, then someone needs to be there with hats ready to go, to pass them out for everyone to put on for the picture."

"Hats." Luz jotted this down too.

"And there isn't much time. All this is done at the end of pit road, as soon as the golf cart brings the owner and crew chief back after the run is successful."

"Thanks for all the information. Now to accomplish all this before tonight." Luz stood up from the table.

"I'll be on pit road. Joe, my crew chief, will know where to find the contingency list, so ask him for it. I'll see you in the stands later."

"Yeah! See ya." Luz walked out of Loctite, slipping her Amberson hat on her head.

When she arrived at the Harwood garage she found Joe Kerr, who quickly located the contingency list. He handed it to her and explained where to find each of the stickers she needed for the car. Luz scurried around the garage area, going from one supplier to another, asking sweetly for the decals and patches for the team uniforms that she needed to fulfill the Amberson contract requirements. She hurried back to the garage and got there just as the pit cart began to tow the chassis to the fuel station. Luz quickly placed the stickers where they belonged on both sides of the nose, and the sides of the rear wing on both of the chassis. With her travel sewing kit she attached the patches to the crew chief and drivers' uniforms as the contingency rules stipulated.

Only four more hours and the qualifying process would begin, starting with that evening's drawing and following at eleven the next morning, when the first car would attempt to make the field. The crowds watching practice that afternoon were everywhere. Every shape and kind of person from beer-bellied red necks to svelte blond models was present at the track. She overheard a group who spoke German, another Italian; there was a cluster of Japanese tourists huddled over at one of the television trailers. It was an international event.

Once Luz reached the pressroom, she showed her ID to the Yellow Shirt and picked up the daily run lists for the day before. Comparing the data collected over the last few days, the Amberson car number 45 ran at 222 mph in practice. The Blackbird car, number 66, showed its best speed was 221 mph, with 215 mph, its worst. Harwood racing's entry ran around that same 221 mph area as Blackbird and Amberson. With so many cars in that same range, the competition would be fierce to make the race and hold on to the position in the lineup once a car qualified.

"You're not reading the rule book this time," she heard Carter Holland say as he walked up to the table where she was sitting.

"No, I'm studying these times to figure out a reasonable speed to accept for qualifying."

"Your crew chief will be there to help you—it would be difficult to make that decision with as little experience as you've had," Carter told her.

Luz looked at him intently, then looked down at the papers in front of her.

"Carter, even with the little experience I've had, I know in my heart to take anything less than 220 miles an hour would be a mistake."

"How can you be so sure, Luz?"

"In my business, I've looked at charts to analyze stock performance. If this were a stock chart, 215 miles an hour would be the low end, here the slow end, and 225 the high or fast end of things. My bet is the fast guys have been driving easy, and probably have a few miles per hour to add to their speed. How fast the pole winner will be, I'd guess about 228 miles an hour. But, as you've pointed out, I don't have much experience," Luz said matter-of-factly. Then she waved at Carter: "Bye now." She stood up abruptly, gathered the papers she was studying, and walked out the door.

Irritated by his comment that she was too inexperienced to figure out a good qualifying range, Luz sat down at a bench near the broadcast trailers to look at the rule book. She remembered reading a formula that required the speed of the slowest car to be a certain percentage of the speed of the fastest car in the field. When she found the section, she made a chart using the top speeds of 228, 227, 226, and 225 mph to calculate the slowest speed a car could run. This exercise gave her a better feel for what speed the Amberson team needed to run to be competitive in the field.

Moving to the outside stands opposite pit road, Luz watched the cars from the covered paddock as they practiced; she timed them and compared their performance. For an hour she timed different cars, making notes of their speeds, including Amberson and Harwood. The Blackbird car wasn't out yet, but its mysterious yellow clad driver with the black helmet waited patiently.

Turning her attention to the drama unfolding in the Harwood pits, Luz watched as Christi Cole and Mark Miller each took turns practicing a qualifying run. With only one car, Jeff had to cut one of the drivers, and Luz could tell who it would be. It was a shame, since Christi was a sponsor's dream, with her perky good looks and her articulate interviews.

From her vantage point in the paddock, Luz watched the Amberson team unnoticed. Walking onto pit road at the gate near the winner's circle, Michelle Amberson approached the scoring stand, where Roger Schneider and the engineer sat with their heads together studying the onboard computer. Her gloved hand tapped lightly on the top of the stand, and a surprised Roger Schneider looked up to find his boss facing him when he least expected it.

With a pleasant look on her face, Michelle beckoned to Schneider to come speak with her. He quickly scurried off the scoring stand to Michelle. Covered by a tarp, the Blackbird car had been out on pit road the entire afternoon. Luz watched as Michelle walked over to the car and pulled the tarp back, revealing the logos of many of the Amberson sponsors. She quickly flipped the tarp back over the car and, with forthrightness apparent even from across the track, emphatically addressed Roger, her hands pointed at the car, and then pointed at him, as if he was a badly behaved child. When she finished with him, she turned and briskly walked away. As he watched her walk away, Roger Schneider snapped his pencil in half with one hand. Luz could tell he was angry.

Luz thought Schneider was a man who when angry turned a pleasant face to the public while hurting his adversary. She remembered the pit cart and the passenger car in front of Trudy's. She asked questions and sought information about Blackbird Racing before those events. The look on his face after Michelle walked away was one of cold fury. Would he go so far as to endanger innocent lives, or was he only interested in hurting the targets of his anger? His past behavior showed he would take the offensive, and that worried her. Luz left the stands to warn Michelle of the fury she'd witnessed.

CHAPTER 22

Luz walked around the entire garage area, past each of the A, B, and C buildings, in front of Loctite, by the pressroom. Finding Michelle would be impossible in this crowd. She walked to the motor home, where a group of sponsors from Vestcom were being plied with snacks and drinks as they listened to Matt Locke, the Amberson driver, who was telling stories about his favorite moments of his racing career. Luz knew she could spend hours looking for her. Every time she dialed the cell phone number, it went to voicemail.

Happy hour started in fifteen minutes. Everyone who thought they were ready for qualifying would be on the track during that time. The media staked claims to locations for their cameras for the next morning. All of the network reporters interviewed drivers and team owners in the pits, and speculation started as to who would claim the coveted pole, with its $100,000 prize.

As Luz went through her mental checklist of the next few days, she heard the loudspeaker in the garage area announce, "Press conference with Blackbird Racing tonight at the trackside press room at six-fifteen. The qualifying drawing will take place immediately afterward."

Ordinarily Luz wouldn't have noticed anything beyond "press conference," since it seemed as if every fifteen minutes another one was taking place in the trackside pressroom, but when she heard "Blackbird Racing" she shivered.

Luz walked out of Gasoline Alley to pit road. Before she reached the Amberson pit, Luz found Michelle talking to Sid Fury, the bulldog of a mechanic, as well as rat-faced Blake Notson, the crew chief. All of them seemed to be engaged in light banter; occasionally a smile or laugh crossed their faces. Luz could not tell whether they knew about the Blackbird press conference or assumed the next major event was the qualifying drawing. Luz walked on to the Harwood pit box, only nodding in acknowledgment to Michelle as she passed.

It was a long way to the Harwood box. Since Harwood was a new team, with no points and no previous record, they were relegated to the next to the last spot on pit road, closest to the pit road entrance from the track at turn 4, right before the front straightaway began. It seemed to Luz that the walk to that box was twice as far as she had already walked to the Amberson pit. When she arrived there, she realized it was next door to the Blackbird Racing pit.

Jeff, Christi, and Mark Miller all had tense looks on their faces. The remaining crew members scurried around preparing the car. Luz hopped up onto the scoring stand, where she overheard Jeff talking very seriously to Christi and Mark.

"We have to clock at least 224 miles an hour to make a decent showing and to stay in the field. You've both known that one of you would be dropped from the team at this point, and I'm afraid it will be based solely on who can drive the car to speed," Jeff said.

When practice ended at six o'clock, Mark's best average speed over four laps was 224.625 mph, besting Christi's 223 mph.

Mark high-fived the crew members around him, whooping for joy. Then he turned to Christi: "It's been good working with you, Christi. Hope you can find another ride."

"Yes, Christi, you've done an incredible job in the time we've worked together," Jeff said. "Thanks for your effort. I'm sorry I don't have two cars to run. If I did I'd run you both."

Christi's eyes glistened and she looked down, took a deep breath, and controlled the tears from flowing further. She blew her nose, dabbed at her eyes, and looked up. "Thanks, Jeff, you gave me a wonderful opportunity to drive for you. You shared lots of great tips, and you helped me be a better driver. I hope we can work together again."

Christi extended her hand to shake Jeff's. She had a brave smile on her face as she said, "Thanks again."

With her helmet under her arm, she turned towards the garage area. After a few minutes, she was lost in the crowd moving towards the stands where the drawing for qualifying order would take place.

Luz wanted to sit in on the Blackbird Racing press conference. As the Harwood team towed their car into the garage area, she hopped on the pit cart for a ride in. When they stopped to allow all the fans to cross at the opening to Gasoline Alley, Luz hopped off at the trackside conference room.

Looking through the small window in the door, she saw three microphones on a table with the league logo backdrop behind it. When she saw Roger, the driver, Matt Locke, and Blake Notson, the Amberson crew chief, all in yellow Blackbird livery, take their seats at the table, Luz showed her credentials to the Yellow Shirt at the door and slid into the back of the room. Flanking both sides of the podium table were former Amberson team members, each wearing Blackbird uniforms. She didn't know whether to be angry or frightened. This could only mean one thing: Roger Schneider was jumping ship, and taking the entire Amberson team with him, including the driver.

Luz remembered Clint saying to her once that the only way racers can win competitions is to drive their own race—to use the qualities of their individual car, drive their own style, follow their own internal rhythm, and look forward and never look back. To look forward, to look to race day, Luz needed an entire team and two new drivers. She knew one young woman who wanted a ride. With help, maybe from the old-timers like Billy Wojinski, and Carter Holland, she would find the rest of the crew.

Now was the time to act, to work on the strategy for the next day. There would be plenty of time later to listen to Roger's story, since all the trackside press conferences were filmed and archived. Qualifying order seemed a moot point now that she didn't even know who would drive the Amberson cars or who would be the crew members.

Luz slipped out the doorway, unnoticed. Once outside, she sat at one of the concession stand outdoor tables, dialed Michelle's number, and hoped for a connection. She was surprised when Michelle answered right away.

"Turn to the press conference on the track channel," Luz said as she heard chatter in the background, glasses clinking and happy laughter coming from the suite.

"Speak up, Luz."

"It's Roger and Blackbird Racing. The entire team has left Amberson."

"What!!??" Michelle put the phone down, and Luz could hear her saying, "Turn on the television and find the track channel. Yes, that one. Turn up the sound." Then Michelle picked the phone up again. "Luz, let me watch this, and I'll call you back."

While she waited, Luz looked for Christi Cole, hoping she would want a ride with Amberson. At least that way, when she drew for qualifying she'd have a driver to announce to the press. The most important thing for her now was to remain calm, resolute, and confident. There was no time for doubts now. She believed in the new friends she'd made at the speedway and in those old friends of Clint and Michelle who'd proven their loyalty.

As she walked towards the Harwood garage, teams stowed their equipment in preparation for the mechanics' party. She heard laughter, teasing, and general good spirits. Luz wished she could feel so happy. Right now she felt she had let her friends down. As she turned the corner between the B and C buildings, Luz saw Christi closing the door to the Harwood garage with a duffel bag in her right hand, her helmet under that arm, and two fire suits draped over her left arm. Dressed in jeans and a white T-shirt, she looked barely over eighteen. When she saw her, Luz waved her arms and called out to her. "Christi!! Christi!! Over here—it's Luz. Wait up!"

Darting in and out of the crowd, Luz caught up to her. Breathless, she said, "Thank goodness you're still here. Christi, I really need your help. I have to put a team together by tomorrow. Would you drive for me, for Amberson Racing?"

Christi looked puzzled. She took her hand and felt Luz's forehead. "No, you don't have a fever. You're kidding, aren't you? You can't really be serious about needing an entire team."

At that moment, two crew members wearing the Blackbird livery walked by. Christi's eyes followed them. She said, "That was Sid Fury and Blake Notson. They've been on the Amberson team for years. What are they doing in . . . ? Oh, you really are serious. Oh, Luz, how awful for you, and qualifying is tomorrow."

"Yes, qualifying is tomorrow. I need to know, Christi—will you drive for me?"

"Of course! What an opportunity! I think. Who are you going to get for the rest of the team?"

"I don't know that yet, but I started with you, and now I have about twenty more team members to go. Any suggestions would be appreciated."

At that moment Luz's phone rang.

"Luz, it's Michelle. We saw the whole thing. The attorneys are here, and they are working on a response. Jonathan Barrow called to say he is on his way over to secure the garage."

"I'm on my way over there now. By the way, I found a good driver. Christi Cole was let go by Harwood today. She was up to about 223 miles an hour during happy hour today. I think she could go faster in better equipment."

"Christi Cole has agreed to drive for us!" Michelle told her guests in the suite. "Good job, Luz. A league official will be with us to change the door combination so we will be secure for the night. Barrow wants to look for anything important that might be left behind. I want a press conference tomorrow morning at ten-thirty, right before qualifying starts. That'll give us media attention too. Are you at the garage yet, Luz?"

"Just got here," Luz said with relief as she turned on the lights, then continued, "Both car chassis are here. There is an engine in a crate over in the corner. The desk in the back is a mess. All of the lockers are in shambles. And there is a hell of a lot of laundry to do. Looks like they took their toolboxes and all their personal stuff out of here earlier, probably during happy hour."

Jonathan Barrow walked in as Luz reported on the condition of the Amberson garage. He looked around as if he expected to find important evidence lying about on the workbench or garage floor.

"Jonathan Barrow just walked in. I've got to go. I'll see you after the drawing and before the party," Luz said, disconnecting the call.

"Luz, you've really stirred things up around here. Seems Mr. Schneider doesn't want to work with you. Probably took any documented evidence with him," Barrow said in a chastising tone.

"Gee, maybe he threw it away or hid it here. Like in this trashcan or laundry bin," Luz responded angrily, frustrated that the head of speedway security was stating the obvious and blaming her. She leaned into the garbage can pulling rags, bottles, and paper towels out of the container. Then she did the same thing with team shirts, pants, and fire suits stashed in the corner bin, only to have a piece of paper that looked like a bank statement fall out of a pocket.

"A wire transfer confirmation. Wow! Over a million dollars was wired to a bank in the Caymans from the Amberson account only yesterday," Luz said as she skimmed it and then passed it to the speedway security chief.

"Good thing they were in a rush on their way out of here. It might have ended up in the laundry, Ms. Dane, if you hadn't found it. At least now we have somewhere to start," Chief Barrow said, scanning the page. "When I first met you, I underestimated you. Now I'm glad you're on our side. It seems like I should be thanking you."

"That's not the only important thing they left. Look at this." Christi held up a notebook with an aluminum clipboard on top of it. Looking through it, she smiled and said, "All the setup data on the cars. Both chassis. I'm surprised. There is data from races earlier this year. Someone is going to need this in the next few days. Where do you want me to put it?"

"Put it in the top drawer of this desk," Luz said as she cleared the jumble from the drawer into a box to go through later. "We'll need it as soon as I've found us a few more team members. Michelle and the attorneys will be here any minute. I need to leave for the drawing. I'll see you later. Thanks, Christi. Good hunting, Jonathan."

"Thank you, Ms. Dane. Good luck with the drawing."

Luz ran through the garage area, only to be stopped at the exit to the track from Gasoline Alley, while the few remaining pit carts came in from the track. As soon as they passed, she wound her way to the stands, where the team managers and owners waited to draw for qualifying order. Jeff signaled her to come sit next to him on the tenth row.

As she climbed the steps upward, people she passed whispered and pointed at her. Others turned away when she looked their way. Luz did her best to maintain a pleasant, confident demeanor as she moved to the seat next to Jeff. Even when she passed Roger Schneider she nodded her head in acknowledgment and caused a flurry of whispers among the assembled crowd.

When she reached her seat, Jeff said, "I'm glad you finally got here. The mad rush begins in a minute, and I was afraid you weren't going to make it."

"I wouldn't miss this for the world. But I did have a few unexpected problems to resolve before tonight." Her voice held a note of irony.

"Luz, do you want to run up there to be the first to draw, like some guys do, the guys who think it's a great publicity stunt? Or do you want to walk down calmly and wait in line to draw our numbers?"

"I'd just as soon wait. With the day I've had, I'd fall and roll down the stairs in a little ball, like a cartoon rabbit."

When the call to draw was announced, one of the team

owners, a fan favorite, rushed down the stairs and proudly became the first one in line. He eagerly hammed it up for the press cameras, and reached his hand into the velvet drawstring bag to draw the qualifying numbers for his four entries. After an interview with the national television commentator, he stepped down from the podium that had been set up to house the television cameras covering the qualifying action the next day.

Other team owners and managers soon followed with everyone lined up in the aisle of the stands. Luz and Jeff stayed in their seats and waited for everyone else to draw their numbers. Eventually they joined the others. Luz continued to smile at everyone and nod to those she knew. Jeff joked around with the fellows he had known for years.

As they approached the table, Luz listened carefully to the questions asked to verify the number of entries and names of drivers. Roger Schneider stood only four people in front of her so she heard his responses. Yes, Matt Locke had chosen to go with Schneider—it was now official. And Schneider only had one entry, whereas Amberson had two. Luz watched as the officials made note on the marker board of the qualifying order. When she saw that Blackbird Racing drew the chance to qualify first, Luz controlled her anger about the publicity his team would receive with his car on the pole, even if only for a few minutes.

Luz breathed a sigh of relief when she drew numbers putting Amberson at fifteenth and eighteenth to qualify. She needed time to put together a team. Jeff was happy to be qualifying sixth. Afterward, as they walked towards the Harwood garage, he said, "Good, it'll be over in a flash. The team will have the day off on Sunday, and I'll relax knowing the car made the race." The press wanted an interview with Luz, but she artfully dodged their questions notifying them of the press conference planned for the next day.

As they walked over to Amberson Racing, a band tuned up in front of the Firestone garage, near the gate Luz came in that day. Once at the garage Luz tried the old combination, but it had been changed. She saw lights on inside when she peered through the glass window, so she knocked on the door. Jonathan Barrow came to the door to let her in, said hello to Jeff, and closed the door. A team of six people each with a clipboard checked parts, engines, and tools scattered around the garage. Luz recognized two of the group as the attorneys she met the day before with Michelle. In anticipation of any questions, she explained, "Luz, we're taking inventory: uniforms, fire suits, parts, engines, even the chassis and rims. We've another group going over the shop. I heard from Jonathan that you found what might be a key financial statement with what might be passwords written in the margins."

"Surprising they were so careless. Hope it's not a red herring."

"Yes, we'll be careful with the assumptions we make," Michelle said as she walked over to the chassis where Jeff stood.

As he leaned over to take off the engine cowling, Jeff pulled out one of the spark plugs to look at it.

"Someone needs to look at the chassis and engine," Jeff said, showing Michelle the condition of the plug. "How do you know you can even run tomorrow? This engine might need to be replaced, and you'd better look at the headers, plugs, and pumps. Otherwise it might blow up on the track."

"We've only had time to compare chassis numbers and engine serial numbers. We'd hoped we could run tomorrow. Clint always wanted to win the pole," Michelle said wistfully.

Jeff removed the side pod from the left side, carefully inspecting what he could see without touching anything.

"You'd better check those parts before you go out on the track," he said. "I wish I could help you, but I promised my guys the day off the minute we qualified. I can't break that promise to them."

"I wouldn't ask that of you. But I think you're right: we'll have to give up the dream of the pole. Better that than give up making the race."

"Yes, it will be a bad day when the Amberson team doesn't make the 500," Jeff said.

"I don't even want to think about it," Michelle said flatly.

The attorneys went over a few things with Luz about the press conference the next day—what they wanted her to say, and what the agenda would look like. The track opened at nine in the morning for practice, then closed down an hour and a half later to prepare for qualifying, so there definitely would be a lot of press attending. After everyone was clear about their responsibilities, she and Jeff left the accountants and the attorneys to do their jobs.

"Have a good time at the party, Luz. Relax and know that what happens next is out of our hands," Michelle said before she walked out of the garage.

She and Jeff had a blast that night. While he talked to his

old friends, she took turns dancing with different members of his team, as well as a few of the Yellow Shirts and the reps from the tire companies and engine manufacturers. The band played songs from the Beatles, Charlie Daniels Band, ZZ Top, and even a few big band numbers from the 1940s. When they weren't dancing, they were eating barbeque ribs, sausage, and brisket at tables set up between the A building and the Firestone tire garage. Unlike the owners who had snubbed her before the drawing for qualifying, most of the mechanics were friendly and glad to see her. A few without dates even asked her to dance and afterward asked her about what her life was like when she wasn't at the track. By the end of the evening, Luz's face was flushed from dancing in the cool night air, and her eyes were bright from the two glasses of red wine she'd consumed. She felt she'd had a good workout that evening, and was ready for a good night's sleep.

After the band played a Rolling Stones song as its evening send-off, everyone said good night and wished each other good luck the next day. Luz was surprised to find that these people whose teams competed against one another had friendships she envied. They might want to beat each other on the track, but when it was all over, they were buddies who cared a great deal about one another.

Jeff walked Luz to her car and gave her a kiss before he opened the door for her. Catcalls came from behind them as others walked to their cars and took in the scene.

"Mmm. I'd like another kiss, but I don't think our reputations can stand it if we stay here making out. I'll follow you home. See you there," he said as he closed the car door

BARBIE O'CONNOR

CHAPTER 23

Luz started her car and dreamily drove back to her apartment only a few blocks away. Jeff followed close behind. When she parked in a spot in front of her apartment, he drove into the one next to it. He gave her a hand with her pack and helped her out of the car. They walked to the front door together. Jeff wrapped his arm around her waist and squeezed her gently to his side. Luz rested her head on his shoulder. When they got inside, Jeff set her bag down, then took her in his arms and kissed her passionately and fervently. Finally they both came up for air, and Luz pointed to the sofa: "Over there. Sit down."

Still embracing her, Jeff held her, dancing her backwards towards the sofa. Luz started to take off her coat and began to unzip his parka. They shrugged their coats off and sat down on the couch.

"Drink?" Luz asked, moving towards the kitchen.

"No." Jeff pulled her back down onto his lap. He turned

her face to him, where he kissed her gently on the lips, then peppered her face with tiny kisses. He stopped at each of her ears to lightly run his tongue over the outer edge, worked his way to her neck, where he began to suckle her skin slowly as he moved towards her breasts. He hesitantly unbuttoned her team shirt, waiting for a sign from her to continue or to stop. Luz answered his query by unbuttoning his shirt while she caressed his neck and shoulders, running her hands along his back, pulling his shirt away from his body and then off onto the floor.

"Um, uh, what about . . . "Jeff ran his finger down the valley between her breasts.

"Protection?" Luz asked, looking up at him.

"Uh huh," Jeff mumbled as he nibbled on her neck.

"I have what you need upstairs," Luz told him.

Offering him her hand, she led him up the stairs to her bed, where they struggled free of their clothes and fell into each other's arms, overwhelmed by their hunger for loving touch. Physical desire and their emotional connection led the two lovers down the path of bliss. Afterward they lay spent in each other's arms and slept undisturbed until morning.

When light filtered into the room the following day, they stirred. Jeff suddenly realized he was not in his own apartment and sat up in bed. Looking around wildly for a clock, he was relieved to see it was only six in the morning. Slowly and quietly he climbed out of bed and tiptoed towards the bathroom.

Feeling his movement, Luz opened her eyes and watched him as he moved around, careful not to disturb her. His nude body in the morning sun glistened as the light blond hairs that covered his skin reflected the light as it filled the room.

"Mornin', Jeff," Luz said, her voice rough from the night's silence.

Startled, he turned around. She beckoned to him to come to her.

"Can't. The track. Qualifying. You'd better get up, too," he said when he moved into the bathroom to start the shower and closed the door.

Content, Luz stretched and felt each muscle in her body slowly awaken. Jeff was a surprise; he gave her more than she expected, patiently waited for her, and then reached his own state of bliss. He was tender with her, yet his passion won out. As her mind slowly woke up, Luz thought about the day ahead of her: arrival at the track, the press conference, the assembly of a team, and the successful completion of time trials.

It was already six-twenty, and Jeff planned to be at the track at seven. Wrapped in her robe, Luz padded down the stairs to make coffee and warm up a couple of muffins. Two full mugs, hers with cream and sugar, his black with sugar, and a plate of breakfast breads for them to share were on the tray she carried up the stairs.

When she came back to the bedroom, he was already dressed. He kissed her cheek and took one of the mugs from her hands.

"Thanks, Luz," Jeff said. "Good coffee; good food; good sex. I can tell it's going to be a great day!" He put on his socks and shoes, then stood up and quickly glanced around the bedroom. He remembered his shirt was still downstairs with his jacket. He kissed Luz on the cheek and said, "I enjoyed last night, and this morning was perfect. I want to spend more time with you, but I've got to run now. Good luck with everything today. I'll see you at the track."

Downstairs, Jeff picked up his clothes from the floor by the sofa. He quickly buttoned his shirt and threw his parka on over it. As he was going out the door, he gave Luz a quick kiss and a hug. She stood in the doorway and waved to him as he drove away.

Luz closed the door; her watch showed twenty to seven. It was going to be a rough day all around with the press conference, finding and working with a new team, time trials, and hopefully qualifying. Dreams of taking the pole vanished when the driver and team walked out the door. Now they just hoped to get a car on the track in time to qualify.

Right out of the shower, Luz automatically put on a clean team shirt, black pants, and black leather tennis shoes with comfortable socks. She braided her hair and threaded it through the hole in the back of the Amberson cap, letting it dangle free. The red shirt complemented her caramel skin, and she wore gold button earrings to dress up a bit for today's events. Carrying a cup of coffee, her backpack, and her carbon fiber briefcase, Luz got in the car, lowered the windows, and drove to the speedway. She was ready for anything.

CHAPTER 24

Luz was surprised at the traffic as she approached the speedway. It was only seven-thirty, and vehicles were bumper to bumper on Crawfordsville Road. Even the intersection at Sixteenth Street was filled with pedestrians and cars. she felt a sense of relief when she finally arrived at her usual parking lot.

Even inside the speedway, the inner loop roads were heavy with traffic. The motor home parking area was almost full, because early-morning breakfast meetings for sponsors were taking place. As she drove by the medical center, she saw the helicopter in place, ready in case of a serious accident. Parked nearby were two ambulances; the others were already stationed around the track. Along the edge of the golf course, Luz saw two huge tents with catering vans along one side and cars parked everywhere, with more coming in all the time. She parked in the Red Lot and entered through the gate, where she and the Yellow Shirts exchanged pleasantries. They wished her team good luck.

Luz entered the Amberson Garage to find mechanics with Hawk Racing shirts poring over the cars. Michelle had called in some help from an old friend of Clint's who owned an Indy Lights team. She felt relief the minute she saw all the work going on—now she knew they would have a chance to qualify and maybe take the pole.

Michelle and Luz walked to the press conference together, along with the attorneys armed with briefcases filled with incriminating files. After the conference Luz wanted to watch time trials until Jeff qualified, then she would join the Amberson team back at the garage. They met Jonathan Barrow outside the door of the trackside pressroom, where he held the door open for them.

The press conference started with the league official introducing Michelle Amberson, who in an elegant sound bite named Luz Dane as her new team manager, gave a quick dossier of Luz's career, and then spoke about the new Amberson driver, Christi Cole, providing more biographical information on her as well. Not a sour note was heard about Roger Schneider. Michelle would let the attorneys and Jonathan Barrow deal with Schneider. She had a business to run, and this was showtime. It was a cheerful, optimistic, and glossy occasion: the three attractive women smiled for the cameras, all of them dressed in Amberson colors.

Michelle returned to the garage, while Luz went out to pit road to find Jeff and wish him good luck. As his was a newer team, the pit assignment was far from Gasoline Alley. She walked past the winner's circle, then to the entrance of pit road. There she leaned against the pit wall watching Jeff and his team members work and waited for him to notice her.

Jeff looked up after making a wing adjustment on the front of the car. He smiled, then walked over to the pit wall and sat down next to her. At that moment they heard the announcement that the first car to qualify was driving onto the track. Matt Locke, now the driver for Blackbird Racing, made the first attempt to qualify Roger Schneider's entry. Jeff looked at Luz, his face serious, his eyes questioning.

"I've done everything I can," Luz said. "There is nothing left for me to do."

"You could always file a protest once they've made the race."

"We'll see what the lawyers decide," Luz replied.

Shrugging her shoulders, Luz crossed her arms and held on tight to control herself. As the chassis made the corner through turn 4, both their heads followed the yellow Blackbird car as it zoomed up the front straightaway. The engine's whine filled the air at the speedway; otherwise, there was a still silence in the Harwood pits. The next time the car came around, several of the Harwood team members looked at Luz and waited for her reaction. It was as if they were in suspended animation: each crew member was drawn into the drama; each waited to see how fast the first car went, how fast they'd need to go to qualify for the 500.

With his stopwatch, Jeff clocked the second warm-up lap at a moderate 223 mph, knowing that this was the windup and there would be more speed from here. After the first qualifying lap of 225.454 mph, the crowd was captivated. Last year's pole winner averaged a speed of 225.10 mph, so this race for the pole from the first in line carried the hope that this team would ultimately take the pole at the end of the day.

Standing at the entrance of the pit road, Luz and Jeff were exactly parallel to the sanctioning body official, standing next to Blake Notson and Roger Schneider as he waited to throw the green flag to accept the run or the yellow flag to wave it off. Luz watched intently as the car passed around again. Hypnotically it captured her attention and moved her from watching the car to watching Roger Schneider to watching the crowd go wild. With over half the Speedway's 298,000 seats filled for qualifying, the hundreds of thousands of fans cheered for the new team showing off all the speed.

Roger Schneider gave high fives to Blake Notson, the crew chief, as the car rounded turn 4 and finished its third lap of 225.828 mph, going towards 226 mph for the fourth lap. Schneider held the green flag out and waved it like he was welcoming conquering heroes back home. His exuberance was reflected in the fans up on their feet cheering for the hometown boy.

As the car finished the fourth lap and sped up the front straightaway, the electronic light boards flashed each lap speed in sequence ending with an average speed of 225.666 mph. Blackbird Racing beat last year's pole winning time, firmly gained the pole position, and was very likely to stay there. When he mounted the golf cart that was to take him to the end of pit road where the car and the team were photographed, Roger Schneider pumped his right fist straight in the air signaling the number one with his index finger.

"You're number one!" started as a chant from the covered paddock seats across from pit road and circled around the first turn. Television cameramen ran down pit road to frame Schneider in their lens, others raced to the end to meet the car and get the first interviews after qualifying pictures. What a story! How would the headlines read the next day—"First Timer Takes First Place," or "Blackbird Racing Gets the Pole"? With all the excitement, the press conference earlier was long forgotten.

Luz hung her head and shook it in disbelief. Jeff, his lips pursed together and gave her an understanding look. "I know this isn't the best news for you and the Amberson team. Don't worry. What goes around comes around. I guarantee it."

Luz looked straight at him and smiled. "I know. Whatever is supposed to happen will happen."

As she looked at him she saw a yellow blur as the Blackbird car passed through turn 4 again, then there was a screech of tires, the sound of brakes locking up, then a crash and crumpling sound. Luz's face changed from a smile, to worry, to fear, her brow furrowed as she screamed, "Look out!"

A careening screeching mass of metal, carbon fiber, and tires hit the outside wall of turn 4 and then ricocheted across the track towards the entrance to pit road, straight at Jeff's crew and car.

"Across the pit wall!" Jeff pointed to his crew members whose faces were stricken with terror. "Kiss the wall! Get down in the crack behind the wall!!" He pushed Luz down by her shoulders to the concrete behind the pit wall and covered her head with his clipboard.

Each of the crew members scrambled across the wall. Some rolled over the top to lie down on the ground with the hope of finding safety and waited for the inevitable to happen. Like being in the middle of a blast furnace, it sounded like thunder when the Blackbird car hit the Harwood chassis in the pits. In a whoosh as it caught fire, the gusty blast of methanol showed no flame but seared the whitewashed pit wall a dark black. A billowing cloud of red flame erupted as the oil line exploded in the crash, adding more fuel to an already big fire.

Jeff lay on top of Luz, careful not to smother her, but protected her from the debris flying in all directions as the cars collided. Pieces flew up fifty feet in the air, across to the paddock seats, up to Gasoline Alley, and over the catch fence next to the pit road. When he first saw her face with her big eyes and wide-open mouth held in a silent scream as she pointed to the car hitting the wall at turn 4, Jeff knew what was next. He had seen it before in practice videos; either the car flew down the front straightaway hugging the wall or it hit at a right angle moving across into the pits to the exact location of his car. Without enough time to move out of the way, the only choice was to hit the ground behind the wall, hoping all the flames and debris would move up and out of range.

The fire crew at the end of pit road was too close to prevent the explosion, so they too huddled behind the pit wall only ten yards from where the flaming mass erupted. The crews stationed at the corners of the speedway raced to pit road with water and carbon dioxide extinguishers to drown the inferno. When teams nearby heard the screams and saw the out-of-control chassis barrel down the entrance to the pits, they scattered, running for the entrance to Gasoline Alley. Some of the Yellow Shirts hopped over the wall separating pit road from the track, looking for sanctuary as far from the accident as possible. Once the explosive flaming debris filled the air, the fire crews with the Jaws of Life and an ambulance standing by pulled the driver, Matt Locke, out of the car. Locke was unconscious but still breathing, his fire suit aflame. The paramedics smothered the flames engulfing his uniform and then loaded him into the ambulance for the trip to the infield care unit, where he was treated for second-degree burns and then sent by helicopter to Indiana Medical Center for more serious treatment. When they removed his helmet, which protected his face and head from fire, the medics breathed a sigh of relief: There were no facial burns that inhibited them from affixing an oxygen mask to his face giving him a greater chance for survival.

After ten minutes of intense work, water pumped over the molten crash site, carbon dioxide sprayed from fire extinguishers to smother the fire, the chassis and engine, now a heap of metal, carbon fiber, and rubber, smoldered on pit road. The fans that before clambered with joy and excitement now stood awestruck in silence and sorrow. Sadness descended on the speedway and replaced the euphoria that only minutes before had dominated the five-hundred-acre racing palace.

The firefighter who removed Matt Locke from the wreckage now stood over Jeff Harwood and grabbed his left arm to help him up. When Jeff pushed himself up from the concrete and revealed Luz unconscious below him the firefighter's eyebrows went up. Convinced Jeff was steady on his feet, the fireman scooped Luz from the ground with one arm, cradled her in his arms, and carried her towards another ambulance where other Harwood team members were treated for smoke inhalation, minor cuts and bruises, scrapes and burns. Luz lay on a stretcher as they checked her pulse and breathing. Except for a minor scrape on her arm and another on her cheek, Luz looked fine. As she regained consciousness, her eyes slowly opened and she coughed violently. She looked around at the inside of the ambulance with its backdoor view of the fourth turn at the speedway, and said to the attending paramedic, "The crash. It happened. I must have passed out."

"Be quiet now. We will be taking you and this crew of guys to the infield care unit to check you out completely."

"Jeff? Is he all right?" Luz tried to sit up to look around, but she felt dizzy.

"Wait here," the paramedic said, his hand on her forearm. "I'll see if I can find him."

He crawled out of the ambulance to look for Jeff, asking, "Is there a Jeff around here?"

Luz could hear him calling out beside the ambulance. She closed her eyes, prayed he was safe, and she heard another voice calling out Jeff's name. Then outside the vehicle she heard his subtle Texas accent and the familiar rhythm of his speech.

"That girl you covered up, she asked for you," Luz heard the medic say, then she heard footsteps outside the ambulance. In a moment, she saw Jeff standing in the doorway, at the foot of her stretcher. Luz pushed herself up on her right elbow.

"I want to get up," she said weakly. "I just don't have the

strength."

"Hey, hey, you stay right where you are," Jeff said, his palm facing her, held out like a stop sign. "Just wait a minute. I know I knocked the breath out of you when I pushed you down on the ground, but I was only trying to protect you."

"Oh, I'm fine, just a few cuts and scrapes. But Jeff, your car! What about your car?" Luz asked.

"My car is toast. One big smoldering heap of carbon fiber."

"Oh, Jeff, after all that work. And the car would have qualified well," Luz said. "The driver? Matt? Blackbird? What happened to them?"

"Matt's on his way to the medical center, but he had a strong pulse and was breathing just fine," the medic answered.

"The Blackbird car was totaled too. No way that chassis will ever race again. In fact, I don't think it could be a show car. So there is some justice in the world, Luz." Jeff's tone was matter-of-fact.

"How are the rest of the guys?" Luz asked.

"Looks like they are all going to be fine. A few scrapes, and cuts. For the most part they made it through the inferno with minor injuries," Jeff said. "Of course, now that we don't have a car in the show, I don't know how I'm going to make payroll."

"Oh, Jeff, can't you get another car?"

"Luz, the entry for the 500 is for a particular chassis. Now that this one is destroyed, I can't just go out and buy another one and try again. Not this year at least. The rules don't allow it. Next year, maybe."

Luz pursed her lips, deep in thought, then she turned to Jeff. "I have an idea. Please come with me—now. It's important."

She hopped out of the ambulance and steadied herself as she leaned on the door.

"Luz, you can't leave. You have to go to the medical center. Where do you think you're going in such a hurry?" Jeff asked.

"To get the Amberson team ready to qualify."

"How is Amberson going to qualify? Why are you in such a hurry?" Jeff sounded confused.

"Jeff, humor me. Your guys are going to be at the medical center for at least thirty minutes. Your equipment isn't going to walk away," Luz argued. "Please give me twenty minutes of your time, and then you can come back to all those things you have to do. I think most of them can wait. Trust me, please. I know what I'm doing." She held out her hand, beckoning him to go with her.

Jeff stood up to his full height, his arms crossed across his chest, shaking his head, refusing to take her hand. Luz put her hands on her hips and waited. They stood opposite one another like gunslingers in a Western showdown. A quiet descended on the track as another car waited in the tech line prepared for its qualifying run. Unaware of the action on the track, Luz and Jeff continued their argument and garnered a lot of attention on pit road and in the stands.

Luz stood looking up into Jeff's face and dared him, her blue eyes flashing with impatience as she shouted at him, "I need to know if you are with me or if you are not! I know I'm not one of the good old boys of the speedway. In fact, I know I'm a virgin at this speedway. But I've asked questions, I've made friends, I've read the rule book. I have done everything

I can to keep from getting screwed, at least everything that an outsider can do. You think you know everything! And I suppose you can't possibly think of a good reason why I am rushing back to the garage area like a Texas jackrabbit, at least not a good enough reason to suit you."

"No, Luz. I can't. I think you might have a concussion or something; your brain is addled. Seems like you are not thinking straight," Jeff said, his nose inches from her face.

"*I'm* not thinking straight? You just lost everything! Maybe you're the one who's not thinking straight. Did it ever occur to you that I might have a really good idea that will help us both out? I am asking you for the last time to trust me and come with me now."

"No, not right now," he said. "I've got a lot to do."

Luz withdrew her hand, took a deep breath, stood up to her full height, and said at the top of her voice, "You are a damn fool, Jeff Harwood. All I wanted to do was offer you and your team members a job at Amberson Racing, but no-o-o. Well if you don't have time for that right now, I'll find someone who does!"

Luz turned around and began walking back to the garage area. The fans in the stands jumped up clapping and cheering. Some whistled at her as she walked down the pits in front of them. Jeff stood looking like he'd been slapped with a pail of cold water, then he realized what she had just said to him. He ran after her.

"Luz, Luz. I, I'm sorry. I didn't think. It never . . ."

"It never occurred to you. Well, I hope it's not too late. If I know that slime Schneider, he's probably already gotten to

Michelle and is sucking up to her big-time, asking for forgiveness, wanting her to take him and his whole team back. That's why we have to hurry. Come on." She turned to walk back to the garage.

Luz motioned to him to come with her, and the two of them made their way through the crowds to Gasoline Alley, and then over to the B building, where Luz hoped Michelle would be. As they walked through the garage area, Jeff was saluted by different crew members who'd seen the wreck on closed circuit television. So many expressed their condolences, patted him on the shoulder, and wished him better luck in the future. Walking together, Luz and Jeff were an attractive couple and a formidable force. Once they arrived at the Amberson garage, they found the garage doors open and Christi Cole signing autographs for the fans circling around her. Her Amberson Racing driver's suit had come in that morning, a rush job by the manufacturer. All the sponsors' logos were embroidered in the proper places according to the contract, and the Indy Car and Firestone logos were positioned on the shoulders and epaulettes. She looked great as she smiled, socializing with the fans in her friendly girl-next-door manner.

Just as she finished signing a Firestone cap for an elderly gentleman, Christi looked up to find Luz standing directly in front of her.

"Have you seen Michelle?" Luz asked.

"Yeah, she was here a minute ago, talking to Roger Schneider. After the wreck, of course, he wants to come back. Oh, Jeff, I am so sorry. How could anything that bad happen to you? You don't deserve it."

"Christi, do you know where they went?"

"I heard them say something about the motor home."

"Thanks. We'll see you in a little while." Luz touched Christi on the forearm before she walked away. "You look great! Keep up the good work."

Jeff was already in one of the golf carts parked outside. Luz hopped on and he drove over to the motor home area. Parking in front of spot 54, Jeff and Luz jumped out of the cart. The patio was deserted, even though tables were set and food ready to eat at the buffet table. The Amberson logo and all the sponsor logos covered the side wall of the tenting set up to shield the patio from wind and rain. The electronic steps leading to the door of the motor home were extended, and Luz climbed them to open the door and walk in. Jeff followed.

All of the walls and cupboards were covered in mirrors, which made it difficult to figure out where everyone was actually sitting. The champagne-colored rug that ran down the center of the vehicle was covered in heavy plastic sheeting to protect it from grease, dirt, and grime. Seated around the marble-top dinette table were the two attorneys, along with Michelle Amberson. Opposite them, on the edge of the beige leather loveseat, was Roger Schneider. When they stepped inside, Luz and Jeff could hear him whining, "But I've got a contract."

The attorneys were mute; they merely stared at Roger with unseeing eyes. Michelle smoked a cigarette as she looked out the window. Luz stepped into the conversation quickly once she sized up the situation.

"Roger, the terms of your contract are no longer valid due

to your actions yesterday and today. There is language that says if you leave Amberson, you leave for the rest of the year. Clint didn't want anyone accusing him of industrial espionage or of stealing employees from other teams. So why don't you leave? We don't have time to listen to your whining," Luz said.

"Bitch. Sticking your nose in my business isn't going to do you any good." Schneider stood up and moved towards the door, then stopped. "Things were working out just fine before you got here, Ms. Dane. Why didn't you stay in Texas where you belong?"

Schneider passed within inches of Luz, growling, "Get out of my way!" He pushed and shoved his way past Luz and Jeff as he left.

Luz sat down by Michelle and sighed. "Glad he's gone. What an angry guy!"

"Glad you rescued us from his yelling and complaining. I was afraid he was about to be violent," Michelle said to Luz, then turned to Jeff. "What a shame about your car, Jeff."

"Thanks, Michelle. I'm lucky, though. All my team is in good shape, no injuries."

"Michelle," Luz said, "the reason I dragged Jeff all the way over here, when he obviously has a lot to take care of, is to ask you—to tell you—to hire Jeff and his team to work for Amberson Racing for the 500."

Michelle looked surprised as she pondered the idea Luz proposed to her, then she smiled. "Luz, what a brilliant idea! Clint would approve. He wanted Jeff to come back to work with him, but knew Jeff wanted to solo. Now after that horrible crash, you poor boy, you must feel like you've lost everything.

All that hard work going up in smoke—I've never seen anything like it."

"Jeff saved my life, Michelle. I was down there when the Blackbird car came in to the pits. He pulled me down behind the pit wall where I'd be safe, and covered me with his body to protect me. Please give him this chance."

Michelle studied Luz's face. Her blue eyes were intense and serious. The bandage across her cheek strengthened her image as a survivor. Her team shirt was mussed from the chaos of the pit road accident. Michelle saw in front of her a very determined young woman who had earned her authority and who had made a well-thought-out, clearly defined decision about how to manage the Amberson race team.

"You've earned the right to make that decision," Michelle said. "We asked you to manage the team. Everything you've done has been in our best interest. I don't see any reason to question the recommendation you are making now. How do you think we should proceed?"

"Appoint Jeff as crew chief. Give him the choice about who to hire from his team and whom he may want to bring back from the Blackbird team. He's very good with people and I think he knows whom he can trust. Amberson has two entries in the race, two opportunities to qualify. I think Jeff can handle that, and I'd like to help him do it."

"If Jeff agrees to take the job, you certainly have my blessing to work with him for the rest of the month," Michelle said. "I actually think you could manage the team without his help. You've picked up a great deal of knowledge about how things work around here."

"Thank you for having so much faith in me, Michelle, but I don't think I've got the mechanical part down the way Jeff does."

"Yes, that's true. But with Jeff as the crew chief and you as the team manager, together you are a team owner's dream. Your talents complement one another."

Luz leaned back in the chair she was sitting in and closed her eyes.

"Luz says you saved her life," Michelle said to Jeff.

"Well, I had to get her out of harm's way. I knew there would be debris, fire." His voice faded away.

"Jeff, I'd like you to be crew chief for the Amberson team for the rest of the month. Hire anyone you'd like for your crew—even your old team. Luz will be your team manager, and at the end of the month we'll talk about the future. What do you say?"

Jeff looked from her to Luz. They were both smiling.

Jeff took a deep breath, and as he let it out, he told Michelle, "I'd love to take that job." Then he looked at Luz. "And I'd like the opportunity to work with all of you."

"*Yes!!*" Luz jumped up from her chair to give Jeff a big hug, "This is going to be so great! I know our team is going to do well. I can feel it!"

CHAPTER 25

With the full backing of Michelle and Clint Amberson, Jeff and Luz went to work with the hopes of qualifying both Amberson team entries on the first day of qualifying. Jeff hired his entire team to work on the Amberson chassis, and selected a couple of Amberson/Blackbird members to help as well. Fortunately the set-up data was available from Jeff's notebook for his own drivers and chassis, and also from the notebook kept by the Amberson team.

Mark Miller, whom Jeff chose to drive for him, was back on the same team with Christi Cole, this time driving for Amberson Racing. Luz rushed him over to the Simpson space in the garage area to fit him for a driver's suit emblazoned with the Amberson sponsor logos. It would be ready in time for the race. The team fire suits were fitted to the new team members, and team shirts were quickly distributed to the different mechanics. While Jeff and his crew, helped by Hawk Racing, combed over the chassis checking for worn-out parts, and made adjustments to the set-up, Luz organized the work environment. She cleaned out the lockers and reassigned them to the new team members. Dirty team shirts and fire suits were relabeled with the new team members' initials and then sent to the laundry to be ready for the next day. After all the toolboxes and parts were in their proper places, Tommy James, the tire man, checked and catalogued the four sets of tires haphazardly stacked around the space, finally centering them in the two garages between the two chassis.

Lunch was brought in for the entire crew, and while they ate, Jeff updated everyone on the status of the two cars.

"The setup data is the same on both cars, and it looks like only one of them had any other adjustments made on it once the setup was complete," Jeff said. "The numbers differ slightly for the Harwood data, so we've tuned one chassis with that data and left the other alone. Both seats have been poured and are ready to go for the drivers. We've checked the hose clamps, changed the spark plugs, inspected the headers, and looked for worn or loose fittings on both cars. Work is finished on the car with the Amberson setup, and within an hour the other will be finished. I think we can get out to practice about two o'clock, unless someone is qualifying and the track isn't open for practice."

Tommy James piped up. "I'm ready with the tires."

"Extra parts, toolboxes, and an ice chest are loaded on the pit cart," added Beau Williams.

"We have our equipment in our scoring stand. Do I move the stand or the equipment to the Amberson pit box?" asked

Sonny Brown.

Jeff looked at Luz. She answered, "Move the stand for right now. You are familiar with where everything is located in that stand. I think there is room for both in the pit box. Can you put one behind the other, if there isn't enough space?"

"Oh, sure. Makes it easier on all of us. I'll go now to move it up," Sonny said, moving towards the door. Beau Williams followed him.

"When you're finished, come back to get the car," Jeff called after him.

There was a friendly, family feeling in the garage now. Luz felt everyone working together, as one unit, towards the common goal of qualifying for the 500. She had not realized how comforting that feeling was in a workplace. Looking around the 35-by-50 feet space, she smiled as she watched one of the mechanics sitting on a stool in the corner as he washed parts in a hideous-smelling solvent. Two others hunched over the second chassis and replaced hose fittings and spark plugs. Another waxed the first chassis to prepare it for its qualifying run, hoping the wax would give them a few seconds' edge on each lap. Jeff and the engineer, Jay, peered at the computer screens and hoped that as they compared data from one team to another, they might pick up a couple of miles per hour when the big moment came. It was a harmonious group, contentedly working towards their goal.

Beau and Sonny came back from moving all the Harwood equipment to the Amberson pit box. Each grinned from ear to ear. Jeff instructed them to hook up the towrope for the first car, and asked Beau to slip into the car to steer it out to the track. Both drivers were suited up, their helmets in hand.

"Once we get this car out on the pit road Beau and Sonny will come back to get the other one. Bob and Joe are finishing up a few details, but they will be ready shortly," Jeff said as he pulled the large garage door closed on one side. Both drivers waited in the back of the golf cart with Luz in the driver's seat. After he hopped on, she drove out the gate leading to the track through the portal under the Gasoline Alley sign. A car was on the track, making its qualifying attempt. Seven cars had already qualified; their numbers lighted up the pole.

As they towed the car into position, a television crew surrounded the golf cart, pushing microphones into their faces, bright lights blazing hotter than the sun.

"Ms. Dane, it's rumored there are new developments for Amberson Racing. Do you care to comment on them?"

Another, shoving a microphone in their faces, queried, "Jeff, Harwood Racing was dealt a tough blow this morning. Yet now you are here in the Amberson pit box. Any comments?"

With microphones in front of both their faces, they laughed. Jeff motioned to Luz that she speak first, so she did her best to respond to the media's intense scrutiny.

"We needed a crew chief and a crew. Jeff and Harwood Racing had everything Amberson needed. He's a loyal friend and former employee of Amberson, so it seemed like the perfect fit. We think it's a winning combination," Luz said.

Jeff added, "For the Harwood team and our sponsors, it's a dream of an opportunity. I'm thankful to Michelle and Clint Amberson for giving us this chance. We will do our best."

"Stories are circulating around the garage area that Roger

Schneider says he still has a contract with Amberson. Any comments?"

Luz was surprised by this line of questioning and wanted to avoid this topic, so she quickly answered, "I am sorry for Mr. Schneider and the Blackbird Racing team. I wish them good luck for the future."

She ducked away from the television crew and mounted the scoring stand, ready to help Jeff in any way she could. Although the press attempted to interview others on the team, they were met with noncommittal responses, along with a few grunts and mumbles. Everyone on the team wanted to focus on readying the car for its qualifying run, and getting on the track for practice was the first step.

Christi was to take her turn in the first chassis, using the setup that was popular with the former Amberson driver, Matt Locke. Mark Miller was going to practice in the second chassis, which had been set up to Harwood specs. Both were going to take it easy on the practice laps to shake the cars down before either of them attempted to pick up any speed.

As soon as the lights around the track went green, both cars were started and went out for practice. Christi liked the setup on her car; it was tight at first, but it loosened up after four laps. She was driving with a half tank of fuel, giving her the feel of how the car would behave during the vast majority of the race. Once they qualified, she'd take it out for full-tank testing, to get an idea of how the weight of forty gallons of fuel would affect the car's steering into and out of the corners of this two-and-a-half-mile speedway.

Luz checked two stopwatches as she kept track of the

speeds of both cars. During her practice laps, Christi actually posted speeds half a mile per hour faster than she had before when she was driving the Harwood car. Mark's speeds were about the same. He had trouble with the setup going into the turns, as the car was loose coming out of both turns 1 and 2 and caused him to wrestle with it and slow down at the very time he should be speeding up.

The track lights turned yellow, signifying there was a car ready to qualify. All cars on the track came into their pit boxes to wait for the next time out, or to get in line for their own qualifying attempt. Christi and Mark brought their cars in one after the other. With the help of the crew, they were both out of the cars in minutes, ready to share and compare their driving experiences. Jeff started with Christi, since she had the more successful run. His plan was to have them switch cars during the next practice session, with the hopes that after he worked with all the data, he'd be able to come up with a setup which would work for each of them, and then be in line for qualifying at happy hour, when the track was the sweetest for it.

It was shortly before three o'clock when the track opened for practice once again. Eight cars had qualified, and only three hours remained to the race for the pole. Christi and Mark were strapped into their cars, once again zooming around the track. Christi wrestled her car back into the pits after two laps, while Mark found more speed in the chassis he was driving. Leaving Mark out to practice until the yellow came on, the second chassis was towed into the garage to make the proper adjustments and check it one more time before a last practice in advance of the four-lap qualifier. Luz stayed out on the track to time the car, and compared the speeds to those Mark reached in the Harwood car. Based on the qualifying run sheets, Luz compared the speeds both Christi and Mark reached with those of other drivers, including those who had already made the race. It was still possible, she figured, for one of the Amberson cars to make the race and take the pole. With a cool track and warm tires, happy hour might make this a special day for them after all.

BARBIE O'CONNOR

CHAPTER 26

Waiting in line to go through tech inspection and then, ultimately, to qualify for the 500 resembled a wagon train of high performance cars trailed by their pit carts loaded with mounted tires, tool kits, ice chests, and extra parts. Teams waited until the last minute to get in line, hoping to hit the sweet spot of the day, when the track would give them the best time. Happy hour was that opportunity, and Jeff, Luz, and and their drivers waited patiently, hoping to get their run in that day.

In line by five o'clock behind five other cars, Jeff prayed they would have a chance to run that first day, giving them a shot at the pole. With all that had happened, no one thought the Amberson team had a chance to take the pole. Jeff didn't want to get his hopes up, but he secretly believed it might be possible.

Each of the five cars in front of them passed the tech inspection. The speeds increased with each car out on the track, but so far no one had topped the 227.212 mph average held by the previous year's race winner and current polesitter, Dan Piper. As the car in front of them moved out of the tech line to prepare for its run, Jeff turned his attentions to the tech inspectors; he listened to any comments they might have about the first Amberson car in line. Anxiously, he looked at his watch and noticed it was already five forty-five: only fifteen minutes remained of this first day of time trials. After they scrutinized the car with the measurement template, determined that the car was the correct height from the ground, and verified that the roll bar was the appropriate distance from the bottom of the tub, the officials certified the car as ready to qualify. As it was pushed into place in the pit box, where the Indy Car officials gave the signal to start, the car in front completed its second warm-up lap in preparation for the first of the four qualifying laps. The Amberson crew pushed the other chassis into place on the tech stand and waited for another review, hopeful both cars would qualify.

Into the second qualifying lap, a squealing sound echoed around the speedway, and the out-of-control car skidded into the wall and crashed nose-first into the second turn. The track lights turned yellow all around the speedway, closing it for cleanup. Jeff looked at Luz and the crew. "If they get this mess cleaned up, there may only be time for one car to qualify today."

"And that means only one more opportunity to take the pole," Luz said, practically finishing Jeff's sentence. The crew gathered around Jeff and Luz and both drivers. The crowd listened to the public address announcer as he assured everyone that the driver of the car was safe and was walking to the ambulance for his routine check at the infield care center. Everyone breathed a sigh of relief.

"I think Mark should take the qualifying run today," Christi spoke up. "He's had better times when we've been out, and he has more experience under pressure on this track. I think he can take the pole in the car that's already in line. It was a really sweet ride when I was in it earlier."

Everyone looked from Christi to Mark, and then to Jeff and Luz.

"Christi has a point. He does have more experience here. What do you think, Mark?" Jeff asked him, while everyone waited.

"I'll do my best. I've never taken the pole before, but there is always a first time." Mark grinned.

"Then it's settled," Luz said. "Better get in that car and get ready."

"Whooee! There is going to be some fun later if you pull this off!" Beau Williams said, slapping Mark on the back, as they walked together to the left side of the car, where Mark stepped into the seat.

As Joe Kerr adjusted Mark's seatbelt around him, Jeff talked to him through the radio to test the headset in the helmet. Luz listened in on her own radio, as did the rest of the crew. The second car was forgotten for the moment, waiting for a tech inspection that would come later in the week. All the team focused its energies on this one driver, this one car, for this one run.

"Mark, I know you will do the very best you can," Jeff said.

"If you feel like something is wrong, don't push it. We have three more days we can qualify."

"But we only have this one time for the pole," Mark responded.

"If you feel good about it, I know you can do it. Go for it."

The track was finally cleared of debris with two minutes to go until six o'clock, when happy hour would end and Pole Day would be over. The team on the pole at the end of the day would win $100,000 and the keys to a fancy high-performance fishing boat. But even more, that team, that driver, would start in the first position to lead the race for the Indianapolis 500.

Settled in the car, Mark took off when the league official gave the word to push the car out of the pits. Luz and Jeff rode the golf cart to the entrance of pit road, where they waited to see the flash of the Amberson car coming out of the fourth turn. After the first lap, Mark drove at 226.9 mph, taking about 39.665 seconds to go around the two-and-a-half-mile track. The second warm-up lap was clocked at 227.212 mph, as fast as the polesitter's average four-lap qualifying run. Luz and Jeff were astonished. Where did he pick up the speed? Would he continue increasing the speed for the next four laps?

Waiting for the car to come around the track after its first qualifying lap, Luz looked for the red nose to flash into focus, her fingers ready to hit the stopwatch button, eager to see the speed displayed on the LCD screen. As it zoomed past them, Luz yelped, "227.5! He's going faster than before! 227.5!"

Hardly able to contain their excitement, both Jeff and Luz were jubilant, the crowd in the paddock stands was on their feet, leaning towards the fourth turn, waiting for the second lap speed. As the car zipped by, the scoreboard flashed a speed of 227.9 mph. Mark drove the car faster with each lap.

"It's time, Luz—let's wave the flag. We've got to take this run and pray he keeps this up and doesn't run out of fuel," Jeff said, dropping the yellow flag in the gutter. He helped Luz wave the three-by-five-foot green flag mounted on a six-foot pole. The crowd roared when the flag appeared. Those fans seated next to the pit road were up on their feet clapping and yelling.

On the third lap, the speed was measured at 228 mph—not quite a track record, but close. Luz was stunned by the experience. Standing in the middle of the front straightaway, in the small alleyway formed by two concrete walls where the signboard crewmen worked during the race, with the track on one side and the pit road on the other, Luz was overwhelmed by the sound of over 200,000 cheering people. With only one more lap to go, she prayed for a safe return to pit road for their driver and car.

When the scoreboard flashed the fourth lap speed of 228.1 mph and then the average of the four, 227.875, the crowd went wild. Amberson Racing had taken the pole! Luz and Jeff hugged each other, then mounted the golf cart that took them down to the end of pit road, where they waited, along with the crew, in anticipation of their car making a safe return. They slapped each other on the back and gave each other high fives as Bob Barton, their team hat man, handed out the Firestone hats for everyone to wear during the first qualifying picture. In a matter of minutes, they heard the sequential *bump-bump* of the downshifting engine as Mark Miller returned safely to the pit road. Steering the car into the spot marked for the picture, he leaped out of the car, took off his helmet, and let out a "Woohoooo!" as the team gathered around him to congratulate him on the triumph that only that morning had seemed so far away.

Television cameras descended on the group, filmed the qualifying photo shoot and waited for interviews until that ceremony was finished. Michelle Amberson joined them for the photos, dabbing at the tears of joy brightening her eyes. She hugged first Mark, then Christi.

"I'm so proud of you, both of you. I can't believe this. Clint must be so, so pleased. I can't wait to talk to him. This was his dream come true," Michelle said. She looked away to hide her eyes, which once again were filled with tears.

For the photo, Mark Miller sat on the edge of the cockpit while Michelle, Luz, and Jeff stood directly behind him. The rest of the crew members stood behind them. They had not yet accepted the honor of winning the pole. Making the race was enough for them. Being first to start, on the inside of the first row of eleven rows, was something they had never experienced before. That morning it had seemed that everything was lost, yet now they celebrated a great achievement.

After six different pictures were taken, each one with the crew wearing a different gimme cap advertising a different sponsor, the television interviews started.

The regular commentators wore their pit reporter hats, eager for the first interview after this momentous event. Michelle begged off the interviews, saying it was an emotional day for her, and declined to comment. Jeff moved the car to the tech inspection line, where once again it would be checked over to ensure that a "legal" chassis had indeed won the pole. Luz stayed behind to handle the interviews, a job that delighted her, as she felt her team had scored a major victory at its darkest hour. That night, her face and the news of Amberson Racing taking the pole for the 500 appeared on the nightly shows of every major sports news entity in the country.

Returning to the garage area, Luz was greeted by the popping of champagne corks and the laughter and gaiety of a happy but exhausted team. Jeff brought her a plastic cup half full of bubbly, and as he handed it to her, he whispered in her ear, "Thank you for the opportunity. I am very grateful. You deserve the best."

Luz blushed, took the cup, and had a tiny sip, letting the bubbles roll over her tongue and slowly down her throat. In all the times she tasted champagne, she never understood why it was the drink called for in celebration. Tonight, she realized that the effervescence in the champagne reflected how she felt after the amazing victory that day. She smiled as she looked around the very full garage, where team members laughed and visited with friends who worked on other teams. Several other team owners toasted Michelle; hanky in hand, she dabbed at her eyes every so often. Bob Barton was teased about his hat dance, since he'd mistakenly handed half the crew one hat and the other half another, causing a delay in the qualifying photo shoot. Luz wanted to remember this moment forever, as she had no idea of how the rest of the month would turn out: with all the surprises they had already had, there was no way to tell what the future would bring.

All of a sudden there was a tapping sound that garnered everyone's attention. Jeff stood in the middle of the garage and motioned to Michelle and Luz to join him. After they congregated together, he raised his cup. "From all of us at Harwood Racing, we are grateful to you for your trust and faith in us. Thank you for the opportunity." Jeff's fellow team members followed up with their own toasts.

Michelle, still a bit teary-eyed, responded, "And to you and your team, we congratulate you on taking the pole for this year's 500. And we are grateful you took the opportunity made available to you." Michelle looked over at Luz, and then at Jeff, who read her mind.

"Please forgive me, Michelle," he said, "but if it wasn't for Luz none of us would be celebrating. To the best team manager any team ever had."

Around the room, "Hear, hear!" and "Yeah, Luz!" echoed. Perched on a stack of tires, Luz smiled and sipped her champagne. Then she spoke. "To Michelle, Jeff, Mark, Christi, and all the rest of the Amberson-Harwood team, I salute you all! Because of your spirit and your hard work, you deserved to win today. And win you did!"

There were cheers all around. Bob and Beau poured champagne from the big jeroboams brought in for the occasion. After years at the speedway, it was known that anything could happen during qualifying, so a cooler of champagne was always nearby in the motor home during the month of May. Sometimes sponsors signed up at the last minute; other times a good friend had a special qualifying run. The Amberson team was always prepared.

Luz made sure she shook hands with all of the crew members, thanking them by name, and reminded them of the dinner the following night at St. Erin's steakhouse, where everyone and their significant other would celebrate taking the pole. A tradition with the Amberson team to celebrate with a meal together; it gave the women a chance to dress up and the men a chance to let their hair down.

Before the team left for the day, Jeff reminded them they had one more car to qualify. Everyone smiled: after today's runs they knew that Christi would qualify at a speed fast enough to make the race without any danger of being bumped off the grid. The weather forecast was good for the next day, so they expected an easy time of it. Even though time trials began at noon, Jeff asked them to be in about eight in the morning.

As team members left, they all stopped to say goodnight to Jeff and Luz, who both sat on the tires, exhausted from the emotional roller coaster of that day.

"What a day!" Beau said on his way out. "Who would've thought we'd destroy one car, and take the pole with another, all in one day?"

"Yeah, this one belongs in the history books," Joe Kerr said as he turned out the workbench lights. "I wonder if we'll get some special award. Voted team least likely to succeed at noon, and then the team to take the pole only six hours later."

"You've had a big day," Jay Jennings said to Luz in his thick Georgia accent. "I heard about that press conference, and then that fantastic run by the Blackbird car. It must have hurt a lot watching that team do well after walking out on you. And then the crash. Jeff here covered you up and saved a few more of us too. You must have nerves of steel, all this up and down all day."

Luz smiled, thinking about the ups and downs she faced everyday in the stock market as she advised her clients. "You might say I've had a lot of practice with swings in the market. I guess it is good preparation for this business. Thanks for caring. I'll be going home in a little while to get a good night's rest. Hopefully tomorrow will be a bit calmer than today."

"You did a mighty fine job today. I'm proud to know you," Jay said.

The day's emotions started to show on Luz's face. Her smile was a bit weaker, and there were circles under her eyes. The scrape on her face started to scab over, giving her a tough look. Her stomach had rumbled from hunger for the last hour, and all she wanted now was something to eat, along with a hot bath and a warm bed.

"Jeff, what about going to the Union Jack for a little something to eat?" Luz asked, picking up her pack and the clothes she had in her locker. She turned to Michelle. "Maybe you want to come along too?"

"You darling girl. I haven't been to the Union Jack since Clint was a sponsor's rep. It might be nice to stop in there once again."

Luz turned out the remaining lights and checked the locks on all the doors. It was time to go. Time for a well-deserved break, for all of them.

CHAPTER 27

After dinner, Jeff followed Luz back to her apartment. Both of them were feeling the pleasure of a busy day with a successful outcome. Luz invited Jeff in, hoping he'd stay the night. In a few short hours their relationship had changed, from that of one friend helping out another to that of two coworkers of equal standing, although one had helped the other get his job. Luz still felt the heat of her passion for Jeff, but she suddenly felt uncomfortable as they stood alone together in the front hallway of the townhouse.

Luz knew Jeff was a truly special guy, but she also knew she had a responsibility to herself to make the best of the opportunity presented to her. She was a newcomer to this business, but so far she had demonstrated that her innate talents and careful decision- making skills brought success to the Amberson team. How she handled the rest of the month might make a dramatic difference in her future. She didn't want to be mistaken for another knight fighter, a girl groupie hanging onto a star team member. She wanted to be taken seriously in racing circles, and at the same time, she felt she was falling in love with Jeff. The next few weeks mattered a great deal to her.

Luz had given Jeff the opportunity of a lifetime. Taking the pole with his best driver, even though it was in another team's equipment, showed the racing community that he had that special something that in racing differentiated the winners from the losers. Luz believed in him and promoted him to where he was at that very moment, and she didn't want anything she did to take that away from him. In her heart, she knew she was where she belonged, where she had always wanted to be—in partnership with a man she respected and now was growing to love. She didn't want to do anything that would endanger that love or that respect.

As they looked at one other, trying to read each other's thoughts, Luz gave Jeff a full embrace. "Jeff, I like you very much. I think I might even be falling in love with you. It felt so good the other night. And waking up with you here was wonderful."

Jeff lightly brushed her lips with his. Then she continued. "I don't think today changed all that, but I think for both of us, this team succeeding means a great deal. It's my chance to show off my entire range of talents. To prove I can make it anywhere. It's a chance of a lifetime. I don't want a lover's thing to screw it up for us. Not now, not for this month, this time."

"It's important to me, too," Jeff said. "Today was the most amazing day of my life. I have never felt so depressed and so happy in the same twenty-four hour period as I did today. But what if this is it?"

"You mean, what if it goes downhill from here?"

"Yeah. What if we can't get Christi in the field? Or the car wrecks in practice?"

"All those things can happen, Jeff. But you don't have any control over them. All you can do is your best. And most of the times when you do your best you have a great outcome. Don't be such a pessimist!"

"Those things don't bother you?" Jeff asked.

"I've worked all of my life in a business where I could not control whether a stock would be up or down. But I pick companies with a better-than-average chance to perform well. You and the rest of the team are just like those stocks: you have a great chance to perform well. I worry more about success going to your head, and you leaving me behind, than I worry about you failing. Maybe I'm too much of an optimist."

"No, I don't think that's it. I think you're a better risk-taker than I am."

Luz laughed. "Right. You are in a business where you can't control the outcome. The cars are going over two hundred miles an hour, and you think I'm a better risk taker. Ha!"

"Ha! Is that all you can say? Ha!" Jeff spun her around and around, till they both landed on the sofa. They laughed.

"I want you so much. And I want us to be happy and successful. And I want us to win the Indy 500," Jeff said, his voice starting low and steadily getting louder.

Luz laughed and started to tickle him. They were playing like children, their exuberance taking over. Luz darted up the stairs, and Jeff followed. They were still giggling with excitement and joy when they fell on the bed.

Quickly shedding their clothes, Jeff and Luz followed the lead of their hearts. In one day they had lived through a desertion, an explosion, time trials, and taking the pole together as partners. When they reached a pinnacle of ecstasy, Jeff and Luz held each other in a shuddering embrace. Sinking into the cloudlike sleep of exhaustion, the long day behind them, Luz and Jeff slept in each other's arms.

CHAPTER 28

Stopping at the donut shop on Crawfordsville Road the next morning, Luz ordered her regular coffee with cream and sugar, along with a blueberry muffin and the two dozen assorted glazed donuts for the team. She felt proud of her team. As she paid, Luz remembered what Jeff said once before when they bought donuts: "It never hurts to have a few more than we need. Mechanics from other teams come by to get a bite to eat, and sometimes they share a few secrets."

It was uncanny to her how easily Jeff made friends, and how comfortable people of any background were with him. She knew very few people like him. She had already learned so much from him: to leave bigger tips, to wave at people sitting on their front stoops, to smile when you said no or when you asked for something you really wanted. He could cajole, encourage, needle, and prod his team to success, all the while being a nice guy. It was a delight to watch him work.

Once she parked in the Red Lot, Luz climbed out of the car, placed donuts under her left arm, and slung her pack over her shoulder. As she turned around to shut the door, Beau Williams caught it, closed it with one hand, and grabbed her pack with the other.

Beau smiled at her. "Beautiful day, isn't it?"

"Yes, it is. Thanks. But with the heat, it's going to be a long, tough day."

"Sure, but Luz, did you ever really think the car would take the pole? I mean, that is what I mean by a beautiful day. That sure is something to be proud of. You think really good on your feet, you know that? Never would have thought a woman would make a good team manager, but here you are!" Beau laughed wholeheartedly when they passed through the gate, with a friendly morning salute from the two older gentlemen who had growled at her before and now looked at her in admiration.

It was different today. People looked at her directly instead of ignoring her or looking away when she walked through the garage area. She was included; she had made it into the club. She had demonstrated her ability to think on her feet. With so much going wrong around her, Luz kept her cool and put together a whole new team, better than the two that had existed before. She showed she had initiative, creativity, and good judgment in the middle of a crisis that would have challenged even the most seasoned racers.

Luz stood up straighter, but felt more relaxed. She smiled as she rounded the corner to the garage building, recognizing just what an accomplishment this was, being at the 500, having her team take the pole, her biggest worry just putting anoth-er car in the show. Only thirty-three cars made the race each year. In the history of the race since 1916 there had only been a little over three thousand cars in the show, and only about a thousand teams qualified to make the race; many teams field-ed two or three cars each year. So out of all the people in all of the teams, in all of the countries, Luz was part of an effort only a very small percentage of people ever experience.

She laughed as she saw the garage doors open, with the two cars in front, waxed and polished, the team waiting, the gloom of the day before gone, replaced by a confidence that wasn't cocky, but accomplished. Everyone looked different. They stood taller, moved freer, and their faces relaxed and glowed. It was a new team; its members all welcomed her with the respect she deserved, glad to see her as she walked in the door, donuts in hand.

As each man selected his favorite morning sugar fix, they asked about Jeff. Luz felt like Snow White with her pack of seven dwarves, their faces falling as they began to worry about Jeff and his whereabouts. Just as she was about to tell them he'd be in any minute, Jeff walked in through the big open garage door.

"Hey, guys! Wasn't yesterday the finest day you've ever lived?" His voice echoed through the garage, and everyone looked his way. Glad to see him, they moved as one towards Jeff, slapping each other on the back, clapping their hands, giving high fives. It was a happy yet sedate celebration, full of the respect and admiration these men had for their leader.

One of the team members—Bob Barton, who worked on

gearboxes—said, "Hey, you just got out of the shower. Your hair's still wet!"

As they circled around him, someone else said, "Yeah, and he's wearing the same clothes as yesterday."

"I can see that. There's cheese dip right here." Joe Kerr pointed to a fingertip-sized smudge right above his third button.

The man looked at each other good-naturedly, then at Jeff. The first said slowly, "I think he didn't go home last night." The other quickly added, "I think he stayed over at somebody's house." The first concluded, "I think he got a little last night." And they all burst into laughter.

The other men joined in with snickers, comments, pats on the backs, and good-natured ribbing. With a wink of the eye, Beau Williams said, "So, one of the benefits of winning the pole is using the pole."

"A knight fighter. I bet she was. Those girls hang around here, just waiting for one of you young fellas to have something to celebrate," said Sonny Brown, one of the older men who had seen it all at the Speedway.

Luz watched it all from the locker area and stowed her gear as she maintained an appropriate distance. Her face blushed pink when they figured out Jeff hadn't gone home. But she didn't think it was a good time for this band of men who adored their boss to find out that she was the one who'd been his lover the night before. Better for them to imagine a sexy strumpet waiting outside the garage area, eager to make it with an Indy star.

Jeff's face turned beet red as he laughed and artfully avoided giving any credence to their questions. He sensed Luz avoiding him and moved away from the topic of his amorous adventures to turn the talk to the business of the day. With one car in the show, there was one to go, and both of them wanted Christi Cole to make it, since she would be the only woman in the field.

Luz realized Christi made a great spokesperson—she was young, attractive and personable. Her lack of sponsorship dollars puzzled Luz, because her times and previous racing experience were comparable to other drivers. Maybe advertisers believed that women weren't interested in motor sports, even though women made over half the buying decisions for consumer products and automobiles. Christi was an untapped resource who needed a once-in-a-lifetime opportunity.

Jeff called a team meeting after everyone had arrived and served themselves coffee and pastries. Mark Miller appeared, as Jeff had requested, and gave Christi a few pointers to help her with her times. The weather forecast indicated that showers were predicted for the afternoon. As it was Mother's Day, Christi hoped she'd have a special surprise for her mom: a qualifying run.

"First, thanks to all of you for the hard work yesterday taking the pole!" Jeff said to everyone in the garage. They all smiled and applauded; there were a few whoops from the fellows in the back.

"It was a full day. Remember, we are the Amberson team now, and with that comes a responsibility to Clint and Michelle Amberson to do our best and give every action our best efforts." He looked around the room at his team members, whom he had known for years. Many were men he'd worked with on other teams, and some of them had started at the same time he did.

"We have sponsors behind us now, and they expect a lot. We won the pole yesterday, but that was yesterday, and today we have another car to put in the show. It's a lot more than some of you signed on for, but with it comes a steady job and a regular paycheck!" The team clapped and whistled.

Luz, standing beside Jeff, nodded her assent to the paychecks and, with a knowing look, took over the meeting as Jeff handed it off to her, a practice becoming more familiar to them as the rhythm of working together became more natural. She hoped the team would give her the same respect as they did Jeff when she spoke. "We are going to qualify the car today," she announced. "Reviewing the data from practice, and based on calculations, it looks like we need a minimum speed of 223 miles an hour to stay in the field and not be bumped off the grid. Checking the weather, showers are expected this afternoon after the day heats up, so waiting until happy hour is not an option. Now, Jeff has more."

Jeff was waiting, leaning against the workbench that ran along the back of the garage. Sipping coffee, he noticed how attentive the team members were when Luz spoke, how much respect his men were now showing her.

"The forecast for next weekend is about the same, with thunderstorms forecast for Sunday, which is the last day to make the race. As soon as the track opens for practice, Christi will be out on the track working to get up to speed. When the speed is over 223 miles an hour, we'll head for the tech line.

Any questions?"

Everyone nodded. Luz stepped forward again. "Before we go out onto the track, I just want to say, that speaking for myself, as well as Clint and Michelle Amberson, we are very proud of the work you did yesterday. Without your help, Amberson Racing would not have taken the pole, which many of you know has been a dream of Clint's since the first time he came to the speedway. Tonight a special dinner is planned in your honor. Bring your spouse or guest to St. Erin's for a celebratory dinner starting at eight o'clock. Everyone has the day off tomorrow, and after that, we get ready for the race."

There were cheers from everyone in the garage. Luz smiled. She had the best job because she got to give the group the best news. Even with the team, it was different today. When she made eye contact with them, team members like Joe Kerr and Jay Jennings now looked her straight in the eye, not away. She felt they respected her judgment and the efforts she had made for the team.

"Some of you were contacted by the press about what happened yesterday. If you want to be interviewed, please let me know, so we can deliver a consistent message. Otherwise please refer any media to me or to Jeff. Thanks again for your hard work, and let's all do our best today."

When Luz finished the crowd clapped and whooped. She was glad they accepted her, and it felt good to be a part of the Amberson Racing team.

It was already nine o'clock when they finished the team meeting. Soon the track opened for practice, so the scoring stand, the bottle cart, and other equipment were moved into the qualifying pit assignment. Yesterday they had been way down at the entrance of pit road, near the opening at turn 4, but today, because the Amberson team had so many points, they were close to the Gasoline Alley entrance. It was different for them, too. The fans who arrived early to get good seats for qualifying cheered when the Amberson team towed the car out to the pit road before practice. Everything had changed overnight for everyone.

Once the track light went from red to green, teams began to practiced. Some had already qualified, and some were running full tank tests. Others still waited to make it on the grid. Mark gave Christi some pointers on how to gain a few miles per hour by using the straightaways to build up speed, and reminded her to shift before accelerating into the corners to make it through a little faster. He checked the suspension adjustments each time she came in to confer with Jeff and the engineer, Jay.

Little by little, Christi drove from a comfortable 214 mph, up to 218, and then to 222. On her last time out, shortly before eleven o'clock, one of her four practice laps was over 224 mph. Jeff felt she was ready, but the track was heating up, getting more slippery by the minute. When she returned for yet another adjustment, this one required a trip to the garage for time on the setup pad; there was a wreck in turn 4 that closed the track to practice.

"I'd like to give you one more practice session before qualifying to see if that new adjustment worked like we hoped. Only thing is, the radar shows storms a few miles away. The clouds will cool the track off, but still, I'm afraid we'll lose our opportunity to qualify this weekend. It's a strong front, with a lot of rain," Jeff told Christi as they walked to the garage area.

Luz kept track of the times for each lap after every adjustment was made. She loved timing and scoring because she was in the middle of everything, watching for the car and recording how many seconds it took.

After making the suspension adjustments, they towed the car to pit road, where everyone waited to do their job. What had begun as a sunny day was now cloudy and overcast, with a light breeze from the northwest. The track temperatures decreased, which made it less slippery and might help them raise the speeds. Jeff looked up at the sky, and then at Luz. "I think we'll take a chance and just get in line. There isn't time to practice. I just heard that it's raining about ten blocks from here, and we'll miss our chance if we don't go now."

"Let's go. Tell the crew what you want them to do. I trust you. You've gotten us this far—take us all the way."

With that, Jeff towed the car to where the tech line started. No one else was in front of them. The car was weighed, measured, and checked over by the tech crew, and once it passed inspection, Christi climbed into the car with her helmet on, plugged in the radio, and adjusted her gloves. The crew chief fastened her tightly in the car with the seatbelt, and Luz gave her a thumbs-up sign before she and Jeff boarded the golf cart, which took them to the entrance of pit road, where they would watch for the car during its warm-up laps.

The rush of the day before had not given Luz a chance to take in her surroundings. As they rode the cart down pit road, Luz gazed at the seats full of fans, the parties on the balconies of each of the suites, and heard the cheering and clapping.

"Christi! Christi! Christi!" the crowd chanted, while the big-screen TVs flashed her name. The sound from the hundreds of thousands of fans swelled, echoing around the stadium seats. When they arrived at the entrance of pit road, and climbed into the alleyway by the track, in preparation for the qualifying attempt, Luz felt her heart speed up, in anticipation of the adrenaline rush of the next few minutes. Seconds later, she heard the whine of the engine as Christi's car approached, and then felt the wind it generated as it flew by them. A practice lap, followed by another, would tell them whether the adjustments had worked and whether Christi was ready to take the qualifying attempt. With her stopwatch in her right hand, Luz clicked off the first lap, at slightly over 220 mph, Jeff looked over her shoulder and grinned when he saw the speed.

Knowing Christi, he figured she'd make over 223 mph for her second practice lap, and follow with an easy 224 mph or better for the next four. A shadow fell over the speedway as she flashed by; it was hard to read her speed, but the numbers confirmed Jeff's prediction of 223 mph or better. Looking up, he saw menacing clouds only a block or two away, with the sun still fighting to be out for the moments that followed. Jeff held the green flag, while Luz had the yellow within reach. In two more laps he'd signal whether they'd take the run or not. All they needed was for the weather to hold until the car was safely off the track.

Each time Christi passed them, they compared their time with that flashing overhead on the big screen: theirs was only a few hundredths of a second off. After the first lap the official timer confirmed that she was over 224 mph, with a time of 224.525 mph. Ticking off the second lap, she stayed between 225 and 224, edging ever closer to the 225 mph mark. Jeff waved the green flag, signaling to take the qualifying attempt, while Luz dropped the yellow one in the gutter, glad they were qualifying before the weather changed. When her fourth and final lap was over, the average speed was 224.762 mph, respectable for the field, and hopefully a speed that would keep Christi in the race. The crowd cheered her name and roared when they saw the qualifying speed, which placed her squarely in the middle of the fifth row.

As they raced down to the other end of pit road for the qualifying picture, Luz was excited. She had helped a woman qualify for the Indy 500 in a year when none had been expected to make the race. It was a great personal triumph for her, and it pleased her to help someone who so deserved it.

Waiting for them was the entire team, along with Michelle Amberson and the attorneys, who attended to legal proceedings all morning. Neither Luz nor Jeff had consulted with them about Christi's attempt, but the decision clearly pleased them. When Christi drove in, Jay helped her out of the car. After removing her helmet she got a big hug from Michelle Amberson and then one from Luz. Jeff gave her a high five, and so did Jay. As they posed for the qualifying photo, a flash of lightning crackled in the air, closely followed by the rumble of thunder. Luz and Jeff looked at each other and laughed. A few raindrops started to fall as they hooked up the car to tow it back to the garage. Christi Cole was the only driver who qualified that day.

CHAPTER 29

Near Union Station, in the block next to the fashionable Chaucer Hotel, was St. Erin's. Famous for tender steaks and giant shrimp cocktails, St. Erin's was always jammed during the month of May. All the big teams and their sponsors frequented the tony eatery, giving it the air of an exclusive club: patrons had to have their names checked off the maître d's list before they could enter the restaurant proper. The long bar, which stretched the length of a city block, was a gathering place for the who's who in racing circles, complete with their entourage of knight fighters in tow. Deals were made for the next round of sponsorship contracts, and beautiful women worked to catch the eye of famous stars.

Past the bar were the various dining rooms, some with mirror-lined walls that reflected the white tablecloths and gleaming cutlery, others with warm wood paneling that exuded the feel of an elegant library. Tuxedoed waiters served with aplomb and discretion. With all its legend and glitz, St. Erin's still welcomed those without a tie and jacket who looked for a great meal and interesting scenery.

Jeff drove Luz to dinner, as Michelle had requested. On the way there he told her, "From the first time I worked a race for Clint Amberson, I've always thought St. Erin's was the place to celebrate. That was the year I was a virgin and had worked days and nights to get that car ready to qualify. That was the year of the engine that spit and balked and singed the hair off your arms when you started the car."

"That must have hurt."

"Yeah, but it felt good at the same time. We got a car on the track that no one said could qualify. It was something, that first-time feeling. I promised myself that when my team qualified for the first time at Indy, we'd go to St. Erin's. It's not completely my team, but after the offer Michelle made me this afternoon, who am I to complain?"

"I think it's great that the new team is Amberson-Harwood Racing. The team members and sponsors you put together, and the sponsors, reputation, and equipment that Clint has developed—what a great future for all of you," Luz said.

"Not to mention the profit sharing and bonuses. A three-year agreement is pretty hard to get these days. I'm really proud of us—qualifying two cars in two days, and taking the pole to boot."

"Yeah, you and your team have a great future ahead of you," Luz said wistfully. Her voice brightened as they turned the corner and she saw the sign for the famous steak house. "St. Erin's! I've heard so much about this place. Can't wait to celebrate with everybody."

"Here we are." Jeff pulled into the valet parking lane, where the doorman helped Luz out of the car.

Luz hesitated as she walked through the door Jeff held open for her. If the two of them were to be seen together as a couple at a team event, the implication of a romance might cause them to lose credibility with the rest of the crew. When she saw Michelle having a drink with the attorneys as the bar, Luz ran up to greet her with a warm embrace. Having walked from the Chaucer Hotel, only a few yards away, Michelle attended to each member of the team as they walked in. As usual after qualifying weekend, the restaurant was crowded when they arrived. Most teams considered it a tradition to celebrate at St. Erin's and, like Michelle Amberson, made the reservations a year in advance. Team members were obviously pleased to bring their spouse or guest to such a special occasion.

After St. Erin's special shrimp cocktail with spicy red sauce, the crew was wowed by tender, juicy two-inch-thick steaks and copious wine and champagne. Several toasts and lots of laughter closed out the celebration for the Amberson-Harwood team.

Before retiring to her suite at the Chaucer, Michelle said goodbye to each couple; she shook hands with the gentlemen and gave a light kiss to the cheek of each lady. When she reached Christi Cole, she gave her a big hug and kissed the cheek of her date.

"I'm so proud of you. I don't know if I'm more excited about your qualifying run or taking the pole yesterday. Race day will be exciting, and I hope Clint can be here then."

Overhearing that comment, Jay Jennings asked, "You mean Mr. Amberson might be well enough to come to the race?"

"Yes, he's taking physical therapy in the pool every day. I talked to him tonight on the phone after he watched it all on TV. He was so excited. Tomorrow I'll be going home, but we plan to return to Indianapolis for race weekend." As the last couple left, Michelle called out, "Goodnight, everyone. We'll see you for the pit stop competitions."

Jeff and Luz drove off to Luz's apartment. Tired and happy, they fell into bed in each other's arms.

The next week, filled with activities for both of them, whizzed by. In the afternoons when she was at the track, Luz recorded track times, met contingency money requirements, distributed credentials to sponsors and other guests, and organized events for the sponsors who came to the track for practice. She approved all the expenditures before they were made, and made sure that Jeff had the parts and supplies he needed to reassemble the cars in time for the last practice before the race. Because of the name change to Amberson-Harwood, new uniform shirts and new fire suits were ordered and embroidered with logos and patches in time for the race. Luz provided the new symbol to the speedway—it would be painted on the pit wall for the race—and updated the accounting information at the sanctioning body office.

On her rounds of the garage area Luz stopped by the Loctite shop to say hello to her old buddy Bruce, who was busy selling special tools to several of the not-yet-qualified teams. Luz helped herself to a cold drink from the ice chest, since the hot dogs weren't ready yet. She sat down at a table near the sales counter and looked over a copy of Speed Sport News. While reading she overheard a conversation one of the mechanics was having with Bruce at the counter behind her.

"We've only been able to get to 223, so we're holding out for happy hour."

"I know for a fact there are three cars that can do over 226, but not many more."

"How the hell did Amberson get so much speed to take the pole?"

"Roger Schneider. Amberson is using his setup. Heard Roger has a brand-new deal. His driver and most of his guys are with him. Car number 65. Heard it's a good one."

Luz felt a chill run down her back on hearing the name Roger Schneider. Bruce had mentioned the new deal loud enough for Luz to hear it, probably for her benefit. She didn't want to bolt out the door, so she read a little longer and said goodbye to Bruce before she left.

"Hey, you can't leave yet. I didn't even get a chance to talk to you. Since last weekend with the big press conference and the team changes and of course the pole, you haven't been around. I guess you don't have time for the little people," Bruce said, taunting her as she turned to go.

"Bruce, you would not believe how busy I've been. I still have my regular job to do for my investment clients, and then I come here and work too. With the two cars, there is twice as much to do. I waited here for more than a half hour to talk to you, but you were too busy. Next week, when qualifying is over, I'll be back and we'll catch up." Luz walked out the door into the cool air and steeled herself against the unknown.

While she was thinking about what it meant that Schneider had a new team deal, Luz felt her phone vibrate in her pocket. She saw that it was Anita, so she took the call. "Hi! What's going on?"

"Wow! You won't believe all the talk going on in the office about qualifying for the 500. And the article in the local paper had a nice picture of all of you, too. A few clients have called who want to hear from you personally. I'll text their numbers and names to you so you can call them back. Oh, and Mauricio called, and he knows where you are," Anita said guardedly.

"Hmmm. I can only guess who told him. Great—the last thing I need now is for him to show up. Okay, deep breaths. I'll deal with it."

"It can't be as bad as having your entire team walk out on you, can it?" Anita was reminding her she could overcome almost any challenge.

"Right! I'll keep reminding myself that I can handle anything. Thanks for calling me and sending me that info. Oh, before you go, could you call Mrs. Reynolds about the municipal bond that's maturing next week and remind her that she also has a sizable cash balance in her account? She may want to add to the ladder of bonds we've created for her when we reinvest this money." Luz added, "It would maintain the asset allocation in her account that's right for her. Let her know I'll be calling her to discuss it further, okay?"

"Got it!" Anita said. "Talk to you again soon."

Walking through the garage area, Luz realized that if Roger Schneider worked on another deal along with his gang of thugs, she was in real danger. First it was the pit cart that raged towards her and then the car on a public street almost hit her as she crossed at Trudy's shop; Luz didn't know what to expect next. Jonathan Barrow had assured her Roger Schneider would not bother her again, but now she wasn't so sure. Now that he had another chance, maybe he wouldn't care about her and retribution wouldn't be important to him. All the same, Luz was going to be careful over the next two weeks.

The second week of qualifying came faster than she expected. The day dawned cloudy and cool, making the trip to the speedway a pleasure. The Amberson-Harwood team members were in full race prep when Luz arrived at the track. Each of the team members took breaks during the day to watch the competition, looking for any speed secrets that could be adopted between now and the race. As the day warmed up and the track grew hotter, the predicted faster speeds actually began to slow down, causing a rush out to the track even at what was normally the worst time of the day. When Luz saw that teams were taking 222 to 223 mph for their qualifying runs, she was reassured their cars were solidly in the field.

Both Christi and Mark practiced full tank tests and different setups in between other teams' qualifying runs. As happy hour approached, only three spots were left on the grid, and a long line of ten cars awaited the opportunity to make the four-lap qualifying run. Not enough time remained for all ten to go through the paces. The team relaxed as they watched the lineup and the last-minute strategies to prevent others from making the race.

Sitting on the scoring stand, they had a front-row view of the startup for each car as it set off to make an attempt. Luz and Jeff were perched atop the stand comparing notes about the different teams when they saw Roger Schneider and his crew tow a car out to get in line. Luz grabbed Jeff's arm to get his attention. When he looked at her, he saw the terror in her eyes and prayed the car would fail to make the race. Jeff hoped Roger would then leave the speedway.

"It's awful, Jeff—he's back. I can't believe anyone would sponsor him now, after all we went through."

"He's very good at his craft. But I hope his team doesn't make the race. I would be worried about your safety all the time until you go back to Texas."

"I'd like to believe he's too busy to have any interest in me now."

"I know it's hard, but do your best to stay away from him. And I'll do my best to watch your back." Jeff patted her arm reassuringly.

They watched on pins and needles as the cars moved through the tech line and out on the track for the qualifying laps. At this point there was barely time for ten cars to qualify before the track closed for the day. The first car averaged about 222.454 mph, and the second one closed in on 223 mph, averaging 222.989 mph. The next two cars did not clear the tech inspection, and frantically the teams went back to the end of the line, making repairs as they waited. Car number 65 slowly moved up the line towards the inspection. Luz prayed they would run out of time and wondered whether Roger would lose interest in his vendetta if his team made the race.

At ten minutes before six o'clock in the evening, when there were still five cars in line, the Schneider car passed tech inspection. All the places on the grid were filled, so that car would have to exceed the 222.454 mph speed of the slowest car in the field in order to bump it out of the lineup and take its place as the thirty-third car in the field.

On the edge of their seats, Luz and Jeff watched as Roger mounted the golf cart to go to the end of pit road, where he would signal to take the run or not. At this point it was merely ceremony, since it was the only run they would have. Of course, if they didn't take it, there would still be time for another team to have a chance.

As the car came around the track for the first time Luz clocked it on her stopwatch at 220 mph—fast for a warm-up lap. The second time around it ran at the same speed. The speed increased incrementally with each lap, and the average turned out to be 222.727 mph, edging out a car already in the lineup. Roger Schneider's team had made the grid for the 500, so Luz would have to watch her back for the rest of the month.

As she walked back to the garage with Jeff by her side, Luz had a heavy heart. Her love affair with the new world of racing was diminished by the hatred of this man who had brought about his own downfall. Even with her dampened spirits Luz said hello to the Yellow Shirt who watched over the opening of Gasoline Alley, kept a smile on her face for the new friends she had made around the garage area, and still gave the illusion of one who was at peace with the world.

"Just forget about him, Luz," Jeff said. "There are too many people around for him to hurt you. He would be an absolute fool to try anything. Remember he has everything to lose by doing something crazy."

Luz countered, "Crazy is just what I am afraid of."

CHAPTER 30

The last day of practice before the race dawned cool, with a light breeze from the north. A few clouds dotted the sky, and the air was dry. Luz had slept fitfully the night before. She clenched her teeth during her sleep and held onto Jeff's hand for most of the night. Several times Jeff was awakened by her sleeptalking: she kept saying, "No, no, no!" like a child not wanting to be hurt. When she woke up she was groggy and sluggish, without much energy.

"I don't know how I'm going to get through today. I feel so tired."

"You talked in your sleep, it sounded like you had bad dreams." Jeff handed her a cup of hot coffee. "See if this doesn't help take the edge off. And here's a little something to nibble on." He placed a small plate with both a bran muffin and a blueberry muffin on her bedside table.

She sipped the coffee and ate a bite of the blueberry muffin, mentally reviewing the agenda for the day. Clint and Michelle were scheduled to arrive at the garage at ten in the morning, then the pit stop competition started at eleven. Practice time on the track started at noon after the competition, and lasted for only an hour. Lunch with the team and sponsors was scheduled directly after practice, and then the drivers had autograph sessions at the Fan Festival from three to five in the afternoon. It was another long day, one performance after another, for one audience and then another. She really was living through the ninety days of May.

When she heard the shower stop, she slowly eased out of bed. Only a few more days of this life remained for her. She and Jeff had been together constantly for the last month, and now it was all drawing to an end. He was protective of her, and at the same time, he respected her judgment. They were partners in a business in which few women were employed, much less as managers, and it worked. What would happen when the race was over, the awards banquet ended, the team moved out of the garage, and she went back to San Antonio to her job at Emerson York?

Luz felt she had grown emotionally during this month, more than she imagined was possible, and now she knew she wanted more: she wanted a three-dimensional life beyond her career. But now was not the time to think about that. There would be plenty of time later, when she was back in her normal life. She'd contemplate the future then.

As she showered and dressed, Luz thought about the day ahead, and the preparations for race day. Being at the track early, making sure the equipment was in place, the team dressed and ready to go, the drivers ready for their prerace interviews, and then all the contingency plans for everything from a major wreck to a win. Her mind swirled.

Jeff left ahead of her after he was dressed and ready. They shared a soft kiss before he walked out the door. Luz couldn't think about this relationship right now—she was focused on the next four days, particularly getting through this last day of practice—but still she wondered how many more tender goodbyes she would share with Jeff. Would there only be a few, or would the rest of their lives be a possibility?

As she placed the new press kits in her pack, with the release about Clint coming for the race, Luz found a pink envelope with her name on it stashed inside. The envelope contained a lovely card with a smiling cartoon couple pictured on the front. Inside the sentiment read, "To the best friend I've ever had." It was signed "Yours, Jeff." He'd written an additional note: "What a great partner you've been. This last month has been the best. Have a good day! I'll see you at the track. J."

Luz was pleased he cared so much that he found time to get her a card and surprised her with it. Her spirits lifted, and she felt she had added energy to face the day. Smiling, she placed it on her dresser so she'd see it each morning over the next few days as a reminder that her life right now was very, very good.

Arriving at the speedway, she stopped for each credential check and visited with each of the Yellow Shirts as they directed traffic. With the beautiful weather, the last day of practice and the pit stop competition was sure to be well attended as it gave the fans their last glimpse at the cars before the race.

Drivers were on hand for autograph sessions and interviews, and there was a festive air to all the events during the day.

The garage doors were already open, and the nut barriers, as Tommy James called them, were already in place, allowing the crowds to see but not touch the high-performance race cars. Brochures for sponsors' products were on the display tables, and the team looked great in their new red-and-white uniforms for Amberson-Harwood Racing. While everyone visited over coffee, Luz stowed her pack in her locker, where she found another envelope waiting for her. This one was a soft blue with her name printed in calligraphy on the front. How nice, she thought, that Jeff was so considerate, leaving her two cards in one morning! But when she opened it, a razor blade fell out of it. As she read it, her eyebrows went up and she pursed her lips.

When she finished reading the note, constructed of letters pasted together, Luz said, "I must be getting closer."

"Closer to who?" Jeff asked flirtatiously.

"Closer to the truth. Here. Read it, but don't touch."

Jeff read the threatening words pasted above the card's "Have a Nice Day!" greeting.

"That's really sick." Jeff looked at Luz. "Where did you find this?"

"It was in my locker. I wouldn't have opened it, but I found that great card you left me in my bag this morning and I thought you sent me this one, too. Of course, the minute I read it, I knew it wasn't from you."

Jeff directed a question to the rest of the team: "Has anyone else been in here today? Anyone? A reporter, or janitor, anyone?"

"There was a reporter who came in looking for Luz yesterday afternoon, when she was out," Sonny Brown said. "He said he had something for her. I told him to slip it in her locker. Why? What's wrong?"

"Sonny, would you remember what that guy looked like if you saw him again?"

"Probably. I guess so. Why?"

The entire team looked at Jeff.

"It's a death threat. An ugly death threat. Let's keep this quiet until security can be brought in. Don't let anyone into this garage unless they are someone you know well and someone you trust. We have too much at stake to take unnecessary risks now."

Luz found a plastic bag and placed the card, razor blade, and envelope in it. She called Jonathan Barrow and told him about the incident, her anger barely under control.

"Jonathan is coming right over with some of his men to fingerprint my locker. What a way to greet Clint and Michelle—with a police investigation!"

"We have to set up the pits and get ready for practice. Someone may have tampered with the cars, and that means I have a lot to do right now, and I don't need to worry about you. So stay here!" Jeff said, his tone harsher than usual.

"I'm not a helpless person. I can help you—this is my team too!"

"Luz, the way you can help is to stay here to receive Clint and Michelle and show them everything we've done. Let the guys do the dirty work of setting up the pits. This team belongs to all of us, and if any part of it is destroyed, then we all lose. Please stay here and do your job." Jeff let his frustration show as he pleaded with Luz.

"Okay, I will, even though I'll feel like I'm not doing much." Luz sighed, knowing that he was right and that this was the best for everyone.

Jeff met with Joe and Jay, his crew chief and engineer.

"I want you to go over the cars carefully. Look for anything that doesn't belong, or something that is broken or missing. I don't know how long this 'reporter' was in the garage, but I'm afraid someone sabotaged one of the cars, most likely Mark's. I know we don't have much time, but do your best. I'd rather not practice than have the car destroyed on the track with the driver in it before the race even starts."

Jeff met with Beau Williams too. "Beau, I want you and Sonny to set up the pits for practice. Get everything ready for the pit stop competition. Check the air guns, make sure the bottle cart is out there, get it organized, and look for anything unusual."

The garage was bustling with activity as the mechanics clustered around the cars, examining every part. Clint and Michelle arrived to find Luz and Jeff deep in serious conversation. Jeff gave Clint a hearty abrazo, then touched him warmly on the right forearm. Clint's face lit up with a bright smile, and his eyes glistened.

"Well, aren't you a sight for sore eyes. I declare, it is good to see you," Clint said as he straightened up in the seat of his wheelchair and gave Jeff a two-handed handshake, then added, "I know this wasn't what you had planned for this year, and that has got to be disappointing to you, but sometimes helping out another guy can make things turn out better in the long run. I expect neither of our teams would have qualified a car this year or made the pole if we hadn't pulled together. I'm mighty proud of you, Jeff, mighty proud."

"Well, thank you, Clint," Jeff said. "You've done a lot of work this month, too. At least that's what Michelle tells us, and you're lookin' mighty good, besides. So I'd say we're both lucky to be here." He smiled at the older man.

"Got my own set of wheels now. Think maybe after the race your guys could hot-rod one of these things for me? We could start a whole new racing series. Just for old racers like me. Heh-heh." Clint's eyes twinkled. The two of them reminisced about the days in the oil field together until they were interrupted by Jonathan Barrow, who walked up to Clint to say hello. "Sorry to be here to spoil your return to the speedway, Clint, but we need to investigate this latest threat against one of your team members, Ms. Dane."

"Another one? Who'da thought our team manager could provoke such anger? Our team must be a real threat this year to win. You go right ahead," Clint said, and added abruptly, "Wrap it up before the race if you can, Barrow."

"Will do. Now where is the man who saw the 'reporter'?"

They pointed to Sonny, who just that moment had walked in from setting up the pit equipment, and Barrow asked him to describe the man he'd seen.

"He had dark wavy hair. Had a good build, like he worked out. He was over six feet tall, wore sunglasses, an orange cap, and a white long-sleeved shirt and khaki pants. Sounded like he was from somewhere else, the way he was talking. And he moved real smooth, like a cat."

Barrow jotted down notes as he listened. "Any tattoos, or jewelry, or other identifying marks you can remember?"

"No, he was kind of far away, on the other side of the garage."

"Dark wavy hair. Tall? No facial hair? Okay. My men will dust for prints on the locker and see if we can find this mystery man."

Luz handed Barrow the plastic bag with the card and razor blade inside it. "Hopefully this will help some too," she said.

"I'll let you know what we find out. Clint's right—we'd all like to have this wrapped up before the race. Good luck in the pit stop competition. We'll have someone around, just in case." Before he left the Amberson garage, Barrow said, "It's good to see you around, Clint. We've missed you this month."

"Thanks, Jonathan. Now find out who's behind all these shenanigans before someone gets hurt."

Luz wasn't sure whether the card came from Schneider via a messenger, but she felt he was acting unbalanced, and maybe he'd go too far. She didn't want to dismiss it; in a sport like auto racing, lives were at stake in the pits and on the track and now, it seemed, in the garage area as well. Glad to hear there would be security around during the pit stop competition, Luz thought she'd relax with her dear friends Clint and Michelle before it was time to go out on the track.

"Well, you certainly are a commanding presence at this place. I was so proud of you that first day of qualifying, when everything fell apart and you put the pieces of the puzzle together and made a better team than the one I started with in the first place. I watched it all on TV. You had those announcers running. They couldn't figure out what was happening next. If your daddy were alive, he'd be so proud of you, Luz. So proud." Clint patted her warmly on the arm.

Luz smiled, but at the mention of her dad, her eyes softened. She'd been so busy that she hadn't thought about her parents in a long time. What would they have thought about what she was doing, about this adventure, this risk she was taking? She didn't have time to think about it now. Only a few more days, when it was all over and she had time, she'd imagine how they would have fussed at her or how they would have been proud of her. Luz knew that the more risks associated with an investment, the greater potential return. She was discovering that every step in life had a risk associated with it, and she was taking quite a few risks these days, living her life to the fullest.

The team left for the track, along with Clint, Michelle, Jeff, and Luz. The garage doors were closed and locked; the garage stood empty. Not one unusual-looking part or disconnected clamp or severed line was found on Mark or Christi's car. Jeff was glad to know that everything appeared to be in order. After the pit stop competition, the final practice began: the ultimate test before the race.

Jeff's team had never entered a pit stop competition before. With Luz's coaching and the study of a few videos of teams with fast stops from past season's races, they improved their times to around 14.63 seconds for a full stop with four tires and a full refueling. Unfortunately, all their practice was outside their garage and not on the track, so the driver element was not taken into account. If their driver missed the pit stall, spun the tires, stalled the car, or hit the wrong gear while leaving the pits, their time would be much slower.

Twelve teams entered the pit stop competition, which was set up with a ladder like a golf or tennis match, where two teams compete against one another at the same time. The fastest team from each pair advanced to the next level, where they competed against another team that had won the first round. There was one final winner, of course, but all the teams who entered had a chance to win the $25,000 prize and share it among the crew members.

Starting promptly at eleven, the drivers for the first pairing of teams roared up pit road, stopped for their tire change and fuel stop, and then roared out again. Both were close as the stop began, but the driver for team number 2 stalled the car on exiting the pits, losing that round for their team. The Amberson-Harwood team fared well for their first round. Mark brought the car in smoothly, and the team performed flawlessly, changing all four tires at once. Mark smoked the tires as he left the pit box, giving the crowd something to cheer about. After the entire first round, Amberson-Harwood had the best time of the first twelve teams.

Once again the Amberson-Harwood team had the best time, so they advanced to the finals. Clint and Michelle basked in their team's success. It was a good feeling, especially after all the disappointments leading up to this point.

Jeff watched each of the other teams in the competition, looked for weaknesses, and watched for shortcuts his own team could use. The team they faced in the finals was the resurrected Blackbird Racing team, with Blake Notson as crew chief. Jeff noticed that the other crew members were recruited from Schneider's team as well. Uneasy that Schneider was around waiting to sabotage them, Jeff scanned the stands in the immediate area and looked out onto the track, but he didn't see him, and dismissed that idea from his mind, again focusing on his own team as it readied itself for the competition finals and their big chance to make a name for Amberson-Harwood Racing.

The last "Gentlemen, start your engines!" sounded for that day's final competition, and when the cars blazed into their pit boxes and each team clambered over the wall to change tires and refuel, it was obvious that something was amiss for the Amberson-Harwood team. All four air guns failed to work. Someone had simply and elegantly turned off the valve to the gas cylinder that powered the air guns and the hydraulic lift. Something so ordinary could easily be done, unnoticed, by anyone with access to the pits. Anyone with credentials could be in position to turn that simple valve: anyone, including Roger Schneider.

This little prank was harmless, not a matter of life and death. It effectively slowed down an opponent and kept them from winning. Was it a warning, a harmless prank? In a few moments, or maybe at the race, would real danger be around the corner? When practice began and the cars started for the first time since they were disassembled and repaired, would there be a problem that would emerge on the track at speeds where evidence disappears?

When the time came for the competition awards ceremony, Roger Schneider beamed as he waited on the podium, with Luz below him in the second-place spot. He happily accepted the $25,000 check for his team. Afterward, during the photo shoot, Schneider muttered to Luz, "Watch your back, missy. This is a dangerous playground for nice girls like you."

Luz felt her stomach tense but kept the smile on her face. When the shoot was over, she joined Clint and Jeff. Clint drew Jeff and Luz close and told them, "It looks like foul play at the competition. Who do you think is behind it?"

"Roger Schneider," Luz blurted out. "He just gave me a warning."

"Angry with himself, so he wants to make others suffer. It's a real shame." Clint shook his head sadly.

"We've gone over both cars. Everything looks okay."

"Good, but keep checking them. Can't stop a good man who's in the right who keeps a-comin'. Next time I see you both it'll be before the race on Sunday. I'll be on the grid in this rig of mine. I couldn't be any prouder of you two than if you'd won the race!" Clint said. Michelle tapped him on the shoulder, letting him know it was time to leave.

"Remember, keep the wheels on!" Clint gave them a soft salute and a wink as he powered his wheelchair towards the garage area, leaving Luz and Jeff to pit road and the final hour of practice.

His heart in his stomach, Jeff fired up Mark's car and gave a short prayer and, with the rest of the team, pushed it out of the pit box onto the pit road, where all the wheels stayed on and the car moved quickly up to speed. Radio contact from

Mark indicated he had no complaints about the car during its first lap around the speedway. After four laps Jeff asked him to come in. They read the data off the engine data port, and quickly reviewed of all the suspension parts to see how they were wearing.

While Mark discussed some minor changes with his crew chief, Christi strapped into her car and Jeff fired it up with the rear starter. The engine sounded good—it growled to a quick start and, with a slight push zoomed out onto the pit road to the track. Christi reported in at each corner, making comments about whether the car was loose or tight.

After six laps, Christi returned to go over the performance of the car, her driving experience, and the statistical data from the engine port. Luz made note of the times as both cars sped around the track. Relieved the cars were still in one piece, Jeff and Luz called it a day.

Jeff was edgy; the safety of his team was most important to him. Tomorrow, after the cars sat overnight in the garage, new information might reveal itself in the form of a leak or broken part. The most important thing for the team was to keep the cars away from the general public and carefully inspect them before they returned to the track.

Even with Jeff and Luz so close to one another, working side by side, neither one of them thought about anything else but the day of the race, and all the preparations for it. They delegated remaining responsibilities to various members of the team. Everyone knew their assignment and when it was to be completed. Beau and Sonny were charged with setting up the pits on Sunday morning. Bob Barton placed the fuel tanks in the correct pit boxes, painted with the livery of each car and properly decaled. Jay Jennings brought a backup computer just in case. Luz kept the official scoring sheet for both cars. Both drivers tested their radios with Joe Kerr, and the helmet mikes worked as expected. All the fire suits fit the team and were embroidered with the proper emblems and decals. Everything was ready for race day.

CHAPTER 31

Race morning dawned cool and drizzly. Luz cuddled up next to Jeff, their bodies spooned together. Together they watched the curtains move in the early shadows of the morning.

"It's time, Luz. We have to get up."

"Yeah, I know, but I just want to stay here. I don't want this to end."

"Neither do I. But maybe it's just beginning."

"I like that," she said sleepily. "It's just beginning. Sounds good to me."

Luz sat up and rubbed Jeff's shoulder. His head stayed on the pillow.

"You moved." Jeff looked up at her, pulled her down to him, and gave her a kiss.

"Yes, I moved. And I'm going to keep moving, all the way into the shower."

Jeff's hand slipped away from her as Luz backed away from

the bed; she frolicked into the bathroom; her hands moved like a ballerina imitating a butterfly. Jeff stayed in bed, stared at the ceiling, listened to the shower, and thought about the day. Very little could be done now to win the race or to stop Roger Schneider. All he could do was pray and hope for the best.

"Hey Jeff, you can't stay in bed all day," Luz teased, her voice sexy and sweet. "You have a race to win."

Jeff laughed. "Really, is today race day? Are you sure? What's the date?"

Luz sat down on the bed with a hard bounce, grabbed his arms, and playfully pulled on them to drag him out of bed.

"I promise you the Indy 500 is scheduled to begin today. Get out of bed!"

With one long tug, she pulled him onto his feet out of bed and then, with both hands, pushed him towards the bathroom door.

While Jeff showered, Luz surveyed the checklist of things she needed for the day. Sunscreen, sunglasses, a camera, pens and pencils, race-day credentials, two stopwatches, a cell phone, the most recent practice sheets with times of all the drivers listed by car: all these items were now in the pack. Wearing a team shirt, black pants, and black tennis shoes, Luz was ready for the day.

Jeff and Luz had agreed to go to the speedway together, simply to avoid putting one more vehicle into the heavy race-morning traffic. At five they climbed into Jeff's truck and began the short trip. The streets were slippery, wet from an overnight drizzle, so they moved inch by inch. On their way to the track they stopped at the parking campground on Georgetown to pick up some old friends of Jeff's who were grunts for race day. They had been in the pits with him every time he'd raced. Known as the General and Al, they had promised to cook the whole team a real Tex-Mex breakfast—sausage, bacon, eggs, and tortillas. All the groceries were already at the track, along with the electric skillet and hotplate.

Luz found these two characters charming. They complimented her on her poise during the press conference they saw on the TV and lauded her for fitting in to the racing community. The General was a heavily decorated Vietnam War veteran who according to Jeff was a strategic deployment specialist who was always in charge, hence the nickname. Al, a lifelong friend of Jeff's, had grown up racing go-carts and now had his own chain of auto-specialty stores. Before they entered the speedway gates Jeff made sure credentials were in hand.

"We've been watching you guys from the stands since the beginning of the month, and those pit stops sure have gotten better," Al said.

"Yeah, and how are those guys doing now that they are going to have steady work?" the General asked. "You aren't going to replace us, are you?"

"Why would I replace you guys? Where would I get two short-order cooks who specialize in race-morning meals and who understand tire camber to boot? You guys must be crazy! Replace you, never! But don't expect to get paid, now, either. Let's not spoil a good thing." They all chuckled. The good-natured teasing certainly helped with race-morning jitters.

Arriving at one of the few gates open early, they waited

patiently as speedway staff checked credentials. A grid access pass was required on the day of the race. Some passes allowed complete access to any part of the track; others allowed garage access or pit access but not grid access. A privileged few who were car owners, team owners, or race-day team members were permitted to walk among the cars as the drivers strapped into their cockpits waited for the call to start their engines.

Entering the speedway, Luz felt the excitement. The streets around the track were crowded with bumper-to-bumper traffic, and the Yellow Shirts were more thorough as they checked and verified the credentials of those who entered the stadium of speed. The parking lots were already filled with the vehicles of team members, sponsors, vendors, and caterers preparing for the day ahead.

After parking in the Red Lot the foursome walked in together, and Jeff introducing the General and Al to the Yellow Shirts who normally manned the central gate to the garage area. Although it was around five-thirty in the morning and sunlight peeked dimly through the clouds behind the stands, the garage area looked like an anthill with so many team members moving around. There was a frenzy of activity. Some people were moving from the tire garages to their team garage, others were lining up to move their equipment into the pits, others were making last-minute purchases: shoes, fire-resistant underwear, and caps at Simpson; tools at Loctite; and helmets at Bell. Everyone wore their game face, and opponents indulged in good-natured teasing as they walked about attending to their various duties.

There was a friendly competitiveness between the different teams, fueled by the knowledge that by the end of the day, the team with the best car, the best driver, and the most luck would win the 500. Sharing, borrowing, or stealing speed secrets was part of the game, as was the clever reading of the rule book, but out-and-out sabotage was considered unsportsmanlike and dangerous to everyone on the pit road and on the track.

As the group walked into the garage area, a harsh, grating voice suddenly called across the broad stretch of concrete in front of the Firestone garage. "Hey, there's Luz Dane, the bitch of Wall Street." There, ambling along, was Roger Schneider. He walked up to within a foot of Luz and pointed a finger in her face. "How'd you like the way we won the pit stop competition? Beat your team hands down. They didn't even change a tire. Fools. Think they can be the best."

He leaned toward her, practically snarling. "Well, we're the best. And we're going to win today's race. And there is nothing you can do about it."

Jeff moved closer to Roger, while the General and Al closed in on either side. As soon as Roger finished speaking, he faced Jeff and started again. "And you, you imitation Sir Galahad, don't think anything you can do will make a difference. This bitch is going to pay, and there is nothing you can do about it. I've had enough of her superior ways, and after today she'll wish she'd never seen this speedway."

As the General and Al started to grab Schneider's arms, Luz yelled,

"*Stop it!* I can take care of myself." Then she faced Roger Schneider, her nose practically touching his.

Al and the General backed away and gave Luz space to make her moves. She grabbed Roger Schneider by the shoulders and pushed him backwards, surprised to find she had the strength to move his body over three feet. As she read him the riot act, Luz pushed Schneider backward down the full length of building A from one entrance gate of the garage area to the next one.

"Look, you bully! I am sick and tired of your blaming everything on me," Luz said, grabbing his shoulders with both hands. "You are the one who set this whole thing up."

She pushed harder this time, making him stumble. She grabbed him by the arm like a rag doll and pulled him up to his feet. Swinging him around to face her, she said, "You are the one who stole sponsorship money and ran it through phony accounts. You are the one who tricked your boss and used his equipment." And with one hand on his right shoulder and one on his left, she held him hard and steady, shouting, "And you are the one who tried to run over me twice, and turned off the valve on the air guns during the pit stop competition. So far no one has gotten hurt, but I swear, if anything happens to my drivers or anyone on my team during this race today, I will make every effort to see you go to jail for a long, long time. *Do you understand?*"

To punctuate her last statement, Luz gave Roger one last push, where he landed against the wall of the garage building. He pushed himself off the wall, spat in her face, and walked away with a furious scowl on his face.

Everyone who was in the Firestone garage and in those on the west side of garage building A stopped what they were doing to watch this tall, shapely brunette push a tubby, balding man down a fifty-foot expanse and then up against a wall. When Schneider spit in her face, leaving Luz to wipe the spittle from her nose and cheek, all witnesses scattered. It had been an ugly fight between the two, and as the whispers and rumors spread, both Luz and Roger were given a wide berth as they walked their separate ways.

The undercover security man, Bart Soules, came in behind Jeff, Luz, the General, and Al. The four stood close by, waiting, in case they needed to jump in, but Luz held her own. After the fight, when she passed by them, they broke into applause, along with the rest of the onlookers, and gave her a few shouts: "All right, Luz!" "You showed him!"

Wiping her cheek with the sleeve of her shirt, Luz did her best to hold back hot tears of anger as her frustration escalated. Why did some men have so much trouble with women who were competent at work? She wanted to scream, loud and long and hard. Pushing Schneider around released a small percentage of the anger and frustration she felt, but she really wanted to go further, letting him know how furious she really was. But Luz controlled herself. She stood up a little bit taller and, holding her chin up, mentally erased the furrows in her brow right above the bridge of her nose, took a deep breath, slowly let the air out of her lungs, and counted to ten to give herself a chance to relax. She didn't say a word, afraid she'd lash out at Jeff, Al, the General, or Bart, spewing her anger on them when they had done nothing wrong.

The fight wasted thirty minutes, added a level of tension to the morning that didn't need to be there, and created a topic of conversation that spread like wildfire to the rest of the garage area. When Luz walked into the Amberson-Harwood garage, all eyes followed her as she walked through the door. Word had gotten back to them that she'd stood up for the team, so they broke into applause, then followed it up with catcalls and whistles. A few of them yelled, "You go, girl!"

The General, further amping up the morale of the team, began his best imitation of Julia Child, simpering and kidding around as he and Al whipped up their special Tex-Mex breakfast tacos. Out of their bags, like magicians pulling rabbits out of hats, they brought homemade pico de gallo, hot sauce, flour tortillas, and refried beans. While the bacon and sausage fried in the electric skillet, the General heated refried beans and tortillas in the microwave. Al scrambled eggs on the hot plate while the team waited, hungry, glad the only work left before the race was to set up the pits and tow the cars to the grid. There would be plenty of time for that after they ate and had a short nap to rest before their day started in earnest at eight o'clock.

The smell of bacon wafted out the door, luring members of other teams to poke their heads in to see if there might be leftovers. Both drivers arrived shortly after most of the tacos were passed around, wishing they could have a taste. Mark was on a special regimen he followed every time before a big race, timing his protein intake and his carbohydrate and fluid consumption. Christi, a former marathon runner, prepped for the race the same way she did for a long run, knowing that she would lose pounds of fluids and her endurance would be tested as she drove those five hundred miles. "Oh, those tacos smell fabulous! That bacon, the pico de gallo, it all smells so good. I want some," she whined.

Beau Williams snapped, "You know you can't have any, so stop complaining. At least you get to drive the car!" He had wanted to race cars since he was six years old, but wasn't able to make the grade. Beau took a big bite of his bean and cheese taco to emphasize his point.

Christi went to the women's restroom to change into her fire suit, hoping that by the time she got back to the garage, all the food would be consumed and she'd be able to avoid feeling hungry around all those delicious aromas. Most of the guys changed in the garage, but neither Luz nor Christi felt comfortable disrobing in front of thirty men. As she picked up her fire-resistant long johns and her fire suit at her locker, Christi asked Luz if she wanted to come with her.

"Sure. Let me get my fire suit." Luz walked over to the clothing rack in the corner where all the laundered team uniforms and the new fire suits hung. Luz grabbed her suit, slammed her locker shut, and walked out of the garage with Christi.

After Luz left, Jeff, Al, and the General cleaned up from their breakfast cookout. Al said to Jeff, "That woman is a fireball! Remind me never to get on her bad side. That Schneider guy is lucky she didn't kick him in the balls."

"She already did that this month when she hired me and my team. I think there is something psycho about him."

"No, he's not psycho. He just has some mighty dangerous friends," Bart said, stepping into the conversation as he helped the threesome clean up.

"What do you mean by dangerous friends?" the General

asked, his voice flinty.

"All I know is that Jonathan Barrow asked me to shadow her," Bart answered. "Said Schneider had been keeping some bad company. So far though they don't have enough evidence to link him to any of the near accidents Luz experienced recently." He paused, then said, "The Amberson attorneys think Schneider might have used the team accounts to launder money through billing from a fake automotive parts company, but they've had no luck finding out who is behind that company, but they are working on it. In the meantime, I'm supposed to watch out for Luz, but after what I just saw, I'm not sure she really needs any help."

At seven-thirty, Jeff called a meeting of the crew. He looked around for Luz, but didn't see her.

Just then the door opened and both women came in, Christi with the top of her fire-resistant long johns showing and the arms of her fire suit tied around her waist. Luz left the top of her suit unzipped, revealing a tank top underneath. Both women wanted to keep cool until they were out on the track.

Jeff assembled the team around him. Some stood, some sat on tires or toolboxes, others sat cross-legged on the floor. Two lawn chairs were saved for Luz and Christi on either side of Jeff. Mark sat next to Christi. Once everyone was settled, Jeff stood and began to speak. "Luz has a few words for all of you today, before you go out to the track for the show."

Luz knew this might be her first and last Indy 500, and her words reflected the intensity of her feelings. "Today is the day we've all prepared for. Some of us waited all our lives to be here, and for others it's merely another day at the track. We've had our glory winning the pole, and our trial by fire, literally. We came together as a team, when most crews would have fallen apart."

She continued, looking each crew member in the eye as she spoke. "Before we go out to the pits to get things ready for the day, I want you all to be proud of the work you have done as a group, and as individuals. Each one of you played a part in our being in this race today, and all of you deserve praise for the work you have done."

Taking a deep breath, her features relaxing, her confidence showing, Luz finished her speech. "Today we're all winners. Do your best and give more than one hundred percent. Stay calm. Be confident. Know you have done a good job in order to be here. Remember: to finish first, first you must finish. We made it to the track; we qualified for the race, and now it's time to win the race. Good luck to all of you. Now, let's go racing!" The team cheered, giving high fives all around.

Caught up in the excitement, Luz walked around the garage, personally thanking each crew member, wishing him the best of luck and giving him a high five. She lifted their spirits, inspired them to do their best. As the team dispersed, taking charge of their duties, the garage was left empty except for the cars, which would go out last that day. Moments later, both crews returned to tow the cars onto the grid.

"Remember, I want two members of each team to stay with each car," Jeff reminded them. "Do not let anyone touch your car unless Joe Kerr is present. I don't care if they are a league official or your best friend. Let's be careful. Let's be safe." Still worried about sabotage, especially now that he knew Schneider or his friends would stop at nothing to retaliate for the disruption of their illegal money-laundering operation, Jeff wanted everyone to be especially careful. That meant not trusting anyone during these last two hours before the race.

Once the cars had been towed to the track, Jeff closed the big overhead doors, grabbed his clipboard, and said to Luz, "It's showtime. Let's go racing."

CHAPTER 32

Walking out to the track through the garage area, Luz and Jeff were intent on their mission, just like the other team members they passed. Everyone was in a hurry; no one wanted to visit. A quick wave or a brisk hello was the only acknowledgment people gave one another this morning. Today was race day. Today everyone's mind was on business.

"Let's make sure the pit areas are set up properly," Jeff said, "and then we'll go out to the grid and check on the cars and our drivers."

He stood tall; his own fire suit was zipped up, with the neck and waistbands professionally fastened. On leaving the garage, Jeff reminded Luz that this was their professional attire, and she could be relaxed in her dress in the garage, but once they were outside, it was showtime. Fire suits, just like costumes, were part of the theater of the day. Jeff was showing Luz the business side of him, putting his best foot forward on the most important day of his career so far.

As the polesitter, the Amberson team had the first pick of the pit stalls. Jeff wanted to be close to the opening of the garage area: that would give him quick access to anything extra they needed and also make it an easy in and out for the driver. Although it was more than halfway down pit road, it was better to have extra room on the exit, without another car in the way. Christi's stall was five spaces down from Mark's, making it fairly easy for Jeff to check on both teams during the race.

Luz was in charge of timing and scoring during the race, to aid in the fuel calculations that would determine when pit stops would be needed. As she climbed onto the scoring stand, Luz taped the scoring sheet down to keep the wind from blowing it around, and placed several pens and pencils on the stand. Jay, the team engineer, sat next to her and worked his calculations on fuel to determine when to take pit stops to prevent the cars from running out of gas.

While Luz set up her part of the scoring stand, Jeff reviewed his emergency inventory of parts, duct tape, and webbers to make sure the team would have what they needed for any adjustment short of a major wreck. The ice chest contained water and soft drinks, and the top drawer of his toolbox was loaded with Snickers and Mars bars for quick energy boosts later in the day.

Jeff tested the squirter bottles, making sure they functioned; they had both been refilled with water the day before. The last thing he wanted was a fire in the pits, simply because they could not water down the fuel spewing out of the car as it was refilled during a stop. Buckets of water with heavy cotton bathmats were inside the pit wall to smother a fire, or to keep the paint on the side pods covering the headers from peeling in the event of an extended stop.

"We're as ready as we're going to be! How about your stuff, Luz? All ready?" Jeff made one quick look around, counting tires under his breath. All four air guns were present and tested in each pit box. The General and Al said hi to the old friends they'd met when working with Jeff at other races. Sonny Brown took last-minute instructions from Jeff to watch over Christi's pit, until the rest of the team showed up after the call to start. Beau Williams watched over Mark Miller's pit, while the remainder of the team stayed on the grid, waiting to push the car at the start.

Once finished with their preliminary review, Luz paused to look around. With a little more than an hour to go before the race, she saw the stands filling up with most people already in their seats. Men and women, boys and girls filled the stands. There were women in bikini tops and short skirts who leaned against the chain-link fence calling to the team members, who looked like superheroes in their fire suits. Little boys and girls reached out to drivers with pens and paper, looking for an autograph before the big race. Teams posed with strangers who wanted a memento of one of the greatest events in racing. It was a day of celebration, and everyone wanted to be with the celebrities.

The morning's entertainment began with marching bands from area high schools, followed by the famous Marion County Sheriff's department Harley Davidson motorcycle team. These bikers balanced on one hand or one foot on their hogs as they circled the two-and-a-half-mile route in the stadium of speed, and the crowd of over five hundred thousand spectators roared, clapped, and cheered in anticipation of the race to come. The introduction of the race queen and her court further entertained the fans, who enjoyed all of these traditions. Luz was amazed by the size and noise of the crowd.

"I can't believe how loud it is, all the people cheering and clapping," she said, standing in the pit box.

"Wait till they start the engines," Beau Williams told her. He stood with his arms crossed, headphones resting on the back of his neck, as he overlooked the crowd. "That's when it gets really loud. There's nothing like it!"

"Luz, let's head to the grid." Jeff beckoned her as he climbed over the pit wall and moved towards the alley wall separating the track from the pit road.

Leaving her clipboard and stopwatches on the scoring stand, Luz signaled to Beau that she was on her way to the grid for the start of the race.

"Good luck and Godspeed," he said, giving her a thumbs-up. Luz returned the good-luck sign with both thumbs up, then saluted before walking towards the track.

First they went to Christi's car, where team members reported no problems at this point. Jeff and the crew chief, Joe Kerr, both serious at first, reviewed the checklist together. Soon they were laughing, and Joe swatted Jeff with his hat after some good-natured ribbing.

Luz spoke to Christi, who was standing beside the car. "After waiting for ten women to change their clothes this morning, now you have to wait behind thirteen men to reach the front of this line, and win the race, right?"

"Yeah, but it may be easier to get in front of the guys than all those prima donnas in the women's restroom. What is it with those women reporters? This is not a fashion show; everyone's wearing the same thing in the pits. It seemed to take them forever to change their clothes. And then when I told them I was a driver and needed to hurry since we had a team meeting, well, they could have cared less."

"When you win today's race, then they'll care," Luz said.

"No, all they will remember is that they changed clothes the same place I did, and that will be the big scoop. I think those networks hire those women as eye candy so the guys watching won't change the channel."

"Who knows, Christi? Maybe you'll get a sponsorship deal with Victoria Secret after they report the details of your unmentionables."

"Yeah, right, I can see the ads now: 'Does your guy think you're too hot to handle? Try these flame-proof-undies.' Followed by pictures of the models prancing down the runway with outfits that look like my fire-resistant long johns. What a hoot! Luz, you've been around racing too long. You're already thinking about sponsorship deals that are pure fantasy! It just doesn't work that way."

"When you win, it will work that way. I know you can do it. Just stay steady. Follow your plan to stay in the top ten for the first half and then put on the speed in the last half. If you stay out of trouble, you could finish first."

"What a rush that would be!" Christi glanced at her watch. "Hey, it's already time for me to get in the car."

Christi gathered her driving gloves and her helmet off the seat of the car. Before climbing in, she turned to Luz. "I'm grateful you took a chance on me. This is an opportunity of a lifetime, and I owe it all to you."

"Everyone makes their own luck, Christi. You're good at what you do, and you are going to do the best you can today." She gave the driver a solid hug. Stepping back from her, still grasping her shoulders, she said, "You have everything it takes to be a winner. Give it your best shot. Stay out of trouble, have a great time, and enjoy every minute of it. I'll see you in a few hours, hopefully in the winner's circle."

Christi slipped her helmet on, adjusted the communication gear, and then, with Joe Kerr's help, climbed into the cockpit. Following the ritual she'd used for years, Christi methodically stepped in from the left side and allowed Joe to secure her six-point seat belt harness until it was snug. Then she carefully put her driving gloves on, first the left and then the right, just as she had since the first time she raced. She checked all the gauges in the cockpit, snapped her visor down, and began to meditate, visualizing the race in her head. From this point on, she wouldn't talk to anyone; instead she would mentally go through the race, from the beginning, through the pit stops, and to the end, visualizing a win for her, her car, and her team. Each time she raced this was the ritual she followed. Her career up to this point had been promising, with many podium finishes and a couple of wins. Her driving coach continually emphasized the importance of visualization to her, and this was her big break, so she would use every tool she had to make the most of it and finish first.

Luz left Christi to her creative process, aware that once the drivers were in their cars, each one had a method they used to center themselves and prepare for the three- to four-hour marathon of speed. Luz, like Christi, was experiencing a once-in-a-lifetime opportunity to be on the grid before the beginning of the race, and now was her time to take in the surroundings. She started with Mark Miller's car at the front of the grid, and moved to Christi's after that, and now she looked down the front straightaway towards turn 4 to see the remaining rows of cars, more than half the field, lined up in front of her. Around each brilliantly liveried car were crowds of people. Some were team members in their fire suits, solemnly waiting patiently for the call to start; others were friends, family, sponsors, celebrities, all talking, shaking hands, shouting best wishes, enjoying being part of this event. She passed Patrick Dempsey moving in the other direction, and then David Letterman bumped into her. He said, "Pardon me" with a nice smile as he walked on by. By the time Luz had walked to the end of the grid and turned around to look up the straightaway towards turn 1, she had seen five television stars, two movie stars, and a handful of supermodels. With the announcement that there was only thirty minutes until the race would begin, herds of people walked off the grid towards pit row, the suites, and the pressrooms. It was time for Luz to return to the front of the grid, to the two cars Amberson-Harwood Racing was fielding for the 500.

As she surveyed the grid, she looked around to the outside stands, then to the infield stands and suites. She could see pit road, with the line of scoring stands, bottle carts, and tires, empty but for lone team members in each of their pit stalls, waiting for the rest of the team to return once the cars moved on the track. The board men in the alley leaned against the wall between the track and the alley, relaxing for one final moment before the cars came around turn 4 and down the straightaway to spray rocks, dirt, and chunks of tire in their faces.

The crowds in the stands were restless, waiting for the singing of the National Anthem, the flyover of the military planes, and the engine roar signaling the start of the race. Luz walked slowly through the cars, lined up three abreast, eleven rows long, more than the length of an entire football field, to get to the pole position. She stopped at Christi's car to shake hands with all the crew and wish them well for the race. Joe Kerr would be starting the car for Christi, and the rest of the team would give her a push to help her on her way. At Mark's car, the crew was huddled with Jeff, who led them in prayer. As they broke, their hands upraised, Luz gave each one a quick pat on the back and words of encouragement.

The music started for the *Star-Spangled Banner*, followed by *Back Home in Indiana*. Then, flying over the crowd, the majestic Flying Fortress caught the fans by surprise; *oohs* and *aahs* filled the air, followed by the loudest round of applause Luz had ever heard before. Finally, the grande dame of the speedway gave the call to race. As Luz heard the words, goosebumps chilled her arms and back. She would never forget that feeling when for the first time in her life she heard, "Lady and gentlemen, start your engines!"

With that, the roar of thirty-three engines came to life.

Jeff was down on his knees behind the car, starter in hand, pushing the power button, giving it a charge, praying it would turn over and rumble to life. As Mark revved the engine, the team breathed for the first time that day, knowing they would be able to start the race they had all been working towards. Slowly they pushed the car off the line in sync with the other front-row cars. The warm-up laps started. Quickly Luz and Jeff jogged off the track, out of the way of the cars behind them. On the radio they were assured that Christi's engine had turned over as hoped. With that good news, the two scrambled over the walls separating the signboard alley from the racing surface and then crossed pit road to Mark Miller's pit stall, where they climbed up to the scoring stand and took their positions, ready to work. The remainder of the team members walked to the pits of their assigned car, ready for the first pit stop, whether in a moment or in an hour.

As they settled in, Luz tested her stopwatch on the warm-up laps and made a note of the weather at the start of the race. Once the race began, Jeff stepped down from the scoring stand to walk between the two pit stalls as needed, and the chief engineer took his seat next to Luz, monitoring fuel consumption and comparing their own timing and scoring data with their competitors'.

Row by row the cars moved off the grid. An orderly warm-up and start to the race had been the major emphasis at the drivers' meeting that morning. Weaving from side to side, warming up the tires, each driver was alert to every nuance in the suspension. The hundreds of thousands of fans stood, their heads following the field down the track, keyed up with anticipation of the wild dash once the race went green.

The cars passed through turn 4 the second time, approaching the yard-long start-finish line, the only stretch still paved with bricks from the original track. Then the green flag dropped. The teams' adrenaline level shot up, and the fans were riveted to the blur of open-wheel rocket cars as the 500 began. Rounding turn 1 in front of the pack was Mark Miller. Amberson-Harwood Racing, at least for a little while, was leading the race.

CHAPTER 33

Intent on the track, Luz focused on turn 4, waiting to see the nose of the Amberson-Harwood car number 54 come around in front so she could push the button to stop the timing on one lap and then begin the next. Luz compared her lap time with that of the data displayed on Jay Jennings's computer merely to test her accuracy against the electronic measurement system on the track. The simple paper, pen, and stopwatch system would be the official record backing up the computer data if the electronic system malfunctioned.

Initially the adrenaline of the start of the race kept Luz energized on the edge of her seat on the scoring stand. The first few laps required her keen attention. All the cars bunched together as they made their way up the straightaway, and at first picking out Mark Miller's red-and-white car was tough: speeding along at over 200 mph, the cars blurred together. But after twenty minutes, Luz was in a routine and was able to relax and take in the scene around her. At this point team members sat on stacks of tires or the edge of the bottle cart or leaned on the scoring stand or one of the large rolling toolboxes as they waited for the first pit stop. There was edginess to their waiting; they counted the minutes until the first stop, anxious to perform at their best. Evenly spaced throughout the race, the scheduled pit stops took place about every fifty laps. Fuel consumption and the timing of yellow-flag cautions often changed the frequency of those stops and gave teams that were quick to take advantage of a change of pit strategy an edge of half a lap or more over the competition.

With the sound of the roaring engines and the vocal emotions of the crowds around them, the only way for the team to hear each other was to communicate via radios and headsets. Short staccato comments were the norm; no one wanted to tie up the radios in case of a wreck and the need for split-second responses. Jeff moved between the two pit boxes at first, but now he stationed himself next to Jay Jennings, looking over his shoulder as the numbers flickered on the computer screen. Pit strategy won more races than faster engines, and Jeff didn't want to lose the lead by not paying attention. As Luz focused on timing the car as it went by, she listened to the silence on the radio and waited for the first pit stop or the first big wreck, hoping their cars could avoid a smashup.

"Yellow, yellow, yellow," Luz heard over her headphones. "Wreck in turn 3, wreck in turn 3."

Luz's eyes darted back and forth between turn 4 and the big closed circuit television monitor showing the wreck, praying that the Amberson-Harwood cars would come around that corner and down the straightaway unscathed. As she saw the replay of the wreck unfold, one car coming from behind another, the ones in front three abreast, slowing down for traffic in front, all she could see was one car on top of another, then the flying parts, clouds of smoke, and the twisting chassis entwined in a macabre dance, first too fast to see clearly and finally appearing to be in slow motion as it stopped on the grassy apron to the lead-in to pit road. She breathed a sigh of relief as Mark's car drove through the clouds of smoke and then as Christi, who skirted a loose tire that came off one of the other chassis, passed through safely.

Both Jeff and Jay feverishly pecked at their calculators, their heads together, deciding if an early pit stop would be a mistake setting them up for problems later. It was a big wreck, with a lot of debris on the track. At least three laps would be yellow caution laps, and maybe even a fourth. It was the forty-fifth lap, and they decided to chance it: there was no telling how much debris was sucked into the intake or what piece of rubble might hobble a tire.

"Mark, pit stop next lap. Christi, go around one more time, wait for instructions," Jeff's voice boomed over the radio.

"Coming in," Mark said.

Like a well-disciplined military unit, the team members took their places, ready to scramble over the wall the minute the car came into the pit box. In front the tire changers lined up first with their helpers, ready to pass new tires over the wall and collect the old ones. Towards the rear of the box, the fueler and vent man were the first to go over the wall; the tire carriers followed. The vent man operated the hydraulic jack, jamming an air wand over an opening located behind the roll bar on the engine cowling. While the car popped up on the jack, the tire changers dropped onto their knees on the ground, air guns ready to remove the lug nuts holding the rims on the car. Just as the fueler finished, new tires were bolted on, then water was squirted on the car to dilute fuel to avoid a fire, and when everyone had finished their jobs, the vent man removed the wand, lowering the car with an abrupt bump. Squealing tires and a smoky exit signaled the end of a nineteen-second stop.

It was fast and clean, with no errors and with time enough to give Mark a drink, clear debris away from the air intake vents, and make a tiny adjustment in the front wing of the car. With most of the top ten coming in for pit stops, Christi was left in the lead. Another first for Amberson-Harwood Racing—both of their cars had now led laps of the famous race. Jeff and Jay strategized again. What would happen if they left Christi out in the lead until the last possible moment? What would happen when she finally pit? Could she at least stay out for one more lap and pit during the final yellow caution lap of that series?

"Christi, how's the car?"

"Fine, I'm doing fine. It feels like I've got a little bit of fuel left, but it's getting close."

"Think you can stay out two more laps?"

"Yeah, it's like my first time here."

Jeff chuckled and gave Jay a thumbs-up. Christi's very first lap at Indy was in a car with very little fuel in it: Jeff had scrimped and saved every penny, not wasting anything, especially with a new driver who might not make the cut. Now that little bit of frugality played a big part in the decision to leave her out on the track. Most of her practice laps had come after the lead driver had finished his, and as a result Christi could differentiate between the feel of a car with enough fuel and one about to run out, as she had experienced once or twice in practice. At least, that was what Jeff banked on as he left her out to run and lead the race during the next two yellow laps.

Mark moved steadily towards the first position as various cars dropped onto the pit road to make their scheduled stops. Towards the end of the third yellow lap, Jeff called Christi in to make a fuel stop, leaving Mark to lead the race. The crowd roared as Christi came in for her stop; only one more yellow lap remained according to timing and scoring. She raced against the clock, wanting to be back on the track before it went green. Her stop went off without a hitch: she drove out as smoothly as she came in, with fresh tires and plenty of fuel until the next stop. As soon as the car sped around the curve on pit road, the team celebrated the two stops with high fives all around.

The adrenalin was intoxicating. Two cars on the same team, leading the race, in sequence—what a thrill! The media already thought it was a great story, especially considering the road all the team members had traveled to make it to the race. Jeff was interviewed by Jerry Punch, whose excitement for the Amberson-Harwood team was clear. Other media reps attempted to talk to individual team members, but it was agreed that Jeff was the spokesperson for the two teams during the race, and only when he felt his full attention wasn't needed for either car. Luz glanced over to see him smiling, answering questions, enjoying the positive attention from the media at that moment.

Out of the corner of her eye, at the beginning of turn 1, she saw one red car flip through the air, and loose tires bounced down the front straightaway. What would become a ten-car wreck began as one driver started to drive over another. Luz knew Mark and Christi were on the back straightaway, and she abruptly spoke into the microphone of her headset, "Wreck in turn 1."

Jeff turned to see how bad things were, distracted, as he was focused on his interview. After seeing that the pit road was open, he barked into the headset microphone, "Come down pit road. Come down pit road."

Helpless to do anything, teams whose cars rounded the fourth turn and speeded up the straightaway watched as their drivers drove into and through the wreck. The smoke and debris masked the exit to the pit road and spread down the front straightaway like ground fog. Loose tires bounced against the catch fences and into the infield. Parts scraped along the ground, their flinty sparks turning puddles of methanol fuel into invisible firetraps for cars that slid into their path. The officials red-flagged the race and directed all cars onto the pit road, hoping further loss could be prevented. The crowd held its breath, fearful that one of the drivers would be dead from such chaos.

Both the Amberson cars made it safely to pit road. Once in their pit box, they remained there, since the officials were afraid to let cars through with all the debris on the exit to pit road near turn 1. The fire brigade and safety crew began the cleanup, and little by little the smoke cleared. Four ambulances were dispatched from the infield care unit to attend to the drivers, many of whom were walking around, albeit a bit dazed. Tow trucks made their way onto the track picking their way around tires, parts, and other emergency vehicles. Five of the cars still had all their tires mounted yet missed a front wing, a side pod, or a rear wing. The other five had virtually disintegrated on impact, their parts absorbing the physical forces of that 5 g-force wreck. Only one of the drivers was still unconscious, and he was taken by helicopter to the downtown medical center, where the trauma experts attended to him. As the Jaws of Life freed the last of the drivers from his car, he waved at the crowd, sending the fans into cheers and applause for all of the wounded drivers.

Watching the wreck unfold, Luz felt her stomach knot. Staring with morbid fascination at the cleanup process, watching the drivers taken away to the infield care center in an ambulance, she was suddenly overwhelmed by thoughts of the danger faced behind the wheel.

Jeff watched her as she stared at the disaster, her face pale and drawn. With his two drivers safe and parked in their pit boxes, Jay downloaded as much information as the rules permitted that might help them for the last half of the race. Jeff relaxed for a moment but was drawn to Luz, sensing that she needed him as she absorbed the chaos in front of her.

"Happens every race here," he said, climbing up onto the scoring stand and sitting where had Jay sat a few minutes before.

"Hmmmm." She wasn't really taking in what he had said.

"They get used to it."

"Get used to what?" she asked distractedly.

"The danger. The risk. Isn't that what you were thinking about? How these drivers can do this over and over again, knowing this might be the outcome?"

Luz looked down at her stopwatch, then over to the spotting point on the fence, and then up at Jeff. Tears welled up in her eyes. She blotted them with a tissue and opened her mouth to say something, but no sound came out. She stared helplessly at Jeff for what seemed like hours, then cleared her throat and said, "My dad didn't drive particularly fast most of the time. In fact, he was very careful behind the wheel." Luz sniffled, dabbing at her eyes with the tissue.

"The day he and my mom died, it was instantaneous. I was thankful they were spared from some lingering, painful illness, but it was such a shock. I had just seen them the night before, and then they were gone." Luz paused, blew her nose, and took a long drink of cold water from the bottle Jeff passed to her. "A semi made a left turn under the freeway just as Dad and Mom were on their way to town from the ranch. The driver didn't see them; to him they came out of nowhere. But I remember seeing the car afterwards. It was broken like these, but with no survivors."

Jeff reached over to place his hand on hers and squeezed it. "I'm sorry, Luz," he said. "I didn't know."

"I'm okay. Just sometimes, things remind me of my losses."

At that moment, Jay Jennings popped his head up in front of the scoring stand. "The officials say it's time to get the cars out on the track; they'll go green in a few minutes. Let's look over a few things before we start the car."

Jeff looked over at Luz and winked at her. "Got a race to win." He hopped down from the stand to huddle with his engineer and decide on any legal changes they might make during the next pit stop.

For a moment, looking around her at the twenty remaining cars lined up, their brilliant colors casting them like abstract metal sculptures lit up by the sun, Luz breathed in the rare air found on pit road at the 500. Up and down the road on both sides of her were mostly men and a few women clad in their superhero-like fire suits preparing for the final half of this marathon, and for the first time, Luz realized she played a very important part in the pomp and circumstance. How different was this than her twelve-by-twelve foot office at Emerson York! How different the risks and how different the rewards! There the games of obfuscation and intrigue mingled with the folly of immature egos and infantile attitudes, while here, the games were based on skill, strategy, and preparation, honest and true in their directness. Luz was proud of her efforts and proud of her part in this passion play. She sat up a bit straighter, and readied her mind for the finale, soon to come for this drama on wheels.

During the red flag, all the teams were prohibited from working on their cars, but now that the race was to begin again, some cars would come in for immediate pit stops, while others would stay out until the last possible moment.

The weather had been cold and rainy earlier, when everyone traveled to the track, and it stayed cold most of the morning. Now, however, a patch of blue appeared in the northwest corner of the sky, and the wind swept the clouds away. The warming of the track, once the sun appeared, made the track stickier, affecting the downforce of each chassis, while the wind from the north felt like a wall on the back straightaway eating away at precious fuel consumption, changing all of the calculations made by every engineer.

The call to begin echoed over the radios, and over the track loudspeaker system. After sitting idle over thirty minutes, most of the cars started; only two remained behind, beset by leaky hoses and cracked headers that had weakened as they cooled. The Amberson-Harwood team members gathered around their chassis during the wait on pit road and looked for any subtle changes, bumps, or missing parts that needed attention the next time the cars made it to their pit stalls. Collectively they held their breath as the starters surging with battery power brought the engines to life on both Christi's and Mark's cars. As the team pushed the cars off the pit road once again, they smiled and laughed with glee in the disbelief they had made it this far.

Back in the pits Jeff gathered them in a circle together for a quick pep talk. "We're a third of the way through, and a third of the field is out of the race." He looked at each team member, locking eyes with each man. "Stay alert, be careful, think about what you are doing when you do it, and keep the rhythm going as each pit stop comes around. We've led the race so far and we can win it, too. Let's keep the faith and act like winners!"

With pats on the back, the group split into the two teams retiring to each of the pit stalls. Jeff checked in with Christi's crew chief, looked over the pit stall, and checked the mounted tires. Noticing that one or two looked out of round, Jeff signaled to Beau Williams to return them to the Firestone garage to be checked by their engineers. Nothing was left to chance today, not where a mistake could be prevented. As he returned to the pit stall for car number 54, the field of cars crossed the start-finish line during its first warm-up lap before the race restarted. Almost a minute later, over the radio, they heard, "Green, green, green."

The cars flew down the straightaway, this time with Mark Miller in the lead and Christi behind him, battling Roger Schneider's car number 65, which worked aggressively to find a way around her. As they sped into turn 1, car 65 slipped around on the back left side of Christi's car and attempted to push her up the track to the high side and then pass her. Christi drove the groove that took her safely through turn 1, down the short chute, and through turn 2. In his attempt to push her around, the number 65 car backed off the throttle, turned his wheels into the grass, and spun towards the catch fencing in the infield. The crowd was on its feet cheering Christi on and waiting to see whether Schneider's number 65 car would lose control or get back on the track. Christi was well on her way down the back straightaway when Jeff called out to her on the radio: "Way to go, Christi!"

In the background she heard the team whistling and cheering on their own for her as they saw her going into the turn and from the monitors watched her slide through to turn 2 like a veteran. Still behind Mark, Christi was careful not to crowd him, but she still defended their territory admirably.

"Good defense," Mark said. It surprised Luz a bit that he

could think about anyone else while in the lead.

The next thirty laps were uneventful. Yet as they approached the halfway point, with pit stops soon to be made, engines began to fail, clamps on hoses broke, and a few more cars dropped out of the race for repairs, leaving them laps behind the others.

Mark and Christi came in for pit stops one after the other, trading off the lead as they had before. The wind on the back straightaway cut into the fuel consumption and changed the calculations Jay had done earlier in the day. After both cars were back out on the track, the engineer and crew chief huddled.

"Our original strategy was to keep out of trouble for the first half and then come to the front in the second half," Jay said. "We're in the front now."

"We've led more laps than anyone else today, and who knows?—we may have a team record for leading the most laps with our two cars. Why change anything?" Jeff asked.

"I'm worried about fuel consumption, but neither car shows the engine to be heating up. We cleaned debris out of the air intake this last time in. Still, what's the point of racing if not to lead the race?"

"Hey, that's why we're here. And the sponsors sure like it." Jeff looked up to the suite balconies above, where he could see the Barbar Beer and ABC Mobile guests cheering as the cars sped by in front of them.

Jay echoed what Jeff was thinking. "Tire wear is good. We made a few adjustments for the change in track temperature based on the data we had from practice a week or so ago, when the weather was the same. Seems like there is no reason to change what we are doing. It makes a good show, and a good story."

With that the two made the rounds of the team members to share their thoughts and keep morale up. Between pit stops it was easy for some of the guys to get sleepy while they waited listening to the rhythmic droning sound of the engines as the cars circled the track. Jeff stocked the toolboxes with candy bars to give the team members bursts of energy and keep them awake, even if it was on a sugar/caffeine high. While they waited and watched, Luz continued her steady recording of the lap times of both cars. Each time she saw the red nose of Mark's car line up with the fence post, she pressed the button, registered the lap time, and then quickly wrote it down before it resumed the display showing the current lap, yet to be recorded. This too became monotonous.

Feeling a little sleepy, at about the 125th lap Luz asked Jeff to pass her a soda laden with caffeine to help her make it to the 200th lap, hoping both cars would still be running by that time. The last pit stop was laps away, and most of the teams felt the effects of waking at three in the morning, now that it was close to two in the afternoon. Like a fire alarm, the voice over the radio called out, "Wreck in turn 3. Oil on the track. Yellow, yellow, yellow."

Turn 3 was back behind the Tower Terrace grandstands, where no one in the pits could see what was happening and who was involved. All eyes turned to the giant monitors hanging from the Paddock grandstands across the track from pit road. Luz glanced up at the monitors, but the smoke and debris pictured didn't give her a clue as to the cars involved. She looked towards turn 4 in hopes that the Amberson-Harwood cars could drive their way through the wreck, but as she waited her heart sank. Not one car appeared through the turn.

"Where are they?" Luz asked, desperation in her voice.

Jay seated next to her, stood up on the scoring stand, as if that would give him a better view, but he shook his head, his face grave.

"How many cars were in the wreck?" Luz asked aloud, looking from one face to the other. No one knew, and nothing came across the radio or showed on the big screen, nothing to give the crew more information than they already had available. A hush descended on the front straight as all of the fans waited for any cars to appear out of the fourth turn.

Slowly a cheer was heard, and the nose of one of the Amberson-Harwood cars appeared on the pit road with a low right front tire. It was Christi's car, and the crowd loved it. She carefully pulled into the pit stall, where the crew went to work changing tires, refueling, and making a quick inspection of the rest of the chassis. Other cars followed her lead, all of them driving on pit road, where most were redirected after the accident. The track was still yellow, and traffic was directed around the track on the apron or pit road, waiting for the debris and oil to be cleaned up. As soon as Christi drove out onto the track, the team saw Mark's car, moving slowly, limping towards the pit stall for repairs. The right half of the front wing was torn off, the nose cone shattered, and the right front tire flat.

The wreck had started when the next-to-last car blew an

engine, spreading a stream of oil down the track near the outside wall on the back straightaway, right in the path of Mark Miller, who was speeding along close behind. As his tires hit the oil, the car became loose and spun across the track and into the infield grass, where he remained stuck until the safety crews arrived, giving him a push back onto the asphalt apron only after all the other cars were directed onto the apron, long before they reached the oily mess left by the other car.

Christi was out in front of the pack when the track went yellow. "Stay out of trouble" was the mantra she heard over the radio as she steered her way around the track during the last two laps of the yellow caution caused by the engine blowout.

Meanwhile, the two pit crews busily patched Mark's car together, hoping to get him back out on the track before the green laps began once again. Fortunately, the integrity of the chassis was not compromised, so the headers and gearbox were still in one piece. New tires were mounted quickly, and a spare nose and front wing, stored on the bottom shelf of the bottle cart, were fitted to the front of the chassis. As soon as the crew chief was sure everything was secure and ready to go, he signaled the jack man to lower the car, and all together the crew pushed the car out of the pit stall onto pit road. Burning rubber, Mark Miller joined the field right before the track turned green. Although he'd wrecked and spent a few minutes in the pit box, he was still on the lead lap, with enough time left to work his way through the field one more time before the end of the race.

With twenty-five laps left before the end of the race, only fifteen cars were left in the race, and only seven cars were still on the lead lap. Most of the teams whose cars had hit the wall, had parts fail, or blown an engine were in the garage area or at the team motor home watching the race on television in air-conditioned comfort. It was the hottest part of the afternoon, the most suspenseful part of the race. Anything could happen before the checkered flag dropped.

CHAPTER 34

With Christi still in the lead, and with only about twenty minutes remaining before the race was over, Michelle and Clint Amberson, along with Jonathan Barrow, left their suite, passed through the garage area and Gasoline Alley, and arrived at their pit box, where they would wait it out, hoping their team took the checkered flag.

Sending Michelle and Clint on out to the pits ahead of him, Barrow excused himself when he noticed Roger Schneider coming out of one of the garage spaces, followed by a tall, dark-haired man wearing a leather jacket who seemed to be pushing Schneider forward. Barrow slipped into the shadows of the hallway by the men's room in building B, where he watched the two men as they trudged in his direction. With everyone watching the final laps of the race, the garage area was deserted. Barrow might be the only witness to whatever Schneider and his cohort had planned. Waiting, he heard the large man say to Schneider, "Let's go in the men's room. We'll need a little privacy for this conversation."

Barrow quickly slipped into the restroom and moved into the shower area right behind the door, his back against the wall. He hid in the darkness and waited. Soon he heard the men's room door slam open against the concrete wall. A low voice with a subtle Spanish accent shouted, "Look, you, you were supposed to win this race! You said it would be *fácil*, easy. You said your driver was one of the best, and what is happening now? This driver no one ever heard of has been leading the race all along. How are we going to get our money back, you bastard? Our partners are leaning on me for the money that was supposed to be transferred out of the country! "

"Look, I did what you told me to do. You set up the offshore accounts where you had the connections. I paid all the invoices you sent me from that company," said a voice familiar to Barrow. It was Roger Schneider. He was trying to sound tough, but there was an undercurrent of fear in his voice. "I let you run the money through the team accounts. You got what you wanted, so leave me alone."

Barrow saw a tall man, a little over six feet tall, with wavy, carefully styled black hair, wearing a fine black calfskin jacket. He had one hand on Roger Schneider's shoulder, pushing him against the wall; the other hand was shoving a 9 mm Beretta into Schneider's face. His heart beating so hard he thought it could probably be heard, Barrow held his breath so as to not reveal himself to the new occupants of the men's room before he could make his move.

"Yes, you let me run the money through the accounts, but

why didn't you tell me my former girlfriend was working on the Amberson team? Luz Dane was always a smart girl, too smart for her own good sometimes. I thought things would be easy, but now, I don't know," the dark-haired man said, stroking Roger's chin with the gun while he talked.

"I didn't know her until three weeks ago when she arrived at the track. How am I supposed to keep track of the women in your life? Or where they work?" Schneider roared back, his temper getting the best of him.

"I never did business with her. She was too thorough, too knowledgeable. But she was easily romanced and so easy to use. She had all the right connections for me, and she was so eager to please. And all the people who worked with her, especially her manager, so easily impressed. It was an ideal relationship until I grew bored with her."

Schneider could tell that this man was getting close to losing it. Beginning with a slow reminiscence about his relationship with Luz, his voice grew louder and more menacing as he thought about the past, then he started waving the gun around, punctuating his displeasure by poking the gun barrel into Schneider's chest. Barrow took slow, even breaths and silently removed his revolver from the holster under his arm.

"Then why didn't you get rid of her, once you found out she worked for Clint Amberson? That accident with the pit cart was amateurish, and then you missed her on the street too. What went wrong?" asked Roger belligerently. "I thought that was your expertise, killing people and making it look like an accident."

At that his nemesis straightened his body, once again all

business, standing tall at six foot two. He tucked the barrel of the gun under Roger's chin, frowning.

"Roger, you are a spoiled child. You always have been since high school. I should have known better than to think I could count on you," Mauricio said, playfully chucking Schneider under the chin with the gun.

Barrow slowly inhaled, centering himself as he prepared to pounce on the swarthy gunman.

"No, no, listen to me. I did what you asked, I really did. Why can't you just forget about me and concentrate on her?" Roger pleaded.

"Before I take care of Luz, I must take care of you," his partner replied, with a voice as cold as the steel of his gun.

Hearing that, Barrow bolted out of his hiding place and hit the interloper on the back of his neck, just as he fired his revolver at Schneider. The sound was deafening in the small concrete restroom. Barrow struggled with the man, pushing him up against the concrete wall, but the strong man moved swiftly out the door, his forehead and neck scraped and bloodied. Looking down, Barrow found Roger Schneider crumpled on the floor, a bullet hole in his thigh, blood pumping out of the wound. Quickly he bent down, checked his pulse, and then wrapped his necktie around Roger's thigh as a makeshift tourniquet. As he covered him with his jacket, Barrow called the infield care center on his cell phone, ordering an ambulance and backup security.

"Someone's been shot. Come to the garage area, building B men's room. His pulse is elevated and he is bleeding badly."

Roger's eyes fluttered, and he tried to say something, but

Barrow cautioned him to stay quiet. As they waited for the ambulance, they could hear the sound of the engines as the cars wound around the track.

Barrow heard the ambulance arrive, the sounds of footsteps running with a stretcher. The paramedic took one look at pale Roger Schneider and quickly went to work. Fortunately, the blood flow had been stemmed by Barrow's quick first aid treatment. Schneider was moaning, complaining of the pain. As they carried him away on the stretcher, Barrow quickly described the man with the black leather jacket, dark wavy hair, and tall physique to the security agent who came with the ambulance. Barrow ran through the garage area and Gasoline Alley down to pit road, looking everywhere for the man who had shot Roger Schneider. He found his way to the Amberson pit stall in time for the last five laps of the race.

"You finally made it!" Michelle said as he ran up to the group crowding around the scoring stand. She smiled and patted him on the shoulder, but he kept looking around, searching the crowd with a worried look in his eye.

"Is something wrong?" Michelle asked, noticing his disheveled, distracted state.

"Yes, Schneider's accomplice is in this crowd somewhere. He's looking for Luz Dane."

"She's right here, up on the scoring stand. But really, Jonathan, there is nothing you can do now, not until the race is over."

"You're right. I've requested more backup. Hopefully we'll catch this guy before it's over," Jonathan said. "So how is the team doing?" he asked Michelle, squinting to see which number was on top of the scoring tower.

"We're leading," she said happily.

"And we're in fifth place," Jeff said.

"Two in the top five," Barrow said. "That's extraordinary."

"Yes, but the race isn't over. And you know how the last few laps can be murder," Jeff said, unaware of how close to the truth his statement was.

At that moment the field of cars streamed down the straightaway, with the two Amberson-Harwood cars in the closely bunched pack at the front. As fast as they moved, it was impossible to tell which car would win the race. The white flag waved as they crossed the start-finish, signaling the last lap of the race.

The crowd was on its feet, cheering the drivers on as they rounded turn 1, into the short chute, through turn 2, and onto the back straightaway. Here they put on the speed and made every effort to pass on the wide-open fastest part of the track. On more than one occasion, drivers eager to be the one to take the checkered flag pushed it to the limit and cars ended up one on top of the other, cartwheeling down the asphalt into the catch fence and the infield, leaving the win to the more cautious drivers farther back in the pack. Today was the exception: the cars flew down the backstretch, through turn 3, and around to turn 4, towards the yard-wide strip of bricks, the finish line, to take the checkered flag.

So close together were the cars, nose to tail, three abreast, that the crowd was going wild. There hadn't been such a close finish since Scott Goodyear and Jacques Villeneuve battled it out in 1994. The Amberson-Harwood team was on its feet, jumping up and down, cheering their teammates on, their fingers crossed, hoping for a victory.

The play-by-play announcer, caught up in the fervor, did his best to describe the battle on the track, talking faster and faster, louder and louder. Finally the checkered flag dropped and he shouted, "And it's Christi Cole, the winner of this year's race! Christi Cole, driving Amberson-Harwood racing number 45, to victory in what has to be the most intense battle on the track. The first woman to win the Indy 500! And the fans are going wild, as history was made today with the first woman to win the 500!!"

On her feet, Luz punched her stopwatch for the last time as Mark Miller finished second. She yelled and screamed, cheering both drivers on. As the cars crossed over the brick line, all she could say was "Yes! Yes! Yes!"

Luz and Jay, both on the scoring stand, hugged each other, then jumped down to hug, scream, and shout with the rest of the team. Jeff grabbed Luz, picked her up, twirled her around, and gave her the most passionate kiss yet. Tears streamed down her beaming face, and she hugged Michelle and Clint at the same time.

"What a rush! I can't believe it. So glad you all gave me this chance!" she said through her laughter and tears of happiness.

"Oh, honey, it's been perfect. You put the team together and made it happen. Without you, none of this would have happened," Michelle said, her arm around Luz's shoulder, as they walked towards the winner's circle.

The whole team was delirious, barely able to believe the miracle they'd just witnessed. Down the pit road, all the other teams lined up to salute the winner, Christi Cole, the rookie female driver, the long shot, who'd never won a major race until now. Jeff walked along beside Clint in his wheelchair, both of them grinning from ear to ear.

"Did you think you'd make it to the winner's circle this year when you started?" Barrow asked Jeff.

"No, and after that wreck that destroyed my car, it seemed a long way off in the distance."

"Yes, but you worked hard, and it paid off."

"I was given a great opportunity, and we all worked hard," Jeff said, looking at Luz with a smile on his face.

Out of the corner of her eye, near one of the scoring stands, Michelle saw someone she thought she knew. Turning to Luz, she asked, "Isn't that Mauricio, that horrible boyfriend of yours, on that scoring stand? What is he doing here? I thought you broke up years ago. You aren't seeing him again, are you?"

"No, of course not. But why would he be here?"

At that moment, the expression on Barrow's face shifted from celebration to serious concern. He looked over to the scoring stand, where the man Luz and Michelle were talking about was perched studying the crowd. On the way to the winner's circle, Barrow tapped Luz on the arm and asked, "Do you know that man?"

Luz looked over and saw Mauricio in his black leather jacket. "Yes, I used to date him. What is he doing here? How did he get credentials for pit row?"

Luz looked straight at her old lover, who hadn't yet spotted her. Then he turned his head and stared straight at her. She gave him an angry glare, as she remembered how he'd used her, trying to gain access to some of her important clients by trading on her reputation, mentioning that he knew her very well.

"He just shot Roger Schneider, and he's looking for you, Luz. Apparently he is the one behind the embezzlement and fraud plaguing Amberson Racing," Barrow said.

Luz heard Barrow, but she wasn't listening. Breaking away from her team members, Luz started to walk towards Mauricio, feeling the anger from so many years before surge through her. Mauricio smiled when he saw her. He casually dropped down from the scoring stand, while Luz marched forward to meet him, her face hiding her true feelings with a welcoming smile. Luz remembered how much Mauricio had liked to romance her before he'd hurt her, so now she would use that trait to get an edge, if she could. Barrow followed her as she walked through the crowd, his hand on his gun, aware that there might not be anything he could do but call for an ambulance if Luz was shot.

When Luz reached Mauricio, her languid smile and open mouth beckoned him towards her, and he bent down to touch her lips. Just as their lips parted for a kiss and she put her arm around his neck, Luz grabbed a hank of his hair, pulled his head back, stomped on his foot, and kneed him in the groin.

"Don't you ever, ever use me again!" Luz growled, stepping back to admire her handiwork. All that anger from years before gave her the strength to do what she'd wanted to do in her previous life but had never felt she could. Everything was different now. She was different now.

Mauricio was still doubled over in pain when Barrow

reached the pair. He finished the job Luz started by cuffing him and calling for backup.

"I didn't know you had that in you, Luz. Good work. Now you better get to the winner's circle, where you belong. Don't worry, I can take it from here." Barrow gestured her away.

Luz turned around and found Michelle waiting for her where they were standing only moments before.

"I'm impressed. You really took care of yourself. Where'd you learn to make those moves, Luz?" Michelle gave Luz a shoulder hug as they walked along in the crowd.

"After the last time, I knew he was no good for me. And he had a habit of popping up unexpectedly. So I needed to be able to protect myself, and I learned how."

The two women walked arm in arm, arriving in time to greet Christi as she drove onto the black-and-white-check-ered winner's circle after her victory lap around the speedway.

As soon as the car stopped, the team crowded around it. Mark Miller stood on the left side of the car, while Joe Kerr stood by ready to help Christi climb out of the chassis after she removed her helmet, earphones, and driving gloves. Once she was out of the car, a wreath of cymbidium orchids was placed around her neck, and a jug of milk was handed to her to drink from, two traditions embraced by the winners of the Indianapolis 500. After her triumphant drink of milk, both Michelle and Luz gave her strong hugs.

The press was eager to cover this story from all the angles. Normally it was a nonevent for a woman to run Indy, as they usually did not finish the race. This race was a first: Christi would be on the cover of every sports magazine and every woman's magazine for the next year. Jeff was inundated with questions from all the major networks. Reporters surrounded Michelle and Clint, always favorites with the Indianapolis press. Luz watched, observing everything as it happened before her, taking it all in, as this was her one and only time at Indy.

From the morning dawn to this moment of stunning victory, it would be a day she would always remember, a time she would never forget. The brilliant colors of the cars as they flew down the track, the carefully choreographed dance of the pit stops, the smell of methanol as the engines started, the thrill of the chase as the cars battled for position, the whine of the engines: Luz absorbed every bit of the sensory feast that was racing.

CHAPTER 35

All night she'd dreamed she was in a race car, but instead of going around a track, she raced for her life. Luz was startled awake at three in the morning by the nightmare of yet another near-miss collision, this time as she piloted an Indy car on the track while being chased by Roger Schneider and her nemesis, Mauricio. On waking up, she found Jeff sitting beside her, holding her hand, with a worried look on his face. "You had another bad dream," he said.

"Yes, I was being chased this time, around and around the track." Luz sounded exhausted.

"Luz, we won the race. The bad guys are in jail. You have nothing to worry about except what you are going to wear to the banquet tonight. Go back to sleep. I'll be here, until I have to go to the track to pack up. You sleep in and come whenever you wake up." Jeff held her and soothed her back to sleep by lightly rubbing her back.

Sleeping late felt good to Luz. When she woke up for the second time, Jeff had gone, but he had left a red rose with a note attached: "You're the best. See you at the track. Xs & Os, Jeff."

Groggily she fixed coffee, turned on the television, and watched in fascination as the news anchors talked about the story involving Amberson-Harwood Racing, money laundering, attempted murder, and the first woman to win the Indy 500. Flipping from one channel to another, she discovered it was the lead story on all the nationally syndicated news shows. To see her own face in the crowd next to Christi Cole as she celebrated the Indy 500 victory was surreal.

It was a cloudy gray morning and began to drizzle before Luz left her apartment. Her own sadness was underscored by the weather, leaving her a bit melancholy. She already missed her routine of working at the track and looked forward to these last moments of the good-natured joking and fellowship of being a part of the team. Knowing this was her last day, she wanted to make the best of it, to remember the experience at its zenith.

From the left-hand turn lane at the speedway entrance, Luz took a long look at the massive concrete pillars that supported the short chute, the stretch of asphalt between turns 1 and 2. She stopped at the entrance to show her credentials and to have one last visit with the Yellow Shirts who greeted her each day as she went to work at the Speedway. A feeling of nostalgia moved through Luz, as she drove the infield loop to the Red Lot. Even though teams of workers were picking up trash, there was a quiet stillness to the area that signaled it was all over for this year.

The team met at the track at nine o'clock to pack everything and clean the garage before getting dressed for the awards banquet. Luz hoped to say goodbye to her friends at Loctite, the guys at the pressroom, and the Yellow Shirts who befriended her. She needed time to see Gena Newman and the rest of the women who had helped her at the credentials office, and Paula Everett, who managed the ticket office. Not knowing whether she'd ever be back, Luz wanted to express her appreciation to all the nice people who helped her help Clint and Michelle.

More than half the transporters already had left the speedway to return to their respective shops to prepare for the next race. At the entrance to the garage area the Yellow Shirts chatted among themselves and security was lax; everyone assumed whoever was there was supposed to be there. Luz waved as she walked by on her way to the Amberson-Harwood garage. As she rounded the corner between the B and C buildings, a transporter was parked between the two buildings, the back door open, with one of the cars positioned on the lift waiting to be stowed up top. Lined up outside were toolboxes, rims, extra wings, boxes of clamps, bolts, and nuts, as well as a small refrigerator and electric skillet. Jeff sat at the desk inside, going through the drawers, reviewing miscellaneous receipts, and filing them in a box as he glanced at them for the last time before putting them on a truck to go back to Texas.

"What can I help with?" Luz asked.

"We have most everything taken care of here, but there

are some items that need to be returned to Loctite, Firestone, and Simpson, if you don't mind being a delivery person." He walked up to her with several papers in hand.

"Happy to help! This way I can say goodbye to some of the friends I want to see before I leave. Thanks," she said as she left.

Crossing through the hallways by the restrooms, she noticed the yellow "Do Not Cross" tape sealing off the men's room in building B where Roger Schneider was shot. What a small world it was: she still could hardly believe the link between Roger and the former lover who had jilted her many years before. How strange it was that she had foiled all their schemes merely by following her instincts and investigating further. Luz remembered something her father used to tell her: "Listen to your gut and follow your instincts." She'd made every effort to live her life in a forthright and honest manner, hoping that most everything would turn out right.

Opening the door to the Loctite storefront, Luz smelled the distinctive fragrance of hot dogs, pickle relish, onions, and warm bread. Most of the displays were removed from the walls, giving the smallish room a barren feeling, yet Bruce still served hot dogs, just as he'd done for the previous four weeks. When he saw her walk in, he came from behind the counter and shook her hand.

"Congratulations! Who'da thought a woman could win the 500? Glad someone had some faith in Christi. She's wanted a chance in the big show since she was a little girl. And she didn't disappoint on her first time out."

"Yes, it was quite a race. I can't believe it's all over now,"

Luz said.

"Over? No way—it's just beginning. She'll get sponsorship, endorsements, photo shoots, who knows? She might even get a movie deal. That little lady has an entirely brand-new career," he said, sitting down at one of the tables as Luz fixed a hot dog for each of them.

"Well, it's over for me." She ladled the pickle relish onto the bun, then handed Bruce his plate.

"Hey, how can you say that? After all the great detective work you did, and the way you put the Amberson-Harwood team together? Are you going to throw all that away?"

"Bruce, you don't get it. I came here as a favor to some friends of my parents who needed my help and didn't have anyone else to help them."

His mouth full of hot dog, Bruce wiped his mouth and tried to talk, yet only whines of protest could be heard from behind his napkin.

"Yeah, yeah. Clint and Michelle have tons of friends here, yet they knew something was wrong and they didn't know what, so they wanted someone from outside who would look after their interests and their interests alone," said Luz.

Bruce finally managed to swallow. "No, Luz, you don't get it. You're a natural. You think well on your feet, you understand the corporate side of things and you work pretty well with men. Maybe this is where you belong."

"Thanks for thinking that about me. But I have to go back to reality, and that starts again for me later this week."

"Well, thanks for stopping by one last time before you go."

"I'm glad you were here. Oh, I'm supposed to give this to

you. It's payment on the account for the tools bought during the month."

"Great! Thanks for paying me now. And Luz, remember, you are always welcome here during the month of May."

"Thanks, Bruce. You've been so nice to me. Hope to see you again soon." Luz shook his hand, then walked out the door.

She stopped at Simpson to leave the envelope Michelle gave her, which contained the payment for new fire suits, and then walked over to Firestone, where they waited for her with a box of new hats. "Your team will need these tonight at the awards banquet."

"Okay, thanks. I'll make sure the right person gets them."

On her way back to the garage, people stopped her to offer congratulations on the win and the superb strategy the team had employed during the race. Luz was happy to give Jeff all of the credit and hoped he'd be back at the garage when she returned.

Walking in the door, she saw Jeff packing one last box. Everything else in the garage had been stowed in the transporter except the plastic lawn chair.

"There you are! I wondered when you'd make it back here after all the errands I gave you to do. Everything is packed up here, and in the Harwood garage. We're even taking the sign-boards to Texas so you'll have a souvenir of your first 500." Jeff seemed as cheerful as Luz was melancholy.

She smiled at him. His boyish good looks were emphasized by his jovial nature, and at this moment he had a right to feel good about himself. Winning the 500 was the dream of any racer. Any crew chief of any race team would be thrilled with the outcome of yesterday's race.

With one last look around, they loaded the two remaining chairs into the transporter and closed the overhead doors to the garage space. Before she turned off the lights and closed the door, Luz took one last look around at what had been her speedway home.

BARBIE O'CONNOR

CHAPTER 36

Dressed in a chic black column dress, Luz stepped out of the car at the convention center where the awards banquet was scheduled to begin in an hour. Jeff, wearing a tux with a Nicole Miller–designed tie featuring an open-wheel car, passed the keys to the valet and offered his arm to Luz. They were ushered up the escalators to the reception area, where the luminaries of racing gathered to celebrate the running of the five-hundred-mile race at the Indianapolis Speedway. As they walked through the room, well-wishers from every team stopped to congratulate them. They were the evening's power couple. When they entered the alcove to the ballroom that overlooked the glass atrium with its stunning view of the downtown lights, Luz took in the scene, wanting to be able to remember it always.

"I think I'd like a glass of champagne. Isn't that what winners are supposed to drink?" She smiled at Jeff, and he steered them towards the nearest bar.

Once they both had glasses of bubbly, Luz took a deep breath, looked at Jeff, and started to make a toast, when Bart Soules walked up to them and raised his glass: "To winning the Indy 500."

Four other glasses joined the toast as Clint, Michelle, Christi, and Mark surrounded them in celebration. All around the glasses clinked together, while all of the teammates hugged, reliving the good luck and happy occasion of the win.

"Congratulations is also in order for resolving the Blackbird Racing mystery! Tell us about it," Bart pleaded.

Luz smiled at Bart, took a deep breath, pulled her shoulders back, and began. "It all started back in high school. Roger and my despicable former boyfriend met when Mauricio was an exchange student here learning English. Evidently the two of them were juvenile delinquents together."

Looks of surprise crossed the faces around her. "Two years ago Mauricio came to Indianapolis for business and contacted Roger. They went out for drinks, and between the two of them they came up with this plan to start an Indy car team and run money through the team books from a fictitious auto parts company posing as a sponsor."

Luz continued: "Mauricio mentioned to Roger that he had dated someone, me, who worked at an investment firm. One of the reasons we broke up was that he started to pressure me to set up accounts with people and businesses I knew nothing about."

"Yes, Clint and I were so afraid for you then, Luz. He was really not looking out for you at all," Michelle said.

"While I was away from the office, Mauricio rekindled his bromance with my manager, who gladly set up the accounts with the promise of millions of dollars eventually being under management at the firm. Of course the auto parts company was really a cartel from south of the border wanting to launder money obtained through illegal means."

"But didn't they take money from Amberson?" Jeff asked.

"Yes, but initially they planned to start a new team. Mauricio wanted Roger to get a new team on the books, so Roger had to meet the April 1st deadline to enter. When Clint had his stroke, it made it easier for them. No one was paying attention to the books, so they just ran the money through Amberson. Then I came along and mucked it up for them."

"And we're so glad you did!" Michelle touched her glass to Luz's and gave her an appreciative smile.

"Amen," said Clint.

"Then what happened?" asked Christi.

"Once they realized someone was looking over their shoulders, they started moving money around so it would be available to them when they needed it. One of the reasons they steered Amberson sponsors to Blackbird was to make it look legitimate, with money coming from other sponsors. The big cartel from south of the border that was laundering money through the race team eventually wanted it back in the guise of its share of the prize money. Of course, that didn't work out too well once the Blackbird car went up in flames." Luz paused as a waiter refilled her glass and another offered canapés to the group.

Bart added what he knew and concluded, "That Mauricio

guy made both the attempts on your life—he drove the pit cart that almost hit you and the sedan that missed you when you were crossing the street. The threatening card was a real warning that he planned to eliminate you and Roger, since both of you could identify him. He planned to kill you at the end of the race, when all eyes would be on the winning car."

Michelle's eyes widened at this information, and she took a swig of champagne from her glass. Luz smiled at her gently. "Mauricio wanted to get rid of Schneider because he was a liability; he wanted too much money to maintain his side of the ruse. He would have gotten away with everything if I hadn't know his character so well."

Jonathan Barrow walked up to the group after overhearing this last comment. "Yes, Luz you have been a great help. Without you we never would have gotten to the bottom of this case. You've been a real asset to the speedway this month. Remember, you are always welcome here."

Luz smiled in amusement. She had gone from an outsider to an insider all in the span of a month. What a wild ride it was! It was amazing what living through the 500 could do for a woman.

Bells chimed: it was time for the dinner to begin. Luz took Jeff's arm, and the attractive couple led the way into the dining room for the banquet and the awards presentation.

This banquet was unlike any other banquet Luz had attended: the end of the meal brought not just dessert but also paychecks, and big ones. Once the tables were cleared, everyone waited in anticipation for the program to begin. Starting with the thirty-third position, the awards were announced.

Even the last-place finisher earned over $150,000.

By the time third place was announced and the second-place winner, Mark Miller, went up to accept the check for Amberson-Harwood Racing, the team was on the edge of its seat. This year the amounts were significantly greater than in past years, as there were an increased number of contingency prizes and the individual amounts were larger than before. Second place came in at $990,000, causing a cheer from the Amberson-Harwood team. Now it was time for the first-prize award and the ceremony that went with the win.

First the emcee unveiled the car, which was in the same condition as at the end of the race, covered in the dirt, bugs, and scrapes of the battle waged on the track. With the spotlight shining on the red-and-white car, the team waited backstage for their cue to take a bow. Jeff and Luz waited nervously for the official announcement of the winning driver and team owners.

"Now it's time to introduce the winning driver of this year's Indy 500 . . . Miss Christi Cole! *She's on it!*"

And the crowd went wild as Christi, in a stunning white gown covered in shimmering crystals, walked to the podium. A variation of the famous saying "He's on it!," coined by Tom Carnegie, the speedway's original announcer, was perfect for her introduction. Christi graciously thanked the audience and listened attentively to the kind platitudes from the master of ceremonies. When it was time for the introduction of the team and car owners, the crowd gave Clint and Michelle Amberson a standing ovation. After all the years that Clint Amberson had entered and participated in the 500, there were many old friends glad to see his drivers win the pole and the race. Looking distinguished in his tuxedo, Clint was in fine spirits as he steered his motorized wheelchair.

Jeff was introduced, and he in turn introduced each of the mechanics to the audience, starting with the tire changers. Luz waited in the wings, elegant and poised, joyfully sharing her new friends' celebration.

Jeff completed his introductions and was joined by Michelle Amberson, who said, "As those of you who followed the Amberson-Harwood team this month know, we had a rocky start with Clint's stroke at the beginning, but we finished on top at the end. So there is one more person we want to introduce now. Luz Dane has her own career as an investment adviser, yet she came to our aid when we needed her. She was new to the speedway when she arrived, but it was her guidance and great decisions that put together the team you see here tonight. Luz, will you join us and take a bow? We are so proud of you."

Jeff walked back to the wings to escort her out to the clapping, cheering crowd. She was overwhelmed by the excitement, laughing, tears streaming down her face. There were so many cameras on her that Luz felt like she had won the Miss America pageant, and the spotlight followed her across the stage as she joined Clint, Michelle, Christi, Jeff, and the rest of the team.

Luz basked in the joy of this sweet victory. More than the five-hundred-mile race, working on the team had tested her in every way, every facet of her life. She'd put her smarts and intuition to work to help a friend. Now she was eager to see what adventures awaited her, what new worlds she would explore. That mystery would be revealed to her day by day, and in her heart, she knew that everything in her life happened in just the right way, at just the right time.

BARBIE O'CONNOR

Thank you for buying this book!

If you enjoyed it, please tell your friends!
Please post a review on Amazon, GoodReads, and other sites.
Read the whole series!

Coming up next:
Virgin at Sonoma
You'll find an excerpt at the end of this book!

BARBIE O'CONNOR

ACKNOWLEDGMENTS

Thanks to all at Indy who gave me a chance to find out what auto-racing at the highest level is all about. Many thanks to Hulman and Company for keeping the grand tradition of the Indy 500 going so all fans can enjoy a dramatic race filled with American tradition over Memorial Day weekend.

To my friends in the San Antonio Public Library Foundation book club, Literary Excursions, led by Coleen Grissom, PhD: Thanks for your thoughtful analysis of so many books, characters, themes, and ideas over the years that served as inspiration for this novel.

Especially, I'd like to thank Anne, Susan, Mary, Pam, Mercille, Evelyn, and Janine for their concise and valuable criticism of my draft manuscript. Eli Miller of Eli Miller Design guided me through the cover design, helping to create the mystery, energy, and dynamism of auto racing in two dimensions. Sarah Nawrocki gave me the final push to get this book out in the world, and Christi Stanforth brought her careful eye to the copyediting.

Again, thanks to my husband, Toby, for the ride of my life.

ABOUT THE AUTHOR

Starting out in the investment field with a major financial services firm, and retiring as a vice president with decades of experience working with clients, Barbie O'Connor was part owner of a team that fielded cars in the 1995 and 1996 Indy 500 races. With *Virgin at the Speedway*, she has realized her dream of writing a novel, but this first novel will not be her last. A fan of all types of auto racing—IndyCar, F1, Nascar, endurance racing, drag racing, and karting—she is writing the Racing Resort Ranch series, which captures motor racing's excitement, romance, and energy. She is also the author of the nonfiction book *MoneySmarts4U: The Basics*, intended to help anyone learn the money management essentials necessary for success in their adult lives. Barbie O'Connor lives in Texas with her husband and two dogs. Please visit her at www.barbieoconnor.com

AN EXCERPT FROM
VIRGIN AT SONOMA

Chapter One

The last supper is never the last one until after it happens. After the breakup has occurred or the family is estranged or the beloved is dead, not until then is it really a last supper. As people interpret the meaning of their loss, then the acting out, the grieving, and the reconstruction of new life begin. Looking around at the carefully set table with its pristine white linen tablecloth and napkins, shimmering crystal goblets, and glimmering silver flatware, Luz wondered if this was the last time she would share a meal with Orval Slattery.

Luz Maria Dane, family investment adviser to the Slattery clan, felt honored to be seated at the head table at the Chateau La Mer wine dinner benefiting the Bexar County Children's Home. She was flanked on one side by Orval Slattery, the patriarch of the family, and on the other by her friend and lover,

Jeff Harwood. She had worked side by side with Jeff running an open-wheel race team the previous May at the Indy 500, while Orval Slattery and his friend Sacha Bernard had founded Chateau La Mer in the spirit of French-American joint ventures that began as far back in history as the days of Lafayette. Other guests at the table were Sara Lawrence, Orval's niece; Julienne and Martin Cohen, the owners of the liquor distribution company cosponsoring the dinner; and Clint and Michelle Amberson, friends of Luz as well as of Orval and Sara. It promised to be a fabulous evening for oenophiles, with a blind tasting of a selection of French wines to compare to the Chateau La Mer creations.

During the cocktail hour, when champagne was served with canapés, Luz made the rounds to meet and greet friends and clients. On her return to Emerson York after her work at the 500, her manager had met with stony resistance any new ideas she had for prospecting new clients or educating old ones. It was almost as if he were jealous of her ability to multitask—to work with her clients via phone, email, and fax in the morning and then focus her efforts at the track in the afternoon getting the car qualified and ready to race. His inflexibility had led her to make the difficult decision to leave Emerson York and start her own investment advisory firm, L. M. Dane, LLC. She'd been told that she'd never be able to make it, that her clients would not move from the big New York firm, but the mortgage crisis and the unforeseen failure of so many Wall Street firms gave her the advantage when she started off on her own.

Now her everyday world was one of evaluating portfolios, rebalancing asset allocations, proposing new investment choices, and listening to the needs of her clients. She missed all the elements of being at the track: the people who worked on the teams, the sounds of the engines, the chesslike strategy required to qualify and win, and the frenzy of getting everything ready in very little time and fixing last-minute problems. Luz had never before experienced the thrill of the sensation of thirty-three high-performance engines starting simultaneously and then forming a synchronized, balletic train as the starting grid of cars shrieked up to speed at the start of the race. It was the rush of a lifetime: she could still smell the methanol fuel when the engines started and feel the wind as it whipped by her when the cars barreled down the front straightaway. By starting a new life for herself with her own firm and the clients she loved, she hoped to combine the best of the two worlds she knew. Seeing Clint and Michelle again brought it all back to her. Luz wanted that balance that love, that excitement, that fulfillment in her life too.

When the bell sounded for dinner, Luz looked around the crowd to find Jeff, who was immersed in conversation with a local banker. She slowly walked towards them, catching his eye, making the wind-it-up signal with her index finger to tell him to wrap up his chat. She almost felt sorry to interrupt, because she was delighted to see Jeff so animated.

"Hello, handsome," Luz said as she leaned towards him to kiss his cheek, and then said to the banker, "Great to see you, Greg. What has Jeff been bending your ear about? Something interesting, I hope."

Greg exchanged a look with Jeff, and a secret smile passed

between them. "He's just letting me know some ideas he has for the future. Pretty interesting ideas, I do say. But he asked me to keep it private for now, so I'll honor his request for the time being."

"Good. He's a visionary. Maybe someday he'll share those dreams with me." Luz's eyes twinkled.

"Luz, you know when the time is right, I'll tell you all about it, but not yet, not yet." Jeff he took her arm, patted her hand, and led her forward into the ballroom.

Once they were seated, Julienne Cohen rose to the podium to welcome the guests for the evening. She shared the mission statement of the Children's Home and thanked Chateau La Mer for their contribution to the evening. In appreciation she invited Orval Slattery to the podium to present him with a set of handblown glass wine globes to commemorate the evening.

"Thank you, Julienne. It is always a pleasure for me to be in San Antonio, especially spending time in the company of such an esteemed group as the supporters of the Children's Home. I'm quite lucky this evening to be accompanied by my niece, Sara Lawrence," Slattery said. "Many of you know her, since she grew up here in the Alamo City. After she graduates from Texas A&M this coming spring with a specialization in viniculture and oenology, Sara will be coming aboard Chateau La Mer!"

There was a collective gasp from the crowd, as there had been much speculation about who would succeed Slattery in his leadership role at the famous winery. Applause followed.

As he stood beaming and smiling, basking in the happy moment, he grasped the bottle of Chateau La Mer Cabernet

Sauvignon and poured about two inches into one of the hand-blown glasses recently presented to him. Swirling the wine in the glass, holding it up to the overhead light, he commented, "Nice legs, eh?"

Laughter at the jovial compliment of a wine he was noted for swept the room, all eyes upon him as he inhaled the bouquet with a practiced manner befitting a renowned winemaker. Then he raised his glass. "To my niece, Sara. May she enjoy the fruits of her labor by creating a wine to rival any of the Premier cru vintages of France. À votre santé!"

A cheerful repetition of the familiar French toast echoed around the room, and Orval Slattery was the center of attention as he drank fully from his glass. Sara looked nervously around at the others at the table, unsure of what to do, as she considered it bad luck to drink a toast to herself. She smiled, fidgeting in her chair, picking at the cuticle of her right thumbnail as she surveyed the candlelit ballroom and looked up at the glowing face of her seventy-five-year-old uncle. He encouraged everyone to make their best guesses during dinner about which wines they were to enjoy, and with that the short program was over. Holding on to the short railing, Slattery made his way down the three stairs from the stage and then to his chair at the head table.

As he sat down, he began to totter a bit, something Sara was accustomed to dealing with as a side effect of the stroke he'd suffered a few years before, which had affected his balance. Rising from her seat to stabilize him and push him towards the center of his chair, Sara found herself falling as well, her uncle's body a sudden deadweight that carried the two of them directly onto the lap of Luz Dane, who yelped in surprise at the avalanche of bodies falling on top of her. At first it seemed like an overcorrection, and as Martin Cohen helped Sara to her feet, they assumed Slattery would jauntily laugh at his own clumsiness, his usual response to his teetering ways, and right himself with a little help from a friend. When Jeff Harwood put one arm around the old man's back and with the other took hold of Slattery's left arm, gently pulling him up off Luz's lap, he found the body slack. Carefully Jeff placed him in a chair, touched his neck, looked for an indication of a pulse, and felt the clammy skin, watching as it turned a pale gray. "Someone call a doctor, an ambulance," Jeff said. "I don't think he's feeling well."

At every other table the guests were eating salad and bread, sipping the wine, discussing how the flavors married with the two wines poured to go with appetizer. Michelle dipped her napkin in ice water and wrapped it around the back of Slattery's neck while Clint wheeled out the nearest door to find out if the hotel had a doctor on call. Julienne, Luz, and Jeff put their chairs together to create a makeshift cot they could lay the old man down on, as he kept falling forward when he was seated. Slattery kept murmuring under his breath. Sara stood by, her face pale as moonlight, wringing her napkin, stunned by the turn of events.

Within minutes, the sound of a siren was heard outside the ballroom doorways, and Clint, on his motorized wheelchair, led a team of emergency medical technicians bearing a stretcher through the door and directed them to the table where Orval Slattery was unconscious. Quickly they loaded him onto the gurney and took him outside, where they verified his thready pulse, placed an oxygen mask over his mouth and nose, and then checked other vital signs as they moved towards the waiting ambulance.

Michelle, Clint, Luz, Jeff followed along, bringing a stunned Sara with them. They decided they would all go to the hospital in the wheelchair-accessible van, with Jeff driving. Once they were on their way, Sara spoke up, her voice hesitant. "I didn't know he was so vulnerable. We just spent the weekend at a friend's ranch and he seemed fine. I don't know what happened. Except for the stroke a few years ago, he's been doing everything right. Vitamins, healthy diet, exercise. I just don't understand."

Michelle had her arm around Sara, holding her close in the back seat of the van. Jeff drove, Luz rode shotgun, and Clint sat in his chair as they drove the five miles to the hospital. Clint turned to Sara: "Honey, I thought I was doing everything right, and look where that got me. Sometimes things happen to our bodies to make us examine our lives, to get us straight in our heads. These little events are God's way of getting our attention. It may be time for your Uncle Orval to retire. Maybe he's been holding onto the reins a little too tight."

Once they pulled up behind the ambulance at the emergency room, Luz walked with Sara into the building to the check-in desk. Sara was instructed to follow the gurney into the triage area while Luz took care of the administrative issues as best she could. Most of the information she already knew from her dealings with Orval concerning estate planning and portfolio management. By the time she was through, Clint,

Michelle, and Jeff were all in seated in the waiting room.

As they perused the year-old magazines littering the tables and chairs in the waiting room, they noticed a pair of police officers come through the emergency room doors, check in at the desk, and then go back to the triage area. Typically many of the patients at this ER were victims of gunshot wounds or stabbings, so they were not surprised to see the law enforcement officers there.

But about twenty minutes later, one of the policemen came out to the waiting room and approached their small group. "I gather from how you are dressed that you may have attended the dinner for the Children's Home this evening. We have a few questions we'd like to ask you and wondered if you could come with me to a more private area."

Clint looked at Michelle, while Luz and Jeff caught each other's eye. Clint spoke up: "What is this all about, officer? Seems a bit unnecessary for a heart attack or stroke."

The officer recognized Clint Amberson from his interviews on television during and after the Indy 500, so he answered his question respectfully. "Mr. Amberson, this is about more than a stroke or heart attack. I'd rather not discuss it out here with all these other people around, so we have a little room back here where we can all be comfortable and out of the way of the other people who are waiting for their loved ones."

The officer led them to a small conference room that was usually reserved for doctors to discuss with families the tough decisions often made in hospitals. Then, one by one, each of them was separately questioned by the two officers, after which they were allowed to return to the larger conference room but asked not to discuss with the others the questions the police had asked. Finally Sara Lawrence was led into the conference room, her face ashen. Bottles of water were passed around to the group.

One of the officers spoke up. "Miss Lawrence we are deeply sorry for your loss. With Mr. Slattery as your only living relative, you are a prime suspect, since you directly benefit from his demise. It is our duty to investigate his death, especially since he died so quickly and apparently was in such good health previously. The doctors here suspect poisoning, as we have told you, and now your friends, upon your request. Everyone here has been questioned, and we have sent an officer to the hotel ballroom to retrieve the glass and bottle of wine from which Mr. Slattery drank shortly before his collapse. Ordinarily we would request that you not leave the state, but since Mr. Slattery was a majority owner in a famous winery in California, which you inherit and most likely must attend to, we ask that you remain in this country and that you check in with us on a regular basis. Once the toxicology reports can tell us what poison killed him and we can test the wine, the glass, and anything else we can think of for the same poison, then we can get down to the business of finding out who killed him."

Luz listened to what the officer had to say and realized that whoever wanted Orval Slattery dead had carefully implicated Sara in his demise. Luz didn't think Sara was a killer. Although she had a great deal to gain by her uncle's death, she still wanted to learn from his experience and knowledge, or at least that was the impression she gave Luz.

Michelle spoke up. "Sara is in the last semester of school. She graduates in May. Her uncle has an excellent staff in place, including Paul Angel, the winemaker. I think she needs to stay in Texas to finish her degree. Maybe she can come check on things when we have a race in Sonoma in March. She can fly out with Luz, and we'll take care of her. I really don't think she is a flight risk."

Luz listened and watched the officer's face as Michelle spoke. He looked a bit skeptical, but seemed to like the idea that Sara would stay in the state except for a brief visit to the wine country. Luz realized it might help if she said something, so she said, "I've managed the Slattery money for years, and I know that Orval intended for the bulk of his estate to go to Sara, but not before she was ready. Sara is aware of this too, so she had no vested interest in losing her uncle too soon. If anything this just makes things worse for her, without his expertise, it may further diminish the value of Chateau La Mer. I'll vouch for Sara, and I'll gladly escort her to and from Sonoma."

The officer glanced at the faces of esteemed members of his community, all of them dressed to the nines in ball gowns and tuxedos. After reviewing the notes he'd made one more time, he said, "Okay, this is the way we'll handle these next few months: Sara goes back to A&M, and then"—he pointed to Clint and Michelle Amberson—"goes to Sonoma as your guest." He turned to Luz. "And you, Ms. Dane, will escort her there and back. Hopefully before she graduates, we'll have this whole thing straightened out."

Smiles shot across everyone's face, and Sara looked relieved.

"I've kept you long enough," the officer said. "I have all your contact information, so you can go now."

Clint led the way, rolling out to the parking lot with Jeff by his side. They boarded the van and brought it around to the emergency room entrance for the ladies to join them. Once they were situated and safely belted in, Jeff drove back to the hotel to get his car and allowed Clint and Michelle to return to their home in Boerne. On the way back, Luz turned to Sara and said, "Why don't you stay at my place tonight? It might be better for you not to be alone. I've got something you can wear tomorrow. Things won't be so bleak when you've had some rest and the shock has worn off a bit."

Sara looked grateful, nodded her acceptance, and followed Luz into Jeff's car. Once they were at her apartment she showed Sara into the guest room, found her a nightie to wear, fixed her chamomile tea, and left her alone with her thoughts. Jeff was waiting for Luz on the terrace overlooking the lights of the city, a small glass of brandy for each of them.

Once she was seated, Luz said, "I know this may seem callous, but I feel like we are so lucky to be alive. I just want to toast to a full life." She held up her glass: "To life, love, health, wealth, much success and happiness!"

"Yes, to all those things and more." Jeff sipped and swallowed the warming liquid as he watched a small jet land at the airport nearby. Luz leaned against the railing to face Jeff, searching his face for a sense of what his thoughts were.

"It's going to be rough for her, isn't it?" Jeff asked.

"Yes, it is. But with good friends she'll pull through this rough time. We all will. Every time someone I know dies, it just makes me realize how sweet life is, and how much we all need each other, and how we just need to appreciate every moment we have to live."

"Yes, every moment is precious," Jeff answered, putting his arm around her waist, drawing her to him, and holding her close. He kissed her passionately, and her warm lips were aroused by his, full of the love she felt for him.

To be continued...

www.ingramcontent.com/pod-product-compliance
Lightning Source LLC
Chambersburg PA
CBHW020241200626
46816CB00001BA/64

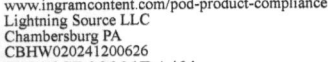